"Jessica Lewis excels in every genre she writes. A departure from the paranormal horror Lewis is known for, this romance is a joy to read. While often lighthearted and funny, the book also earnestly explores complicated family relationships. Lewis masterfully captures the complicated feelings of being a teenager, especially the confusing, overwhelming feelings of a crush. I'm so glad kids today get to read books like this."

—MERYL WILSNER, *USA Today* bestselling author of *Cleat Cute*

"More than just a love story, *Nav's Foolproof Guide to Falling in Love* combines all of my favorite parts of a rom-com—humor, wit, complex characters, a brilliant platonic support system, and a swoony romance that will have you squealing in delight and throwing your copy against the wall."

—EMERY LEE, award-winning author of *Meet Cute Diary*

"A hilarious delight, packed full of charming characters who make mistakes but still treat each other with so much love. Nav captured my heart from page one with her clumsy confidence and hard-earned vulnerability. I was cheering for her love story the entire way!"

—BRIDGET MORRISSEY, author of *That Summer Feeling*

"Lewis crafted a foolproof book that I immediately fell in love with. Funny, tender, charming, and extremely relatable, *Nav's Foolproof Guide to Falling in Love* is a swoony sapphic masterpiece."

—JUSTINE PUCELLA WINANS, award-winning author of *Bianca Torre Is Afraid of Everything*

NAV's Foolproof GUIDE TO FALLING IN LOVE

JESSICA LEWIS

HARPER

An Imprint of HarperCollinsPublishers

For Grandma, always. And to all the messy, unique, anxious queer girls who feel like they can't have their own love story—this is for you.

CHAPTER 1

When Hallie sits down next to me at lunch, eyes puffy and red from crying, I know it's about to be a long twenty minutes.

"Nav," she sniffs, wiping her nose with a crumpled tissue. She's got that hangdog look of a kicked puppy. "I need you to kill someone for me."

"Anytime, babe." I put my half-eaten PB&J away, because I can already feel this is gonna be a counseling session. Luckily, the cafeteria is so loud and choked with students that no one will hear us. "Peter?"

I scan the crowd of high schoolers at the haphazard collection of round tables, but I don't see his limp, greasy hair anywhere. Not that Hallie's arrogant ex would be caught dead in the cafeteria with the normies. He's probably eating in the library to make himself look broody and smarter than he actually is. I was always thankful for that; at least I didn't have to see his dumb face while I was eating lunch. I already have to guard our table like a rabid Chihuahua or else some of Hallie's basketball friends will migrate over and talk to me about sports (a fate worse than death, I swear).

Hallie's dark brown eyes fill with fresh tears, and a pang of hurt stabs my chest. I wish I really could kill that dickweed. She aggressively tears open a bag of honey-barbecue chips (her only lunch—yikes) and starts inhaling them before speaking. "I saw him just now, talking to Leslie. Like, *already*, Nav! It's only been a week!"

Twelve days, which is almost two weeks, but she would strangle me if I said that right now. I take in Hallie's appearance today before I respond. Usually, she's wearing fashionable shirts and designer jeans, but it's been sweatpants and pajama shirts since the breakup. Today is her rubber-duck-wearing-sunglasses shirt, which means she's feeling extra shitty. Her light brown skin is flushed from crying too. I waffle between sympathy and tough love. She probably wants me to pat her hand and tell her it'll be okay, but she's been crying nonstop since they broke up. Maybe it's time to retire Nice Nav.

"Listen, Hallie. You're better than him, okay? He sucks. How he even formed the thought in his worm brain to cheat on you, I'll never know."

Hallie sniffles again, nodding into the now-empty chip bag. "I know, I know. But it hurts so bad. I mean, I thought he was the one."

I resist the urge to roll my eyes. She always thinks her current partner is "the one." I don't get the appeal, honestly, because all relationships end up like this—in tears. I'd be more sympathetic if Peter was actually decent, but he wasn't. He's a loser who constantly mansplained everything to Hallie, even though she's literally on track to be our grade's valedictorian. Hallie just got distracted because he's a drummer in a band and conveniently forgot everything else.

"The first time you met him, he puked after three beers," I say.

"So what, he can't hold his alcohol! He was so sweet. You remember when he gave me flowers for Valentine's Day?"

"That's the bare minimum."

"Okay, well, what about when he took me out for my birthday on that boat ride? And when he asked me out for the first time? That was so romantic."

"Just admit you were dickmatized so we can go."

Hallie kicks my shin under the table, but she snorts out a laugh. At least she looks a little happier now. "You have to admit, he was cute, though."

"No, I don't have to admit that." Hallie may be bisexual, but I definitely am not. I wouldn't date a dude if someone paid me—especially a dude who can't hold his liquor and smells like old cheese.

Hallie's grin gets bigger, and she almost seems back to normal. "Fine! God, you could agree with me a little."

"I never lie, especially about idiot boyfriends . . ." I trail off as someone approaches our table. It's a girl; she's tall (taller than me, anyway, which isn't hard to do), with long, wavy black hair and cute thick-rimmed black glasses. She seems familiar, but even after racking my brain, I can't place her. That's a surprise. Our high school isn't huge, so it's hard not to know everyone from seeing their faces day after tedious day. She stops a few steps from us, backlit by the big windows lining the cafeteria walls. I wait for her to say something, but she doesn't. She stares

3

at me and Hallie for a few seconds, brown eyes wide like she's seen a ghost, then turns like a robot and practically runs away from us. I watch her flee the lunchroom, stunned.

"Huh." Hallie blinks in surprise, still staring at the empty space where she stood. "That was weird. Do you know her?"

"No." As soon as I say that, her face clicks in my brain. "Wait, yes I do. Her name is Gia Flores. She's in art with me."

"That name sounds familiar," Hallie says, tapping the table thoughtfully. "What kind of art does she do?"

I think hard about seventh-period, but I really don't know. She moved here this semester, and she's really quiet. So quiet I can't remember her ever saying anything in class for five months.

"Oh, wait, *that* Flores?" Hallie gasps. "Isn't her mom this year's sponsor for Carnegie?"

My mood instantly sours. Hallie winces a little.

"Sorry," she hurries to say. "I didn't—"

"No, it's fine!" I force a grimace into a smile. Hallie and I applied for the annual Carnegie Camp for Young Scholars, a six-week summer camp that's full of boring as hell study sessions and SAT prep. It's two hours away, and at the end, the top performing kids get a scholarship to a college of their choice. We applied on a whim because I heard those nerds threw *great* parties, but Hallie got in . . . and I didn't. I'm not bitter about it, I swear. Well, okay, I am a little bitter, but I know I'm not exactly a "scholar." I just thought Hallie and I would get to spend the summer together. Like we do every summer. What am I gonna do by myself for six weeks? Work and stare at the ceiling? And I'll have no escape from Dad's watchful eyes either . . . I hold in a shudder.

But I don't tell Hallie that. We got the news yesterday, so it still stings, but Hallie deserves to go. Even if it's without me.

"Anyway," I say, trying to ignore the thought of Hallie having fun with her new, not-me friends, "the camp'll be a good distraction. You can hang out with cute nerds."

Hallie seems uncertain but settles on a small smile. "It's still a month away. I could really use a distraction right now."

I suggest murdering Peter in our spare time, and Hallie laughs. We chat until the bell rings, and we stand, headed to class. Me to regular history and Hallie to honors precalculus. Not a bad twenty minutes after all.

We mill out of the cafeteria, and I'm about to wave goodbye when Hallie touches my arm to stop me.

"Nav," Hallie says quietly.

I glance at her, and I'm dismayed to see more tears in her eyes. Still? If I find Peter in a Waffle House parking lot, we're fighting.

"Hal, Peter is a—"

"Do you think something's wrong with me?"

I stare at her, slow horror leaking into my system. This breakup is worse than I thought. A lot worse. "What? Stop!" I take her face in my hands, ignoring the irritated kids having to move around us. "You are perfect. And gorgeous. A ten. An eleven! Hot girls don't worry about what fuck boys think."

"Thanks, Nav." Hallie smiles at me, but it doesn't reach her eyes. They're the saddest I've seen in a long time. "See you after school?"

"You know it." I squeeze her cheeks until she laughs and squirms out of my grip. I move back and we wave goodbye, but my stomach feels like I've swallowed rocks. She's taking this one really hard. I wish I could fix this for her. I think of how, soon, I won't be there with her if some other idiot breaks her heart at that stupid camp, and my mood dampens even more. I wish I could fix things for us both.

♡♡♡

When I get home from Hallie's, I start swearing under my breath. Dad's car is in the driveway.

I stand outside my house, the sheer amount of dread in my gut rooting me to the pavement. What the hell is he doing home? It's only nine p.m., and usually he works until midnight at the plant. I only came home because I thought he wouldn't be here. Well, that and Hallie literally sobbed herself to sleep in my lap, and I thought it would be better to let her sleep off the breakup hangover.

I chew my bottom lip, studying my house like I'm about to start a heist. Back door? That's risky if he's in the kitchen, and there's no way I can sneak upstairs without being seen. I could climb in through my window . . . No, I'd probably fall and break my neck. I better get this over with. I sigh and walk up the porch steps to open the front door, which is already unlocked. Yikes.

Dad's standing in the middle of the living room. He looks

up when I walk in, his sharp brown eyes narrowed. He's not in his work jumpsuit, so he's not just getting home. Why is he here so early?

"Hello, Naveah." His voice is deep, neutral.

"Hey, Dad." I shuffle my feet, aching to go upstairs. But maybe this is fine and not the beginning of a fight. Maybe he's not still mad at me for this weekend. Okay, sure, I came home a little drunk and covered in hickeys, but in my defense, I didn't think he'd catch me. Who knew he'd be awake at five a.m. on a Sunday? How am I supposed to plan for that?!

"You're out late." His voice is still irritatingly calm.

"Yeah, I was—"

"Don't say work," he cuts me off. "I know your schedule."

"I wasn't gonna say that." I definitely was. I fold my arms, a little angry now too. When'd he get so good at catching me in a lie? "I was at Hallie's house."

Dad's eyes narrow. "I told you, you're grounded. You're supposed to come straight home after school and work."

Okay, yes, but he doesn't know about Hallie's breakup. He doesn't see how upset she is. And why am I grounded, anyway? I haven't been grounded in literal years, even though I've been going to parties since I started high school. It's not like he's been here for me; he's been checked out for a long time. I do everything for myself—cook, homework, actual work that pays me. I couldn't even get him to look over my job application. I left my résumé on the kitchen table, hoping he'd notice. After it didn't move for three days, I gave up and asked Hallie and Aunt

Cathy for help. They nitpicked it to death, which was annoying, but at least they tried. And I ended up getting the job anyway, without him. That was the last time I ever asked him for anything, and he never even mentioned it or apologized. So why does he suddenly care what I do?

"It was a party, Dad. I got back in one piece. What's the big deal?"

"The big deal is that you're disobeying me."

Oh, wonderful, here we go. Anger lances through me like a wildfire. "I'm not a prisoner. I have other shit to do than stay at home and stare at the wall—"

"Enough." Dad holds his hand up, and I want to yell at him some more, but he continues. "We'll talk about this later. I have something else to discuss with you."

"What?" I know I shouldn't snap at him, but I can't help it. We can't ever have a normal conversation.

Dad gives me a reproachful look but answers anyway. "I got a promotion."

Some of the anger dissipates and is replaced with shock. "Really? Like for real?"

The edge of his mouth quirks upward. He's barely smiled in three years, so I'm a little stunned. "Yes, like for real."

"Oh wow." I suddenly don't know what to do with my hands. I kinda want to hug him? But he's still mad at me, I'm still mad at him, I think, so I don't. "Congrats, Dad!"

"Thank you." He actually does seem a bit happier. Dad has a permanent serious expression, so it's nice to see a hint of joy on his face. "And with that promotion, I got a new schedule."

I'm half listening, thinking about what extra money can do for us. No more cheap toilet paper! "Oh yeah?"

"Yeah." Dad's tiny smile grows a little bigger. "I'll be home no later than six p.m. every night. No more coming home at midnight."

I nod happily at first, but as what he said sinks in, I freeze. His schedule is changing. Which means . . . he'll be here more often. And it'll be a lot harder to sneak out. "Oh."

Dad raises one eyebrow. His ghost of a smile is gone. "You don't seem excited."

"No, I am! It's cool! I just—"

"If you're thinking you won't be out at five o'clock in the morning anymore, you're correct."

Ah, shit. I knew it would circle back to that stupid party. "Dad, you're overreacting. And I'm always with Hallie when we go out, so it's not a big deal."

Dad's posture straightens, and he crosses his arms. "I've been meaning to talk to you about that. You spend too much time with Hallie."

"*What?*" I can't help but stare at him, open-mouthed. He *told* me to spend time at her place. At least at first, when he picked up second shift, I always stayed with Hallie after school. By the time he got home, I was getting ready for bed. "You want me to just sit at home by myself, then?"

Discomfort passes over Dad's face, but it quickly disappears. "I'll be home now, so I would like you to be here more, yes."

I shake my head in disbelief. I almost want to laugh, but I know that'd piss him off more. "This is so ridiculous. Why am

9

I suddenly in prison over one party? Like, Dad, come on—"

"Enough," he barks. "No more chances, Naveah. You're to come straight home after school, so I can watch you. You're out of control."

Out of control?! I go to school, I do my dumbass homework even though I couldn't care less, I go to work—why can't I have *one* night a month where I get to have fun? "This isn't fair, and you know it."

"I know you need to go to your room," Dad says. His voice is low and stern—no room for arguments.

I'm burning. He ignores me for three years and now suddenly I have to do whatever he says? I grit my teeth so I don't say anything I'll regret, turn on my heel, and march upstairs in frosty silence. When I get to my room and close the door, tears fill my eyes.

It wasn't always like this. We used to have fun. When I was little, we were inseparable. He'd take me to the park, birthday parties, the skating rink. We'd share Coke floats, and he'd help me with my homework when I was stuck. I used to look up to him, and every conversation wasn't full of tension. And now . . . I don't know what happened. I don't know why he doesn't trust me. Okay, well, I know he hates me going out, but I'm always with Hallie, and we watch each other's backs. I don't get it. It's like I don't even know him now. I haven't known him for a long time, I guess. I collapse on my bed and blink tears out of my eyes. This sucks. This sucks so much.

My phone buzzes, and I blink until I can read the screen. It's from Hallie.

> You let me fall asleep!

I sniff and smile miserably at her text. At least I have Hallie. For now. Until she goes to Carnegie Camp and leaves me alone with Dad for six weeks. God, this day is horrible.

> You needed your beauty sleep

> I thought you said I was an eleven?!

I laugh and send her a few kissing emojis. She doesn't reply right away, so I close my eyes. How am I gonna make it without her? I already dread coming home. It's too much. This is too much.

My phone buzzes again.

> I'm going back to bed. Love ya Nav

I hover my thumb over the keypad. I should tell her about Dad, but I can't. She's having a hard enough time already. And she's already hesitating about the camp, which she earned and deserves, so I shouldn't give her a reason to turn it down.

> Love ya babe.

I turn my phone over and close my eyes. It hasn't even started yet, but I feel like this might be the worst summer I've ever had.

CHAPTER 2

As I watch Hallie dribble a basketball, I try to figure out how to fix my life.

Every Monday, Tuesday, and Thursday, Hallie has basketball practice until five o'clock. I am not athletic or even remotely interested in sports, but I wait on the bleachers in the echoey gym because I don't have anything better to do. Okay, I'm supposed to be at home per Dad's new authoritarian regime, but he can't complain if I say I'm studying for finals. I'm not, but he doesn't have to know that.

Hallie shoots a free throw and misses it by a mile. Coach Underwood barks at her, and Hallie nods, her shoulders slumped. I frown, a little anxious. I'm worried about her. She's never taken a breakup so hard, and she's had six of them. Hallie is my best friend, but she has the absolute *worst* taste in partners. Douchebag guys and emotionally manipulative girls are the name of the game for her. It's infuriating because she gets so attached; I've told her a million times to just do something casual. That's what I do! I've never had an official girlfriend, but I've damn sure had my fun. But Hallie always gets super invested and then, inevitably, her heart broken. This time is different, though. She's never let it affect basketball, which she loves and is damn good at. She's never been in the "cry off and on" stage for so long. She's never asked me if something is wrong with her.

The bleachers squeak as someone climbs them close by, but I ignore the sound to glance back at my phone. A text from Dad.

Where are you? I'm at home.

Ugh. My torture has started. My thumb hovers over the text, unsure. I should tell him I'm at practice with Hallie, but he'll probably chew me out about that too. I've been thinking about what he said, that Hallie and I spend too much time together. What a load of horseshit. Hallie's been my best friend since we were in diapers, but now suddenly she's a bad influence? I swear it's like one day I'm minding my own business, doing my thing while he works and ignores me, and the next he's suddenly interested in being a parent again. But I'm not thirteen anymore; I don't need to be micromanaged. No one told him that, I guess.

The bleachers squeak again, and I look up. I blink in surprise—

Gia Flores is standing next to me.

We stare at each other for a second, both speechless. Twice in two days? I've never even talked to her before. I study her face a little closer this time. Tan skin a few shades lighter than Hallie's, dark, long wavy hair, those really cute glasses. She's wearing a white summer dress with a strawberry pattern, which is impressive since I can't ever be bothered to wear anything except jeans and a T-shirt. And her face is bright red, like she's about to pass out.

"Uh." I watch her warily. Maybe she wants to sell me something. I hope it's food because I could use some sadness snacks right now. Dad is stressing me out. "What's up?"

Gia opens her mouth, then closes it again. This happens several times, and she looks more and more distressed each time.

"Umm . . . are you okay?" Oh shit, is she in trouble? "Do you need help? Should I call someone—"

"No!" Gia finally speaks up, her voice high and squeaky. She takes a shuddery breath. "Y-You're Nav."

This is getting weird. But I'm also a little concerned she really might faint. "Yeah, I am."

"In art, seventh period."

I nod, confused. Does she want to talk about art? Sadly for her, I barely pay attention in there. We're on pastels right now, and I'm way better at painting with acrylics, so I've been doodling on my unfinished math homework the whole time.

Gia takes a few more breaths. She's standing so straight, knees locked, rigid. "I . . . can I ask you something?"

I frown up at her. "Yeah, but sit down first. You're scaring me."

She blinks, like she's just heard me talking. "Oh yeah, okay." Gia sits down next to me, several seats away. She already looks a bit better. "Sorry. Sorry, I'm . . . sorry."

"It's okay." I have no idea what's happening, but this is kinda fascinating. Way better than glaring at my phone. "What's up?"

Gia takes a shaky breath. "Sorry, we've never talked before.

14

And I'm going to ask for a huge favor, but I don't know what else to do." She fidgets, picking at the bottom of her dress with manicured nails. I wait for more, but she keeps staring down at her lap, fear frozen on her face.

Okay. Clearly whatever she's about to ask is a big deal. She can't ask me to help her cheat on exams, because I'm coasting through everything. Maybe she wants a hookup at the ice cream shop? I could do that, but it won't be free, I know that much. Either way, I need to wait. She looks like if I push her, she'll crumble to pieces.

"Take your time." I try to sound encouraging, even though I'm dying of curiosity.

Gia shoots me a quick, grateful look. She has really pretty brown eyes framed with long, dark lashes. "Sorry. I can do this." She closes her eyes for what has to be thirty seconds, but when she opens them, they have a determined glint. "You're friends with Hallie."

I glance at Hallie in surprise, who is running punishment laps for missing her free throw. She looks so pissed off it's kinda funny.

"Uh, yeah. I am."

"She helped me earlier this year." Gia's face is still tomato red and deeply serious. "And she's really good at basketball."

"Yeah," I say slowly. What on earth is this about?

"And she's really smart, and kind, and . . . pretty."

A light bulb goes off in my head. Oh, what do we have here? A secret crush on Hallie? My Thursday just got so much more interesting.

"You're into my friend, huh?" I can't keep a huge grin off my face, even as all of Gia's determination turns into raw panic. "Relax! Tell me more."

Gia really does look like she's gonna pass out. She's so nervous, it's adorable! "I—I think she's really cool. And, umm, I've been trying to ask her on a date for a while, but I chicken out every time."

I'm beaming. I love this shit so much. This has happened a few times before, but never with a girl! It's always idiot guys trying to get her number. At least Gia is cute. Ah, but wait . . . The image of Hallie crying herself to sleep last night pops into my head, and I hesitate. She might not be ready for a new relationship yet.

"I know it's a lot to ask," Gia babbles. Beads of sweat dot her hairline, poor girl. "But I know, I mean I've heard, you're good at flirting and stuff. I was hoping you could give me some tips. I . . . I'm not good at this."

"Well, I would love to introduce you two, but Hallie's actually having a hard time right now."

"Oh." Gia's face falls, and I feel a twinge of sympathy. "But maybe you could still give me tips? I know she's going to Carnegie soon, and I was hoping . . ."

Great, that damn camp again. I can't go anywhere without being reminded of it. "Well, you're probably going too, right? You can talk to her then."

Gia shakes her head. "Mami wants me to go, but . . . it's not really my, umm, thing. I think it's cool that Hallie is going, though. She's really smart."

I start to change the subject but freeze instead. Wait a minute. If Gia said no, there must be an extra spot open. Gia's mom is a sponsor for the camp . . . so if she said I could go . . .

I stand up, scaring Gia into silence. "Gia! Do you think you could get me into Carnegie Camp?"

Gia blinks. Her big brown eyes are wide with shock. "Probably not. I mean, it's full. No one ever drops out."

"But you said you might, right?"

Gia nods, and I can't keep the grin off my face. This is it. This is it! This will legit fix everything. I help Gia get a date, she gets me into Carnegie so I don't have to stay with Dad all summer, and Hallie gets a rebound so she's not crying all the time! I don't know if Hallie is ready, but she did say she wanted a distraction . . . And hey, this is a take-one-for-the-team moment. If I can get into Carnegie, we can party all summer. I can stop her when she falls in love with the wrong person again. Nothing has to change if I can make this happen.

"I'll do it." I grin at Gia's shocked face. "I'll get you that date, and in exchange, you can give me your spot at Carnegie Camp."

"I don't think it's that simple. Mami will murder me. But . . . if I drop out last minute, maybe the day before, maybe . . ." Gia trails off and I can practically see the gears turning in her head. She looks up at me, like a doe caught in a tractor trailer's high beams. "Can you really get me a date with Hallie? I mean, I don't want to bother her, but can you really?"

"Yes, ma'am, I can." I'm practically singing. This is it. This will all work out.

Gia twists a ring on her finger nervously. "But if I give up my spot, she'll be at camp all summer and I won't be there."

Hmm, true. I think for a second, tapping my foot. "Yes, but can you get a date without my help? Even if you spend six weeks with her at the camp, will you make a move?"

Gia's shoulders sag, and that twinge of sympathy returns. "No. I wouldn't."

"Okay, then. I'll get you a date, you spend four weeks hanging out before camp, then you do long-distance while Hallie and I are at camp. Sound good?"

The determined glint returns. Gia staggers to her feet and holds her hand out to me, a serious expression on her face. She looks like she's ready for war, not just going to the movies or something. "Okay. Deal."

I shake Gia's (very sweaty) hand and grin up at her. Thank you, Gia Flores, for saving my summer.

CHAPTER 3

When Hallie gets done with practice, I'm vibrating with energy. It was absolute torture to wait for five o'clock knowing I have the secret to saving our skins in my hands. I meet her by the locker room as she packs up her gym bag and backpack.

Hallie's changed into her normal clothes now (sweatpants and a K-pop shirt), but her hair is still wet with sweat. She wipes her face with a hand towel, groaning. "Nav, I'm gonna quit the team. I can't play anymore. I'm all washed up."

"No, you're not. You're just depressed because you let a dickhead trick you into thinking he was decent." I grin when she shoots me an annoyed glare. "Also, I have good news for you."

Hallie raises her eyebrows. She grabs her backpack from the floor and joins me at the door. "What is it?"

"You know Gia Flores?" I look for her, but she's already fled the gym.

"The girl who stopped at our table yesterday?"

"Yep. I know why she stopped." I can barely contain the glee swimming in my chest. "She has a crush on you."

Hallie's face lights up like the sun. "Shut up. You're kidding!"

"I never kid, babe."

Hallie's cheeks get a little pink, and she smiles, a genuine, delighted grin I haven't seen since that idiot broke her heart. I can't help but grin too as we walk down the empty school hallway, toward the parking lot. This really might be good for her. And me too, but she doesn't need to know that right now.

"How do you know?"

"She told me. While you were running laps." I hesitate. Hallie looks happy now, but I need to be sure. I don't want to hurt her to get away from Dad. "She gave me her number, but you don't have to take it."

Hallie's face turns thoughtful. "I don't know, it might be fun. She's kinda cute, right?"

I think of Gia's big, nervous brown eyes, a mushy feeling in my gut. She's adorable. *You're welcome, Hallie.* "Yeah, she is."

"Let's do it." Hallie looks at me, her expression a little more serious. "I can't mope around forever. I need to get back on the horse. Get out there, meet new people."

"And stop dating fuck boys."

Hallie laughs. "That too!"

"So it's a yes?"

"It's a yes. Give me her number."

I send it over in a text, practically singing at my good fortune. We end up talking about class and more about Hallie quitting basketball as we go out to the parking lot, so it's not until I'm home that I check my texts.

Hallie:

I texted her! It's a date for tomorrow!

Gia:

Thank you so much Nav. I owe you my life.

I smile at my phone. I text them both—Have fun!!

I lie down on my bed, hands resting on my stomach. I haven't felt this good since before the Carnegie Camp results were posted. It's smooth sailing from here on out.

♡ ♡ ♡

My manager, Ethan, yells at me to clean the front, and I groan. I don't have time to clean up a little kid's spilled ice cream; I'm waiting for Hallie or Gia to text me about the date.

It's Friday, and every Friday I work at my part-time job at Sweet Teeth. Yes, it's the worst name I've ever heard; yes, I've discussed with the owner that it sounds like Hannibal Lecter runs the place; no, she will not change it. It's an ice cream/sweets shop/bakery with bad decor and even worse staff. But the kids like it, and the owner, Shirley, makes a damn good red velvet cake. Somehow that combination keeps them breaking even every month.

I go to the front, and Ethan nods at me. "Man the register. I'm gonna go smoke."

AKA, dick around for an hour. "Fine. If you go to McDonald's, bring me a sweet tea."

Ethan makes an ugly face at me and doesn't answer. He goes to the back, and I hear the door open and close behind me. I drag a chair to the front and sit down behind the glass cases displaying ice cream and sweets, and stare at the soft yellow walls and horrible cartoon stickers adorning them. It's just me now, so I can do whatever I want until Ethan comes back.

I people-watch, my mind far away. I've been at Sweet Teeth for a while now, and I'm still in the same position as when

I started—all-purpose girl. Janitor, cash register attendant, cupcake maker, and occasional clown when Ethan doesn't feel like dressing up for the kids' birthday parties. I don't mind. I mean, okay, I would be a *way* better manager than Ethan, and everyone knows it, but he's Shirley's grandson so I know I'm not getting that promotion. I haven't even asked. Still, it hurts that I can't get recognized for the really freaking good job I'm doing. If I got sick or something, this place would be underwater. And Ethan would still find a way to blame me, I'm sure. I glare at the sickly yellow wall in front of me. I hope he spills my sweet tea all over his car.

A group of girls my age walks in, and I greet them, pushing the bitterness to the back of my mind. One of them meets my eyes, and she looks away, a shy smile on her lips. Oh, I think I know her. I search my brain, but all I can come up with is a hazy party with heavy bass and dim lights . . . and the taste of smeared lipstick on my tongue. I grin back at her, and she giggles a little but doesn't say anything as her group approaches the counter.

"Can I have some rocky road?" one of them says.

"For you? Absolutely. Cup or cone?"

I fill their orders and ring them up, and they all sit down at a nearby table. The girl from the party lingers at the register, almost like she wants to say something. I smile and wait, and I'm rewarded with a small, "You're Nav, right?"

"Yes, ma'am, I am." I'm remembering a little more of the party now. That was the one with the horrible country–hip-hop mash-up music. That was also the one where Hallie nearly killed me because she slams down beer like a frat boy and I could barely keep up. Worst hangover of my life. And then there was this girl from out of town, staying with her aunt, loves cute dogs and kissing me . . . "Rebecca, right?"

She brightens immediately. "Right! I didn't think you'd remember."

"I always remember the names of pretty girls."

Rebecca blushes a deep red, and my smile widens. Hallie would kill me for this. Says I'm leading people on. But what's a little harmless flirting? What's a little dancing at a party, a little drinking, a little kissing a stranger under blurry lights? Better than Hallie's strategy of getting into a relationship so deep she's depressed after it's over. Nothing's worth that kind of pain. I've never cried over a girl in my life, and I don't plan to start any time soon.

We chat for a few minutes, and she asks if I'm going to another party coming up, and I make a noncommittal promise that I might. Her friend group hovers near the door, making angry eyes at her, so I cut the conversation short. She waves shyly at me, and I wave back, watching them leave with my hand under my chin. Now, see? Fun, short, a perfect time waster. Maybe we'll meet again at the next party, maybe not. There's no need to fall in love with everyone I meet.

Speaking of which . . . I glance at my message-less phone, reminded of the date. It was supposed to start at seven, at our rival ice cream store, Ivan's. I would normally object to anyone going to Ivan's ever (they don't even use real milk!), but I didn't want to spy on their date. They can bond over how fake the "ice cream" tastes.

After that, I get so busy cleaning counters and serving cupcakes and winking at a new girl that I forget to check my phone. It's 8:06 before I look again, and I still don't have a single text. They must be having a good time! My chest swells with happiness and pride. This is the easiest thing I've ever done. I should monetize this. I should be a matchmaker *and* ice cream server.

I text Gia first. tell me how it goes! She doesn't answer, which is good. I bet they're having a fantastic time. Matchmaker Nav, I charge $20K per hour.

I text Hallie next. tell me how it goes!

I turn my screen off, but it lights up a second after.

Hallie:

Omg can I call you??

Oh shit. That does not sound like a having-a-fantastic-time text.

I sneak into the back and touch the phone icon under Hallie's name. She picks up on the first ring.

"Nav, oh my *God*." She sounds slightly out of breath, but not panicked or anything.

"Umm, you okay? What happened?"

"Yeah! But that was the weirdest date I've ever had."

Oh shit, that is not a having-a-fantastic-time sentence. "What do you mean?"

"Gia didn't talk the whole time."

I can't even comprehend her words for a second. "I . . . what?"

"Yeah. *Yeah.* The whole time, Nav!" There's a little

bewilderment in Hallie's voice, a little amusement too. "I met her at Ivan's, and she was wearing this super cute dress and the cutest sandals. And I thought she was just nervous, but she legit didn't say a word for the whole hour. I even had to order her ice cream."

Oh my God. "Oh my God."

Hallie keeps talking, but I'm feeling kinda lightheaded. I knew Gia was nervous, but I didn't think she'd mess it up this badly! The plan is falling apart before my eyes. The opportunity to get away from Dad and spend the summer with Hallie is crumbling through my fingers.

"Can I call you back?"

"Oh, sure. You okay?"

I mutter some reassurances and hang up. I call Gia immediately, but she doesn't answer. I try again, no answer. I send her a text.

> answer your phone right now or I'll kill you

She doesn't text back, but when I call her the third time, she answers.

"Gia, what the fuck?"

"I—I—" Gia's voice is muffled and far away. "I'm s-so sorry, Nav. I don't know." She sniffs delicately, and the smallest sob escapes her throat.

Wait a minute, she's *crying*. All the shock and anger are replaced with pity in an instant. "Okay, okay, calm down. Don't cry."

25

"I can't!" Gia wails. "I g-got there and she was so p-pretty and I felt like garbage even being near her."

Jesus. I didn't know it was this bad. "Okay, stay calm. Give me a second."

I keep her on speaker while I text Hallie.

> if she talked next time would you give her a second chance?

Hallie texts back immediately. Yeah! She was cute. Maybe just nervous?

Okay. I take a deep breath. Not dead in the water yet. "Gia? You still there?"

"Y-Yeah." She sounds so miserable, the poor girl.

"I texted Hallie. She said she'd give you a second chance if you can talk next time."

I hear a slight gasp. "Really?"

"Really. But that's probably your *last* chance." I pace the length of Sweet Teeth, ignoring the merry tinkle of the front door, signaling customers. "We've gotta do something. We need to make sure you don't freeze up next time."

"I can't do a next time, Nav." The pain in her voice threatens to break my heart. "Let's forget it, okay? I'll go to camp like normal and maybe there . . ."

Fear rushes into my system. No! I can't let her give up. Horrible images of me fighting with Dad and staring at the wall for weeks on end float in my brain. I really need this to work out for my own sake, but a small tug of pity makes me want this to work out for Gia too.

"No, we will not be giving up. It'll be fine. We're gonna practice." I nod feverishly to myself, still pacing. "That's it! I'm good at this, like you said. I'll teach you."

"Teach me what?"

"Romance. Confidence. Whatever it takes to get you a good first date."

Gia is silent for a long time. Then, she sniffles again. "A-Are you sure?"

"I'm sure. I'll meet you after school. We've got this, Gia."

She's quiet but then she says, very softly, "Thank you, Nav."

A customer aggressively dings the bell near the register, and I take a deep breath. "You're welcome. Romance lessons start on Monday."

I hang up and rub my face with both hands. Okay, not as easy as I thought, but I can do this. I can coach Gia; I know how to flirt. Even better, I know Hallie, what she likes, what she responds to. We can do this. We have four weeks between now and when Hallie leaves for camp. Four weeks to take Gia from silent horror to can't-resist-a-date material. Four weeks to make sure I can get my ticket away from Dad and save this disastrous summer from crashing and burning.

Okay, Nav. Here we go.

CHAPTER 4

stay here after the bell.

I send Gia a text near the end of art, balancing my phone on my knee under the table so Mrs. Finch won't catch me. Though she probably wouldn't care; we're done with our final projects, which count as our exams, so this week we're just doodling and listening to her tell the story—for the thousandth time—of when she went to Paris.

I sit behind Gia, who sits near the front of the class, bless her, so I see the exact moment when she gets my message. Her shoulders go rigid, and she immediately starts bouncing her leg and chewing on her left thumbnail. She turns slightly toward the door, like she's thinking of bolting from the room mid–Paris speech.

Great sign for upcoming romance lessons.

By some miracle, Gia doesn't run from the room screaming for the rest of class. The bell rings, and everyone gets up to go, except for us. Gia turns to look at me over one shoulder as if she were facing a firing squad.

I shake my head and go to her table. We're the only people in the art room now; Mrs. Finch tries to escape quicker than we do. I sit on the tabletop and smile. Hopefully it'll put her at ease and not make her pass out.

"Calm down, Gia. I'm not gonna kill you."

"I know." Gia looks up at me reproachfully, like she's not the one quaking in her very cute boots. "I'm just nervous."

"I haven't said anything yet!"

"I'm scared of what you *will* say."

Jesus. This is gonna be a long session.

"All right, let's get straight to it. What happened Friday night?"

I'm surprised and horrified when Gia's eyes fill with tears. "I—I got to Ivan's and I froze. I choked. She was so gorgeous and I'm just . . . me. So I couldn't say anything to her because she deserves better."

Okay, lots to unpack here. "First of all, Hallie is gorgeous all the time, so you're gonna have to get over that."

Gia's face pinches, like she's having a particularly bad stomach cramp, but she doesn't say anything.

"And second, what does 'just me' mean?"

Gia shrugs, avoiding eye contact. She's looking directly at my chin, where I know a pimple resides. Rude. "I don't know. Like Hallie is perfect. And I'm not."

"You don't have to be perfect to get with Hallie. If you're not a sociopath or an asshole, you're miles ahead of the competition." I shudder as I remember Ashley, who, I kid you not, threatened to stab me with her hair clip if I didn't stop hanging around Hallie so much. Never mind how many times I explained to her that I was not and never will be interested in Hallie; we were raised together since birth so it would be like dating my sibling. My explanations meant nothing to Ashley's murderous tendencies, though. "But you do have to be able to talk to her."

Gia sighs, her gaze dropping from my chin to her lap. "Which is impossible."

"Not impossible. You're talking to me right now!"

"Yeah, but I don't like you."

"Umm, *ouch*, Gia. Break my heart, why don't you?"

Gia finally meets my eyes, hers huge and round. A blotchy red blush creeps up her neck and into her face. "Oh God, I didn't mean that! I mean like, romantically. I do like you, in a neutral way? I mean, we don't really know each other that well because this is only the third time we've talked, so I can't really say if I like you as a person or not—"

I hold up a hand to stop her from digging her grave further. I guess I can add socially awkward in all ways, not only romantic, to my list of things I know about Gia. "I get it. This is business. I help you woo my friend, you help me get into Carnegie. Maybe it'll help us both if we think about it that way."

Relief flashes over Gia's face and she nods. "I can do that. Thanks again."

"No problem. And hey, you're paying me, right?" I wink at her, but she just blinks owlishly back. Jeez, I guess I'm genuinely not her type. "Okay, first things first—I need to know how bad things are. We know you can't talk to Hallie face-to-face, but what about calling her?"

Gia shakes her head so hard I'm scared her neck will snap.

"Okay, how do we feel about texting Hallie?"

"Bad. Real bad."

"Okay . . . can we *think* about Hallie?"

Gia is silent, but her face turns that splotchy red again, so I have my answer.

This may actually be a disaster.

"All right. New plan. Finals are coming up, so we really don't have time to address this right now anyway. When's your last one?"

"Wednesday."

"Good, mine too. Text me your address and we'll meet at your house after school."

Gia's brow furrows. "Why at my house?"

Well, really it's because I don't want Dad to see me not studying or whatever, which would end up in another verbal boxing match. But she doesn't need to know that. "You'll probably feel more comfortable practicing there."

"Oh! Good idea." She gives me a small, timid smile. "I really appreciate this, Nav. And I'm sorry for what I said earlier. I do like you. In a business way."

I let out an involuntary snort. These will be a long four weeks, but maybe not bad ones. "I like you in a business way too, Gia. See you on Wednesday."

♡ ♡ ♡

I paint my toenails, the tip of my tongue stuck out in concentration, while Hallie rattles off biology vocab words.

"What's a biome?"

I carefully dab a drop of blush pink polish onto my pinkie toe before answering. "Deodorant. The extra-strength kind."

Hallie giggles, and I grin at my bare feet. We're in her room, where I spend most of my time. It's really my second home, if

I'm honest. I know the random assortment of K-pop posters, light pink walls, trophies for everything from spelling bees to every sport Hallie's ever tried, and plain blue comforter as well as my own home. Those are the constants, though; everything else in the room changes depending on who Hallie's with. For a while, it was full of old-school horror movie memorabilia, which I gleefully helped trash when Hallie broke up with one of her girlfriends. There's been western themes, space themes, really obscure anime figurines that cost a fortune for some unfathomable reason. I'm relieved that Peter's mark—bonsai tree shaping, like *why*, Hallie—is absent and hopefully in the garbage where it belongs.

We're supposed to be studying, but I'm bored and vaguely anxious. Dad's at the house right now, waiting to pounce on me. He told me to come straight there from school, but after hanging out with Gia, I wanted to be around my best friend. And not him. Which, if his angry texts mean anything, he does not understand.

"Come on, be serious." Hallie smacks my arm with her rolled-up notes. She's a meticulous notetaker—the kind of nerd who has highlighters and tabs in her binders. I used to tease her about it, but that's just Hallie. "Where is the bicuspid valve located?"

"I don't know, but it sounds gross."

Hallie groans as I laugh. "Nav, you're gonna fail if you don't study."

"I've already studied. Just not that particular gross word." I lay back, my head on her lap, and do my best impression of a puppy dog. "Come on, I'm bored. Let's take a break! Please?"

I expect Hallie to laugh and agree, but her frown deepens. "We need to study, Nav."

My smile fades too. This is how our study sessions usually go—Hallie tries to lead, I distract her with fun things, she caves. Why is it different today? I must look troubled because Hallie's expression softens, and she taps my forehead with her notes. "Twenty minutes. And then we're going over the parts of the heart again."

I grin up at her. Maybe I'm reading into things too much. "Deal. Tell me something interesting. Is Sarah still having her wild birthday party?" Sarah Knight is on Hallie's basketball team, and her parents are out of town a lot for work. They also buy lots of beer and have a bad memory, so she's thrown some really great parties.

"Yep. It's a little later this year because her parents are actually going to be in town for her birthday. For once."

I grimace at the ceiling. Don't I know how that feels. My birthday's in August, and I'm lucky if Dad manages to dig up an off-season Christmas card.

"We have to bring her a present, though. Last year she cried because everyone wanted the free beer and didn't bring her anything. And she's still upset about Jakobe."

Now I feel bad. I'm definitely one of the ones who just wanted the free beer. "Deal. Are she and Jakobe still broken up?"

"Yeah, but it's been a real shit show. You know he showed up at her house to beg for another chance?"

"Eww! Creepy!"

33

"You think? It's kind of romantic." Hallie gets a wistful gleam in her eyes. "I wish Peter would do that."

"Hey," I say, a warning in my voice. "We're not doing that tonight."

Hallie sighs, a deep, heavy one that makes her sound a hundred years old. "I don't know, Nav, this one hurt."

"But why? He wasn't even the best-looking one."

"It's not that. I just—I believed him, you know? When he said it would be forever." Hallie's face falls, and she looks to the floor, like she can't bear to meet my eyes. "I tried so hard to be the perfect girlfriend, and it didn't matter. It's always like this. And it's like—what am I doing wrong?" Hallie's voice breaks and she takes a shaky breath. "Maybe I'm not good enough for anyone."

I sit up, my teasing mood gone. How can she think this, when that idiot cheated on her? How can she think this, when Gia is somewhere out there probably hyperventilating over the mere thought of their date? I've been Nice Nav for two weeks, but maybe she needs another dose of Real Nav.

"Hey, look at me." I wait until she does, and then I stare straight into her eyes. "I don't ever want to hear you say that shit again. You *are* good enough, Hallie. I don't see the point of dating, but even I know you just haven't found the right person. Of course you're not gonna be with worms-for-brains forever. But listen, like really listen to me, okay? You don't need him. You actually don't need anyone. You're trying to fill a void, but that void doesn't exist. You're a whole ass beautiful person all by yourself. You're smart, you're talented, and you don't need

34

anyone to say that to validate the truth. Hell, you don't even need *me* to say that. Nothing is wrong with you. You're fine as you are."

I stop, unsure if I've overstepped. Hallie doesn't say anything at first; her eyes are huge, like saucers, and she's still looking right at me. She doesn't seem sad or upset, though. She looks kind of stunned.

I wait, fidgeting. And shit, I said all that and I'm supposed to be setting her up with Gia! God, I'm stupid.

"If you still want to find someone," I add hastily, "I'll support you. I just wanted to, umm, say that." I shut my mouth, and Hallie blinks. She smiles at me, a rare tentative one.

"Thanks, Nav. I . . . No, never mind. Thank you."

"Are you sure?" I pick at the brand-new paint job on my nails. "You can tell me if I went too far and was an asshole."

Hallie laughs, and the weird, nervous energy in the air pops like a balloon. "You're always an asshole, so there's no point in saying that."

"I'll add that to my résumé: 'perpetual asshole.'"

Hallie rolls her eyes and smacks my arm again. "I'm about to turn into one if we don't study."

I complain, but eventually, I open my biology book to study the parts of the human heart. Hallie snuggles close to me, and even though I hate biology, I don't hate this. I don't hate being close to my best friend in the world, horrific taste in partners and all.

CHAPTER 5

I glance at the address Gia texted me, and then at the house it allegedly belongs to, mouth hanging open like a fish. It's Wednesday after my last final and I'm free of school for the next two and a half months. Thank the summer gods. Now I'm at Gia's for some romance practice, like I promised. Except . . . I'm sitting in front of a mansion. I'm not kidding—this house has to have at least eight bedrooms and a million bathrooms. There are seventeen windows; I count them three times to be sure. It has fancy topiaries shaped into oblong shapes near the porch, a huge, immaculate front yard, a circle driveway, and a *fountain*?! There's literally a stone fountain merrily spitting water to the sky in her front yard. No way.

I call Gia. She picks up on the second ring.

"Hello?"

"Hey. I think I'm lost."

"Oh no." Worry hangs heavy in her voice. "Did you take a right or left by Dairy Queen? That always messed me up at first."

"No, I'm at the address you sent. But this cannot be your house. There's a *fountain* in your front yard."

Gia pauses for a second, and then lets out a loud laugh in my ear. She doesn't say anything, but fifteen seconds later, the front door of the mansion opens and Gia appears on the porch.

I shake my head and get out of my car. I'd heard the Floreses had money, but I didn't know they had *money* money. I can't believe I'm about to step inside a real-life mansion. I wander up to the front porch, which is quite a hike from her driveway, and Gia gives me a shy wave. She's wearing a plain orange sundress with a white ribbon on the waist, and dinosaur-patterned black leggings. Wait, are those dinosaurs wearing sunglasses? How is Gia so cute? Hallie is so freaking lucky.

I smile at Gia, trying to recover from the whiplash of information assaulting my brain. "You could have told me you were ultrarich."

"Sorry," Gia says, opening her door wide. "I forget sometimes."

"That's just what a rich person would say."

Gia rolls her eyes, which surprises me. She actually looks annoyed. Normally I'd apologize, but this is kind of good, isn't it? So far, the only emotions I've seen from Gia are terror and I'm-about-to-faint. It's a good thing that she's comfortable enough to be irritated with me now.

We don't say anything else as Gia leads me inside. I kick off my shoes at the door and wander behind her, starstruck. The floor is covered in gray and white tile that probably cost more than my entire house, and there's a giant, wrought iron staircase in the middle of the room, probably leading upstairs to bedrooms. A cavernous living room sits behind it, full of weirdly eclectic furniture, including a green couch and three cozy-looking gray chairs, with a magnificent stone fireplace in the middle of the wall. Every room is full of warm sunlight thanks to the massive windows I spied out front. I'm overwhelmed. I haven't even seen the kitchen yet.

"Let's go to—" Gia starts, but something moves at the top of the staircase and startles me out of my dumbstruck stupor. A dog barks and runs down the steps to greet us. When it gets close enough for me to see, I gasp. It's a corgi! A tan, black, and white loaf of bread with cute triangle ears and stubby legs!

The dog barks again, and I almost push Gia out of the way to tackle it with a hug. It jumps into my arms, and I can barely hold in a delighted scream.

"Look at this!! Look at this baby!!"

Gia watches me, an amused look on her face. "I guess you like dogs."

"You bet your ass I do!" We used to have a dog, but Cuddles the miniature poodle is no longer with us. Not dead, but gone all the same. I hug the corgi tight, burying my face in its soft fur. It wriggles and tries to lick me all over, and I'm pretty sure I'll die of happiness if it continues. "What's its name?"

"Her name is Jordan."

At the sound of her name, Jordan looks at Gia, bat ears twitching.

"Sorry, Gia, Jordan is my dog now. I'm stealing her."

Gia rolls her eyes again, but this time there's no trace of irritation. She has a small, tentative smile instead. "Come on, let's go to my room. Jordan too."

I follow Gia up the steep staircase, placing Jordan on the ground halfway because I need my hands to help haul my big ass up these steps. Jordan hops up the steps happily, cute pink tongue lolling as she waddles to the top. God, I love Gia's life.

Gia leads me to the first room on the right and pushes open her door. I pause in the doorway, stunned again. Gia's room is huge, at least twice the size of mine. But it's also a wreck. She has a collection of beanbags surrounding a TV with a shiny gaming console underneath, and they're surrounded by half-eaten snacks. There's a desktop computer next to her window, which is also covered in snack bags, and there are dirty clothes and blankets thrown in the corners of her room. Notes and textbooks and highlighters litter her floor. She did not clean up for me at all, which I kind of like. I feel like I know her better now. Gia Flores, socially awkward and messy as hell.

"Sorry," Gia says, gazing at her room like she's seeing it for the first time. "I guess I should have cleaned before you got here."

I laugh and sit down on one of her beanbags. "Don't worry about it." I pat the beanbag beside me, which is in the shape of Snorlax. I'm sitting on a purple Pokémon whose name escapes me. I haven't seen *Pokémon* in a while, but I recognize the face. "Come sit, let's chat."

Nervous Gia is back. She fidgets with the bottom of her dress but sits next to me anyway. "Do you . . . have a plan?"

"I do. I think we jumped the gun a little on Monday. Let me ask you a few questions."

Gia nods, her brown eyes wide and worried. Jordan wanders to her and nudges her hands, and Gia pets her head absently. "Okay, I'm ready."

"Relax, it's not an exam. I just want to ask: Why do you like Hallie?"

Gia blinks at me, and then a dreamy smile blooms on her face. "Hallie is so cool, you know? And she helped me out one time."

"You mentioned that before. What happened?"

"Well, you know I'm new here, this year? And it's hard moving in the middle of the semester, in the middle of junior year. I should be used to it because Mami and I move a lot, but it sucks. Everyone has their own friends by the time I get there."

A pang of sympathy aches in my chest. I didn't try to talk to her when she first got here either. I should have. I could have at least been friendly in art.

Gia continues, oblivious to my guilt. "One time, in March, I was having a really shitty day. Mr. Carter yelled at me for being late, and I'd left my biology homework at home, and my sketch wasn't going well. And then all my books fell out of my locker. Like, *all* of them. There were pens and stuff everywhere. I was about to cry."

"And Hallie helped you?"

Gia nods, fidgeting with her ring. "Hallie helped me pick everything up. She didn't have to, but she did."

That's definitely something Hallie would do. She was always the kinder of us both, and she's friendly in a way I can never be.

I have a lot of acquaintances, but Hallie has a lot of friends. I have exactly one friend, so that should say how I feel about that.

"That's so sweet, Gia."

Gia smiles at her hands, redness creeping up her neck. "And—there's something else."

"Oh yeah?"

"You can't laugh."

"No promises."

Gia shoots me a reproachful look but continues anyway. "Hallie is . . . well, she, umm, fits . . ."

"Fits what?"

Gia takes a shaky breath and closes her eyes. "She's my dream girl."

My eyebrows shoot to my hairline, and a loose grin slides onto my lips. "I'm sorry, your what?"

"I said you can't laugh." Gia groans. She hugs Jordan to her chest, and the dog licks her chin.

"I'm not laughing, I'm just interested!" I'm lying. I'm laughing. What on earth is she talking about? "Explain it to me."

"I mean, everyone has a dream girl, right?" In response to my blank stare, Gia sighs. "Okay, maybe I'm weird. But in my head, when I think of who would be the perfect girl for me, I always think of someone like Hallie."

"Like . . . kind?"

"Yes, but also athletic. I'm not athletic at all, and when I watch people play sports . . ."

I nod sagely. "Athletic girls are hot."

41

Gia grins at me. "You get it. And Hallie is taller than me. That's pretty rare because I'm tall too. I always wanted to be the little spoon."

It's hard to hold in a laugh at that, but I manage. This is kind of adorable. "Okay, so we agree that you are physically attracted to Hallie."

Gia's blush deepens, but she nods.

"And you think her personality is good too."

"Right."

"Anything else?"

Gia's eyebrows furrow like she's deep in thought. "I don't know, it's . . . everything? I love that she's so smart. She gets the best grades, and that makes me want to try harder too. And she's always reading a new book every week, and when I look them up online, they all sound really fascinating. And she does this thing with her hair when she's taking a test, where she tugs on her bangs when she's thinking . . ." Gia trails off, suddenly nervous again. "Umm, is that enough?"

A slow smile spreads on my face. If Hallie heard all this, she'd have a heart attack from happiness. She's moping around about not being good enough, and here Gia is failing her tests because she's too busy watching Hallie stress-pull her hair out.

"That's enough. I can work with this." I nod to myself, thinking of a plan. I wanted to know what exactly Gia liked about Hallie and if this was a throwaway crush or something more, and obviously this is something more. Gia is full-blown smitten with Hallie, which is great because Hallie is always looking for that deeper connection. Plus, Hallie already had a positive interaction with her, and she agreed to give her a second chance. We're off to a good start.

"What do we do now?" Gia asks after a moment of silent thinking.

"Let's practice." I stand up, and Gia mimics me, frowning. "Dates are off-limits right now, but we have to work on conversation skills."

"Okay," Gia says, but she's shaking a little again.

"All right, I'll pretend to be Hallie. Just talk to me like you would her." I search my pockets for the hair tie I brought along. I don't use them often, since I chopped off my hair and buzzed the sides (now *that* was a great day. I swear Hallie's mom nearly fainted); I don't have to do much maintenance for the fuzzy mess that's on top. I pull my loose curls into a horrible ponytail at the crown of my head, which I'm sure looks hideous. Close enough to Hallie's long one, I hope. "See? I'm Hallie now."

Gia laughs, but it's strained. "Okay. Wh-what do I say?"

"Whatever you want."

Gia stares at me, so I elaborate.

"Normal stuff! Here, I'll start. Hi, Gia, fancy meeting you here."

"We're in my room?"

"No, we're at Ivan's, on a date!"

"Oh. Then that means we walked in together."

Jesus. Tough crowd. "Focus on the conversation, not where

we hypothetically are. *Anyway*, I'm Hallie, as you know. How are you?"

"Umm." Gia shifts from foot to foot, staring down at her hands. Jordan looks up at her, ears pressed against her skull. "I'm, umm, good."

Well, that's a lie. She looks like she'll collapse any second. I wait for her to ask me how I am, but it never comes. She keeps her gaze focused on her feet.

"Okay . . . how were your exams?"

Gia opens her mouth to answer me, but nothing comes out. She starts shaking, her hands tangled in the bottom of her dress, and her shoulders heave up and down at a rapid pace, like she's just finished running.

No, like she's having a panic attack.

"Shit, Gia, are you okay?" I run to her side, and Jordan does too, whimpering and barking. Gia falls to her knees and Jordan jumps into her arms, licking her face and forcing her to hold her. All I can do is put a hand on her shoulder. "Gia? Gia, talk to me."

"S-Sorry." Gia's voice is so quiet I can barely hear her. She hugs Jordan tight, and the sweet dog doesn't try to get away. She whines and licks Gia's chin.

"It's okay, we can stop. I'm a terrible actress anyway."

Gia laughs, and even though it's quiet, it seems to help. Her breathing gets better, and soon, she's able to look at me. She gives me a wobbly smile that threatens to break my heart. "Sorry, Nav. I . . . I don't think I was ready to pretend to be on a date."

"Yeah, no kidding." I stand first and offer my hand to Gia. She takes it, and I help her to her feet. "First, are you sure you're okay? Do you need anything?"

"No, I'm good now. Promise."

"You sure? Really?"

"Really. Let's try again." She hugs Jordan one more time and then puts her down. Jordan doesn't leave her side, looking up at her intently. Oh—I get it now. Jordan must be a therapy dog. She's probably trained to help Gia through her panic attacks.

I look at Gia, who is still shaking slightly, and my respect for her goes up by a thousand percent. She's trying so hard at something that has to be so painful for her, and she's not giving up. Warmth fills my whole body. I don't believe in love, but damn do I want to make sure Gia finds some version of it.

"Okay. But I'm not Hallie." I tug my hair out of the ponytail and smooth it down. "I'm Nav. We're just talking, like we've done before."

"Got it," Gia says, frowning fiercely.

"Good. Tell me three things about yourself. I'll start—I'm Nav Hampton, I work at Sweet Teeth, and I definitely failed my bio exam."

Gia lets out a breathy laugh. "I'm sure you didn't fail."

"Oh, I definitely did. But your turn."

Gia takes a shuddering breath. "I-I'm Gia Flores. And I have a dog named Jordan. And I . . . really hate spaghetti."

I smile and nod at her. "Good. That's a start. We're done for today."

Gia's brow furrows. "That's it? But we only have four weeks—"

"Pushing now won't help you later. We made progress. You told me you don't like spaghetti, which I didn't know five seconds ago. We're doing fine."

Gia looks at me, right into my eyes, and gratitude blossoms all over her face. "Thanks, Nav."

"You're welcome." I back up a few steps, and Jordan watches my movements, panting happily. She's calm, so Gia must be calm too. "Now, are you gonna be a good host and show me around your manor?"

Gia smiles. She strokes Jordan's head and goes to the door, still a little shaky but calming down by the second. "Let's start the tour."

CHAPTER 6

I sit in my car for a while after I get home, staring into my illuminated living room. I can see Dad's shadow through the translucent curtain, passing in and out of view. He's pacing.

I'm in trouble.

I spent an hour gawking at Gia's house. She has a *pool*, an actual pool with clear blue water, lounge chairs, and a separate pool house, a hot tub, and a sauna. I won't step foot near that watery death trap, but I was still stunned speechless. Talk about rich bitch energy. I wanted to stay longer, but I could tell Gia was exhausted from the panic attack, so I left right after the tour. It's not even dark right now. But I also didn't text Dad to tell him where I was going, which I'm now seeing was a big mistake.

After Dad makes his third lap around the living room, I close my eyes for strength and unbuckle my seat belt. I have to get it over with quick, like ripping off a Band-Aid. I walk to the front door and turn the knob. It's open, again. Oh boy.

When I round the corner, Dad isn't pacing anymore. He's standing in the middle of the living room, arms folded. He's still in his work jumpsuit, so he probably just got home. I was so close! If I hadn't gotten distracted by the tiny soaps in Gia's guest bedroom, I probably would have made it.

"Hey, Dad."

"Naveah." Dad's voice is even, but he's standing still as stone. "You're out late."

"Good thing it's summer," I joke.

Dad's eyes narrow, and I wince. Wrong move.

"It's Wednesday," Dad barks. "A school night."

"Normally, yes, but I finished all my exams. So it's summer for me."

Dad blinks, like I've surprised him. I'm surprised too—I get a tiny twinge of disappointment. I guess I wanted Dad to know my school schedule. I shouldn't be shocked that he doesn't.

"Anyway," Dad says, his voice shaking a little, "I told you to come home straight after school. If school is out, you shouldn't have been studying."

Well, he's got me there. My shoulders slump wearily; I'm not in the mood for this. "Maybe I wanted to unwind after finishing my finals?"

Dad shakes his head. "You're always unwinding. I tell you, you spend way too much time with Hallie. You're at her house more than your own home."

I stare at him for a second, at a loss for words. Why does this always come back to me and Hallie? "Dad, I wasn't even at Hallie's house."

Dad blinks again, seemingly stunned. "I . . . oh. Where else would you be?"

Where else would I be? Seriously? It's like he doesn't think I have any other friends. And I'm mad that he's right!

The anger rises in me like a pot of water coming to boil. "It's none of your business where I go."

The confusion evaporates from Dad's expression, and it's replaced with fury. "You're not gonna talk to me like that."

"Why not? You don't get to tell me where I can and can't go."

"I can, and I will, because I'm your father—"

"First time you've started acting like it in a while."

I wince internally. I didn't mean to say that. It's true, but I shouldn't have said it. Now I *know* Dad's gonna be pissed, and we'll be in an all-out screaming war in a few seconds. I steel myself, standing straighter, arms to my sides. I wait for Dad to start yelling at me, like always.

But he doesn't.

It's a tiny moment, one I might have missed if I wasn't looking right at him, but the anger melts from his face and is replaced by an emotion I hardly ever see on him—

Hurt.

Before I can comprehend what just happened, Dad steps away from me. "Go to your room, Naveah." His voice is terribly quiet. And I'm so shocked and confused that I listen to what he said and climb the carpeted steps to my room without another word.

I lean against my closed bedroom door, too stunned to even think. Dad's expression sticks in my mind and guilt twists in my gut like a coiled snake. I didn't know he'd be hurt by what I said. Mad I was disrespectful, yes, but hurt? I don't understand. He's the one who ignored me for three years. He's the one who never showed up for any award program at school, who never so much as wished me good luck on a test, my first day at Sweet Teeth, the application for Carnegie Camp. I'm the one who tried, so many times, to reach out; he made it clear that wasn't what he wanted, so I backed off. Gave up. He's the one who set the pace, and I've been following his lead. Until now, for some reason. I don't understand him at all.

I collapse on my bed and turn my phone on, feeling low. I don't have any texts, and I'm not in the mood for doomscrolling, so I open the Galaxy Cat app.

Galaxy Cat is quite possibly the worst game in existence. It's not even a game really; it's just collecting as many cats in the same sitting position with different skins as humanly possible. It's the oldest game on my phone. It's survived two new phones and a dunk in the toilet and several cracks in the screen. I have over a hundred cats now, though I don't even like the things. And the skins are so stupid—why do I have to collect not only the green alien skin but also the red, blue, and yellow ones? It's the same fucking cat, but in a different color. If I think about it too long, I fly into a rage.

But despite all that, I play it because I started it the day Mom left us. There's a huge counter in the top left corner, proudly announcing how many days I've played in a row. How many days I've spent without her. We're up to 1,136 now. When I got to a thousand, I threw a pathetic party for myself, which ended in me getting horribly drunk and waking up face down in my empty bathtub. Looking forward to day 1,250.

I do the mindless mini game I've done literally hundreds of times to collect galaxy scrolls to summon more repeat cats until a text from Hallie saves me from death by boredom.

Just woke up from my post finals crash.
I AM FINALLY FREE

I smile and tap her text. Galaxy Cat mercifully disappears in favor of her chat. I type out a reply. time to get shitfaced to celebrate

Not yet. Let me get a few more naps in. She adds a snoring emoji, and I laugh. I'm about to tease her when she texts again. Where'd you go after your exam? I waited but Mr. Kelso said you were gone.

I hesitate. I could tell her about Gia, but damn do we have a long way to go. I'm scared if I say anything, I'll jinx the little progress we've made and my fragile plan will go belly-up.

it's a secret. I add a kissing emoji. She sends an angry devil face back, and I laugh.

You know I hate surprises

yeah but not this one ☺

We end up talking about how we did on our exams (I passed everything, though that D was real close to an F in biology for me, while Hallie got all A's on everything, the bastard), but somehow we circle around to Dad. I tell Hallie what happened today, and she sends me a stream of curses.

> He's got a lot of nerve acting like you're the bad guy. When was the last time he cared?

I wince. She's right, and it's exactly what I've been thinking, but it hurts to see it in writing. Dad doesn't care about me, and I know that, but his sudden interest is so . . . weird. Is he sick? Did he have a near-death experience at work? I don't get it. I don't say any of this to Hallie, though. Hallie and I don't talk about Dad often. My mom, ever. It's a taboo between us, and for almost three years, I've been fine with that. Now, gnawing worry eats at my chest. I wish it wasn't taboo, just once.

But instead, I type: forget it. wanna watch movies tomorrow to celebrate surviving?

Deal, Hallie types. My turn to pick. Halloween here we come.

I groan and make such a big deal out of Hallie's horrible taste in movies that I forget about Dad altogether.

CHAPTER 7

"We're out of bonbons," Ethan grunts at me.

I pause in my balancing act of tipping back in my chair. I'm behind the counter, staring at an empty store. Now that it's officially summer, I can take the grown-up, all day shifts Ethan is too lazy to do. More money, but also more mornings like this, where I stare at my reflection in the ice cream scoopers for three uninterrupted hours. I'm so bored I could die. "And this is my problem, why?"

Ethan mimes kicking my chair out from under me, but I don't flinch. He won't. He doesn't have the guts. "It means someone has to replace them."

Ah, the mythical "someone." AKA, the only one of us who can make sweets. "Eventually, you're gonna have to learn how to do this job by yourself. What happens when I graduate, huh?"

"I'll hire a different dumbass, I guess. Though we all know you're not going anywhere after high school."

Man, I hate this guy.

I almost rip him a new one, but I grudgingly refrain. Shirley is a sweet old lady who is fiercely protective over her useless grandson, so she'd probably fire me if he complained. Which he won't do unless I push him, because he can't bake himself out of a paper bag.

"Fine. I'll make the bons, *if* you bring me an egg McMuffin and a coffee. Two cream, two sugar."

Ethan sighs. You'd think he had the weight of the world on his shoulders and not that he's twenty-seven years old freeloading in his grandma's bakery and making a high schooler do his job. "Just the sandwich, no coffee."

"Sandwich plus a hash brown."

"Deal."

Got him! I don't even like coffee. I hold in a grin as Ethan stomps to the door and out of Sweet Teeth to buy my sandwich. I put the "Be back soon" sign in the middle of the countertop and head to the back, smoothing my hands on my apron. Time to do some baking.

I'm not a great cook, but I'm not bad either. Dad burns water, so after Mom left, I had to step up and be the chef of the household. I don't even know if Dad enjoys what I make; I always have to leave it in the fridge because he works second shift. Worked. Worked second shift. With a jolt, I realize now he'll be home when I get there. And we could actually eat together.

I shake my head as I pour sugar for the caramel centers into a measuring cup. I think I'll stop by Wendy's tonight after work instead.

I make bonbons for the next hour and a half. I'm proud to say these are all my idea. I looked up a recipe online, bought some $2 molds off Amazon, and practiced until I got them right. These are caramel, so the hardest part is heating the sugar. You have to watch it like a hawk while it heats, because it'll burn in seconds. And even when you have the dark, amber color you're looking for, things can still go wrong when you add the butter, heavy cream, and sea salt. Too hot—game over. Too cool—a mess. Crystals? To the trash the batch goes. I spent several days of practice swearing and sweating in my kitchen, but eventually, I got the rhythm down. And I presented them to Shirley, heart swollen with pride, and she goes, "Wow, Ethan! These are fantastic!" Kill me.

But I don't mind, not really. Cooking, baking, and making tiny, intricate sweets are some of the only ways I can relax. I found this hobby all on my own; no memories with anyone to taint anything. It's all me. My own skill and knowledge and steady hands not melting the chocolate. So if I have to let Ethan take a little credit to keep doing this, I will. I'll complain the whole time, though.

After the bonbons are safely in the fridge and cooling, I stare at my finished work with a sort of fond pride. Not worthy of a Michelin star, but they're enough to keep a small-town bakery's lights on for another month. Good enough for me.

The bell attached to the front door tinkles merrily, and I wipe my hands on my apron. I should change into a clean one, but they don't pay me enough to bake *and* look presentable. I pause when I reach the front, and then a slow smile spreads over my face. A customer isn't waiting for me—it's Hallie.

Hallie lounges at the bar, one hand under her chin. She looks like she's melting into the granite countertop.

"I demand free food!" Hallie yells. "This girl is so mean and rude!"

I put my hands on my hips and fix her with an exaggerated, stern glare. "That's not very mature of you, babe."

Hallie cracks up, and I do too. The "babe" thing is a yearslong inside joke. The summer before eighth grade, Hallie fell madly in love with some guy we met at a summer STEM camp. They talked for weeks, and he always called her "babe" in this disgustingly fake-suave voice. He put her down but in sneaky ways, like "Oh, you're wearing that today, babe? Interesting." She changed her whole wardrobe for him, and then at the end of the summer, we found out he kept calling her "babe" because he didn't know her name! I started calling her "babe" to make fun of him, and it stuck. I've gotten in trouble about it before (this was a precursor to the Ashley-threatening-to-stab-me incident). It's funny as hell, though, so I'm gonna keep doing it until one of her partners really does kill me.

When we get done laughing, I lean my elbows on the counter. "Want a bonbon? I just made them."

"Umm, obviously."

I grab one out of the fridge and toss it at her. She catches it and pops it into her mouth. She lets out a contented squeal.

"Nav, marry me. Marry me and cook for me for the rest of my life."

"I don't believe in marriage. And if I did, I wouldn't come cheap." I'm teasing, but it's hard to keep a smile off my face. Hallie, at least, appreciates my cooking. "What's up? You come to harass me?"

"Sort of." Hallie pulls her phone from her pocket and taps

on the screen for a few seconds. She turns it around to show me. A colorful flyer with a cartoon woman curled up like a pretzel takes up the entire screen.

"Look, there's a free yoga class at the rec."

"Okay . . . ?"

Hallie raises her eyebrows. "Hello, I'm inviting you to go with me!"

Yoga? I hate exercise. Hell, I hate sweating. That's why I work in an ice cream shop. "Hallie, come on. Look at me. Do I look like I want to do yoga?"

"You look like you'd never let your best friend down, who I remind you, you love very much." Hallie waggles her eyebrows again, which is so funny a laugh escapes my bewilderment.

"Do you really want to go? Like seriously? This doesn't seem like your thing."

Hallie's smile slips, just for a second. But long enough for me to notice. She shrugs and smiles again. "Maybe it could be my thing."

Huh. Something is off about this. Hallie's thing is basketball. And falling in love with douchebags. Not . . . yoga. "I don't know, Hal. Dad's really been on my ass about coming straight home after work or whatever."

"That's true." Hallie frowns at the countertop, tapping it impatiently with one painted nail. Thinking. "Okay, how about we say you're helping me get prepped for Carnegie Camp?"

I know I'm making a face, but I can't help it. I can't escape that damn camp wherever I am. It's haunting me. And when

I think of Gia, who is definitely not ready for our switcheroo plan, I feel sick.

"No?" Hallie looks at me with her best puppy dog eyes. "Please, Nav?"

This is so weird. Why does she want to go exercise so bad? I'm confused, but by the strangely hopeful expression on Hallie's face, I'm sensing that this is important. So I put all thoughts of Dad and that infernal camp out of my mind and shrug.

"All right, I'm in. When?"

Hallie's face lights up like the sun. "It's every weekday at noon. You're off tomorrow, right?"

I am, but tomorrow I have to go to Gia's. She's hopefully calmed down by now, and maybe I can get something more than "I don't like spaghetti" out of her this time. "Yeah, but let's go Monday instead. I have something to do tomorrow."

Hallie looks curious. "Oh yeah?"

I grin. "Yeah."

Hallie is clearly waiting for me to elaborate, but instead I hand her another bonbon. "Eat this and go away. Ethan will kill me if he sees me dicking around."

Hallie still looks curious, but takes the sweet anyway. "Okay. See you Monday!"

I wave at her as she leaves, her long ponytail swaying behind her. Yoga does not sound fun at all, but if Hallie likes it, fine. At least I can complain about it if it sucks. Silver linings, truly. I pop a bonbon in my mouth, shivering in delight at the sweetness, and return to the kitchen to start a batch of macarons.

CHAPTER 8

"First lesson: flirting is all about confidence." I tap the white-board on Gia's wall with a blue dry-erase marker. Gone are all the math formulas and vocab terms. It's romance time.

Gia frowns at me but nods, scribbling a note in a random notebook she grabbed from the (still cluttered) floor. She's wearing her black-rimmed glasses today, which are surprisingly cute in a nerd way. It's afternoon because I try to make a habit of not waking up before noon on my off days, so there's no time to waste. I fished a marker out of Gia's junk pile, and we're getting straight to it. I write *confidence* on the whiteboard and tap it again with the pen. "What do you think that means?"

"Fake it till you make it?"

I point at her dramatically with my marker. "You're absolutely wrong."

Gia's mouth presses into a thin line and I laugh.

"Listen to Professor Nav. Everyone always says if you fake feeling confident, you'll eventually believe you are. You know what that's called? Brainwashing! We can do better than that. I'm talking about building real confidence here. And that's all about knowing your self-worth."

Gia frowns at me again. "How? I thought it was about courage. Like I'm too scared to talk sometimes."

"Nope. How you view yourself affects how other people view you." I stand straighter and give Gia an easy smile. "Do you think I'm confident?"

Gia nods wordlessly, her pen poised to scribble furiously in her notebook.

"That's because I know what I'm about. I know I look good. I know I dress good." I give her a flirtatious wink. "And I know I'm a good kisser."

Gia has no reaction at all. She stares at me, expression blank. "That's good for you, but I can't do that. I'm not confident in anything."

Jeez, it's like she's immune to any charm whatsoever. If I spend the day with her, *my* confidence will be eroded. I pinch the bridge of my nose between my pointer finger and thumb. "Okay, what are your good points? We can build confidence off that."

"I don't know if I have any." Gia twirls a strand of her hair absently around one finger. She's not looking at me, but she doesn't seem nervous or embarrassed. Just deep in thought. "Maybe I only have regular points."

"Give me those."

"Umm . . ." Gia taps her pen against her notebook. "I can memorize facts really well. But only for, like, a day."

Okay, that's a start. "You did well on the bio exam, then?"

Gia meets my eyes and grins. "Ninety-eight."

"What's a bicuspid valve?"

Gia gives me an exaggerated thumbs-up. "No idea."

I can't stop a laugh from bursting through my chest. Gia laughs too, and for a second, I forget I'm trying to train Gia to get with my best friend. She is genuinely hilarious. It wasn't like this before—maybe Gia's getting used to me? And this is her real personality? I tuck that away to think about later as I regain my composure.

"All right, give me another one, Einstein."

Gia crosses her arms, notebook forgotten. "I'm bilingual."

My eyebrows raise by their own volition. "That's definitely a good point. What's the other language?"

"Spanish. I'm bicultural."

"What does that mean?"

Gia shoots me an amused glance, her concentration momentarily broken. "Mami and I are Mexican American and my father isn't. He's Italian."

Ah, makes sense. Gia's last name is Flores, and now I remember seeing her mom's picture in an article online; it said she was the first Latina sponsor of Carnegie Camp in Mapleton's history. But now that I think about it, I've only ever heard her mention her mom. Maybe she and her dad butt heads like I do with mine.

"Well, this is *definitely* a good point. Two languages is very sexy."

A slight blush creeps up Gia's neck, and I can't help but laugh.

"Anything else?" I ask.

Gia is quiet for a few seconds, but then says, "Does Hallie like games?"

"Like video games or like Monopoly?"

"Video games."

"Oh, no, I don't think so. She doesn't have a console or anything."

Gia's face falls, and for some reason I want to comfort her. "Why? You like them?"

"Yeah. And I'm good at them."

I smile at her. "Then that's a good point. You don't have to like everything Hallie likes. I hate sports, and we're still friends."

Gia doesn't look convinced. And now Jordan has stopped chewing on her ball and is staring at her, so I better wrap this up quickly.

"Show me this game you're allegedly good at."

Gia's tense shoulders relax a little. "Really?"

"Yeah. Is it on the computer?"

"No! Come here." Gia gets to her feet, and I follow her to the beanbags near the TV. She turns on her console (PS4? 5? No idea) and grabs a controller from a messy box full of cords near the wall. She also grabs a headset and loops it around her neck. The game boots up while Gia chatters to me happily.

"I play a lot of things, but my favorite is called *Briar's Blaze*. It's a mash-up of an MMORPG and a first-person shooter, which is, I know, wild, right?! And there are teams, or guilds, you can join to do PVP and mini games if you want."

I nod dumbly, not understanding half of what she just said. Galaxy Cat it is not.

Gia continues as she types in log-in details. "The story mode was really fun, and there are bosses that you can invite your friends to help you defeat, which I think is cheating because if you grind enough, you can easily beat them on single play—"

Gia is cut off by a muffled cheer as the game boots up. Gia's character is a charming green-haired dwarf, with a beard and an axe and everything. Gia puts on her headset with an apologetic glance at me.

"Hey, can y'all be quiet for a minute? My, umm, business person is here."

Business person? I crack a grin. "Who's that? Are you talking to real people?"

"Yeah, these are my guild members. Kenny and Takara are harassing me right now, but there are other—"

Gia cuts herself off, and she stares at her little dwarf guy intently for a few seconds. Then she rolls her eyes.

"Shut up, T. No, I'm muting you." She touches the side of her headset and then lowers it to her neck again. She gives me a sheepish grin. "So, umm, do you want to try playing?"

"Gia, I'm gonna be real with you. Playing this game sounds like a nightmare."

Gia smiles at me. "It's a niche game, so I get it."

"But I'm glad you told me about it." I return her smile. "Everything you just said? No nerves at all."

Gia blinks at me, stunned. "Oh. Really?"

"Really. That's confidence! You know the game, you know you're good at it, and you're sure in your knowledge. So now you just gotta be this confident in everything else."

Gia turns to the TV but there's a flicker of hope in her gaze. "Yeah. Maybe."

I stand up, inspired. This complicated game has given me some ideas; Gia can do confidence, given the right environment. "Now, let's try it on yourself. What do you have to be confident about?"

Gia seems nervous. She looks everywhere except in my eyes. "I—I don't know. Like I said, I don't have any good points."

"You do. You told me two minutes ago."

Gia fidgets in her chair. She thumbs her controller nervously, sending the little dwarf running in a tight, endless circle. "Those aren't that great. Not worth thinking about."

"Gia."

Gia won't look at me. Her gaze is firmly on the TV, where the poor dwarf is running his marathon. A fairy in a blue robe stands beside him and a question mark pops up over its head.

"Why rush, right? We have time. And I mean, I can always think about it tonight and I'll tell you tomorrow."

I stare at Gia's quickly reddening face and Jordan pawing at her leg, and I know I've been defeated. She's close to another panic attack, and this time I didn't even mention Hallie. We were doing so well! Frustration and my own bit of anxiety wells up in my chest. We don't have time for this. Three and a half weeks is not enough time. The horror movie of Hallie leaving me behind and spending my miserable summer here, alone, plays on repeat at the back of my mind, always. I need her to focus. I need Gia to be able to do this.

But she can't. I can see it, even as she picks up Jordan and takes a few shallow breaths to calm down. No, I'm thinking about this wrong. She can't do it *yet*. I've been too pushy; I have to be patient and go at Gia's pace. I take my own calming breath, and smile at Gia. "Okay. You think about it and get back to me."

The relief in Gia's face is borderline heartbreaking. "Okay. Great idea."

"Yeah, because it was yours." I chuckle to myself and gather up my things. "I'm heading out. But next time, we'll make some progress. I promise."

Gia looks slightly sick at that, but she nods. "Okay. See you later, Nav."

I wave and leave Gia to play her game. When I get to my car, I lean my head back against the headrest and stare up at the mysterious stain in the ceiling. I'm trying to be positive, but if I don't figure something out fast, both Gia and I are in big trouble.

CHAPTER 9

Monday morning, Hallie meets me at my house. She's wearing black athletic shorts and aviators, and clutching some sort of strange tube under her arm. "Yoga time!"

I smile, but it's more of a grimace. I don't want any part of yoga time. I'm kind of tired because I stayed up late brainstorming on how to help Gia get over her phobia of talking about anything other than a video game, so exercise at high noon isn't high on my priority list. But Hallie wants me to go, so I'll go. I even half-assed some exercise clothes: a huge T-shirt I stole from Dad a while back and some comfy cotton shorts. It's not Hallie's wardrobe full of color-coded athleisure wear, but it'll have to do.

"I'm ready. Let's do it."

Hallie and I walk to her car. Hers is a newer SUV, but I'll take my rust bucket any day. I was using Sweet Teeth money to save for it, when last Christmas Grandpa matched my savings. It only cost $5,000 and the heat doesn't work, but I love it to pieces.

Hallie climbs into the driver's seat, and I get into the passenger side. I buckle my seat belt and we're off to the rec center twenty minutes away.

"I can't believe I have to work out on my day off," I grumble.

Hallie shoots me a grin. "It'll be fun!"

"Yeah, sure." Fun for who, exactly? The closer we get to the rec, the worse I feel. I should be sleeping until four p.m.

I'm about to complain again, but my phone vibrates with a text. At first, I'm confused; Hallie is the only one who texts me for real, and she's right next to me. But when I look at my phone I'm surprised into a smile—it's Gia.

I took this picture of Jordie, her text says. Thought you'd like it.

I open the text, and a little gasp escapes my chest. Jordan is collapsed on her back by the pool, dead asleep. She's wearing pink heart-shaped sunglasses. I think I'm about to die of cuteness, like oh my *God* what an adorable creature—

"What're you grinning at?" Hallie asks.

I want to lie, but I can't. "You gotta see this dog. I'll send it to you." I send her the text, and her phone dings merrily from the cup holder. I probably would have snuck a look at the red light, but Hallie is deeply serious about road safety. She ignores her phone and keeps her eyes straight ahead as we pass decrepit gas stations, cookie-cutter houses, and endless trees on the way to Mapleton's only good feature.

"Someone sent it to you?"

Uh oh. I hesitate for a moment too long. I don't know why I want Gia to be a secret, but I just feel like she's not ready. If she crashes and burns, and I don't get to go to Carnegie, it's a lot less painful if Hallie knows nothing about it. I clear my throat and look down at Jordan's picture.

"Yeah, I got it from someone."

Hallie is silent, waiting on my elaboration, but I keep my gaze stubbornly on my phone.

Finally, as Hallie pulls into the rec center, she says, "Hmm. Okay."

I breathe a sigh of relief. She's letting it go. Thank God. I jump out of the car and type a quick reply to Gia:

> PLEASE TELL HER I LOVE HER

> also have you been practicing your confidence ma'am?

Then I drop my phone in the gym bag I brought for show and smile at Hallie. "Ready?"

Hallie smiles back. "Ready. I think you'll love it, Nav."

"I thought we knew each other well. I guess not."

Hallie snorts out a laugh, and we approach the rec. It's a huge brick building that serves as a community center for anything from sports to old ladies doing crafts. I follow Hallie aimlessly and let her do all the talking, and then I'm in a bright room full of mirrors and about ten middle-aged moms. Ugh. Hallie trots to a closet near the giant mirror wall like she's been here before.

"Here's a mat." Hallie returns and hands me an off-color pink atrocity. It's got crease lines from age and I swear to God someone has taken a bite out of the corner. There are *teeth marks*. I hold it aloft between two fingers, speechless.

"Where's your mat?"

Hallie holds up a brand-new blue one with shiny green leaves at the edges. The weird tube. "I brought my own!"

Oh hell no. I frantically search for an escape, but the doors are closed, and a tall, lean white woman in spandex leggings dims the lights.

"All right, everyone!" she yells to all the women, plus me and Hallie. "You ready to sweat?!"

God, please kill me now.

I let out a soft stream of curses while this lady makes my body move in ways it's never moved before. I'm sore within minutes and out of breath right after. Then she has the nerve to say, "That was a great warm-up, ladies! Now the fun begins!"

"Please, Hallie," I beg. "Let's run away. There's still time."

Hallie gives me an amused look. She's not even sweating! Fucking athletes, I swear. "Hang in there, Nav."

It gets worse from there. I have to get into a bridge position that I can barely hold, and do some sort of pretzel with my legs. I'm wheezing while these middle-aged moms are all chatting softly and smiling like we're in an ad for medication that has "death" as a side effect. How can Hallie stand this?!

After thirty-five more torturous minutes, the class is over. Instructor Lady wants to do something called a "cool down," but as soon as the music stops playing, I book it out of there. I collapse on a bench outside the rec, away from nosy yoga enthusiasts. I need to wheeze out my lungs in peace.

Hallie meets me outside, grinning. "Loved it that much, huh?"

"I'm never going anywhere with you again." I take a few shuddering breaths and stand, and we wobble to her car. She hops into the driver's seat and turns on the air full blast.

"That was so fun," Hallie says.

I glare at her out of the corner of my eye. "Fun?! How?! Lady had me in positions I've never even heard of."

Hallie chuckles. "Maybe that's good for you. Change of pace!"

"I don't want to change paces. I want to be able to breathe." I'm still struggling, Jesus. "And the music was so loud and awful. I'll never get that stupid song out of my head."

"Yeah, but the—"

"No, nuh uh, no sugarcoating this. It was terrible. Pretty sure I saw April Flannigan's mom in there, and you know she hates me for making out with April on their dining room table." Great party, but she came at me with a *broom*, like I was some kind of stray cat. I shudder at the memory. "And isn't yoga supposed to be relaxing? I am not relaxed. I feel like boxing a wine mom."

I stop, expecting Hallie to laugh and agree, but there's just silence. I look over at her in surprise and she's frowning at the road with a hard to read expression on her face.

"Hallie?"

Hallie looks at me, finally. She's smiling, thank goodness. "That's okay. We won't go back."

"Good." I can't hide the relief in my voice. She looked kind of upset for a minute. "Let's stick to horror movies in your room, yeah?"

"Yeah," Hallie says, still smiling. She gives me an exaggerated wink. "*Texas Chainsaw Massacre* tomorrow?"

"Oh God," I groan. But I say yes because if Hallie wants to do it, I will. At least it's not exercise, so silver linings.

Hallie drops me off at home, and I wave at her. She waves back, and I dig in my bag for my phone. I have one text, from Gia.

> I'm practicing my confidence right now.
> I've never texted you first before.

I roll my eyes, and a smile springs onto my lips without my permission. Gia is such a goober, but she's tenacious and funny too. I was worried, but maybe things will work out after all.

I head into my house, sweaty and exhausted, but somehow my bad mood has disappeared.

CHAPTER 10

When I pull up at Gia's house, I'm on a mission.

I stayed up late last night planning our meeting today, and I think I've finally got it. I know how to get Gia more comfortable without stressing her out. I'm so proud of myself, I could burst. Could be a bit of sleep-deprived manic energy, though. Hard to say.

Gia opens the front door after I send her an I'm here! text. She's wearing black sweatpants and a coral shirt with a bunch of crows on it. Glasses again today. She gives me a tentative wave, and I return it, already in a great mood.

"Gia, I think I've got it."

"Got what?"

I don't answer; instead, I climb the steps to Gia's room, only pausing to pat Jordan's sweet little head. I sweep open her bedroom door, dodge the debris collected on Gia's floor, and march right to her whiteboard. Gia pokes her head into her room, hovering like she's terrified to go in.

"Come on! I have a perfect plan."

"You seem excited about this." Gia hesitantly steps into the room, Jordan trotting behind her.

"I am! This is today's theme." I write the words *LOVE THEORY* in big block letters on the board. Gia frowns at them, and even Jordan cocks her head to one side, like she's confused. "You're not ready for practical applications of love, which is my bad. But we can talk about it in a theoretical sense. Like love science."

Gia sits down on the floor, still frowning. Jordan hops in her lap immediately. "Okay . . . I don't know how just talking about it will help, though."

"Ye of little faith! Listen to Professor Nav." I scribble on the board before presenting my idea to Gia.

Confidence

Communication

Getting to Know Them

Open and Honest

Quality Time

I smack the board with my pen. "These are the five things you need to fall in love with someone. We're not trying to fall in love with Hallie because we're on a time limit here, but we can use these five to get you a damn good first date."

Gia nods, gaze focused and determined on the whiteboard. Finally, my genius is recognized!

"Can you explain the first one?"

"Yeah! I was trying to get you to be more confident last time, but I spooked you. I'm sorry."

"It's okay," Gia says. She gives me a small smile. "I'm always spooked. It's the anxiety disorder."

I smile back. At least we can joke about it now. I think Gia's slowly getting used to me, which is ideal for this plan. "Even so, I didn't do it right. Really, confidence takes time. The more you feel comfortable with yourself, the easier the date will be. But we can't force that."

A troubled expression crosses Gia's face, and Jordan stops panting to look up at her intently. Uh oh.

"How do I get confident quickly? We only have a few weeks—"

I hold up a hand to stop her. "Don't worry about that for now. Today, we're talking about this." I tap my marker against *Getting to Know Them*. This is the easiest one; I just need Gia to talk about herself for ten minutes without throwing up. But I have to trick her into it. I can't mention Hallie at all or we're dead in the water.

Gia looks from the whiteboard to me, an adorable crease between her eyebrows. "That's me getting to know Hallie, right? Are you going to tell me about her?"

"Let's forget about Hallie for now." I sit across from Gia and fold my legs. Jordan sprints to me, and I laugh as she licks my chin. A bit of worry eases from Gia's face. So far, so good.

"If we forget Hallie, what are we going to do?"

"Theoretically, getting to know your date helps you understand them. But I don't actually know that much about you, which is why I messed up the first time."

"Oooh." Gia nods, understanding. "We're practicing."

I wince at the word *practice*. We definitely weren't ready for that the first two times. But this time, Gia doesn't seem anxious. In fact, Jordan is trying her best to chew a hole into the lapel of my shirt, so she must be doing fine. Okay, I can work with this. "Yep, we'll do some get-to-know-you training for now. No pressure!"

"Right. Umm . . ." Gia looks lost for a second. "What's your favorite color?" she blurts.

I hold in a laugh. "I meant like . . . romance related questions."

"Oh." Gia's brow furrows again. "Do you want to know mine still?"

A soft chuckle escapes my chest this time. "Go ahead."

"It's flamingo pink. Not only good for flamingos. It's the best for animal noses."

I nod, because I know exactly what shade she's talking about. I had to paint a calico cat in art, and I almost ripped the thing up when I couldn't find the exact shade I wanted for the paw pads. I was cycling through lemonade and watermelon and fandango like I was going nuts. "It's good for sunsets too, like when the sun has just gone down."

"Oh yeah!" Gia brightens. "And it's really good for pastels, like if you're doing something off model? It's a great background color."

I nod again, and I start to tell her about the perfect color combination I found for sunsets but stop myself. We're off topic already! "Okay, enough about colors. What's your ideal date?"

Gia frowns like she's deep in thought. "Maybe . . . a movie?"

"Classic first date," I agree. "But you have to have dinner afterward, so you can talk about the movie."

Gia's brow furrows even more. "I don't like that idea."

75

"Dinner? Everyone does dinner after a movie!"

"What if she watches me eat?" Gia suddenly seems distressed. She chews on her thumbnail, which I'm noticing is ragged already. "What if I eat weird? Is that a thing?"

Jordan's head snaps up from drooling on my shirt. She climbs out of my lap and sits by Gia, nudging her. Gia pets her absently with one hand, still gnawing on the other. All right, that's my cue for damage control.

"Everyone eats weird. The whole process is weird if you think about it. You shove food in a hole in your face and mush everything into baby food. And then you keep doing that until your jaws gets tired."

"Oh God, that's disgusting." But Gia's laughing now, so mission accomplished.

"Movie and dinner aside, anything else?"

"Maybe an aquarium?" Gia's tone turns wistful. "I haven't been to one since I was a kid."

"Why do you wanna stand around and look at fish?" I complain. "That's boring."

"No, it isn't!" I'm a little surprised by the passion in her voice. "It's very educational. And better than a zoo because the animals in zoos make me sad."

"Who wants to be educated on a date?"

"Me! And it's cool because there are so many different species of marine life there. It's a microcosm of the ocean. *And* there might be a shark."

I can't help but laugh; this girl is hilarious. I can never predict what's about to come out of her mouth. "Maybe on a tenth date, but it's a nightmare for a first one. Someone has to be really into you to look at fish swimming in circles for an hour. I'm vetoing this."

"Fine," Gia grumbles. Then she looks at me, directly into my eyes. I'm momentarily stunned because that doesn't happen often. She's usually looking over my head or at my chin. "What's your ideal date?"

Huh. I rack my brain, but I can't think of anything. I wave my hand in the air dismissively. "Doesn't matter. I don't date."

Gia's eyes widen. "What?"

"I don't date," I repeat. "In fact, I'm against dating as a principle. I'm not into how messy relationships are. No offense to you and Hallie."

Gia's eyes widen even more, if that's humanly possible. "So you don't actually know what you're talking about? You're pulling all of this out of your ass?"

We stare at each other for a shocked second, and then we're both laughing, full on cackling and not-cute snorts from me. Jordan starts barking, probably trying to join in.

"God, Gia, you continue to break my heart. Listen, I practically have a PhD in romance."

"Right." Gia rolls her eyes, still laughing. Her neck has that blotchy blush again, but I'm glad it's not from embarrassment or panic. Just amusement and laughter. It's a nice change.

"No, I'm serious. I don't date, but I have a bunch of casual encounters. Hookups, if you will." I try to look serious and wise, but it's hard because I'm still wiping tears from my eyes. "Hook-ups are like mini dates. Same basic principle, just shorter and has a firm—way more fun, I'll add—goal. So you could say I've been on, like, thirty full dates."

Gia raises one eyebrow. "I think you need to check the math on that one."

"I barely passed math, so I'm ignoring that." I lean back on my hands, in a good mood. Today has gone well. I've never seen Gia laugh so much, or be this relaxed. I don't want to push her, so we should be done for today.

"We can—"

"Can I—"

I stop, and Gia does too. I grin at her. "Go ahead."

"I was going to say . . ." Gia fidgets with the ring on her finger. I'm just now noticing, but it's a smooth glossy black, with a silver section in the middle. The silver has raised blue rhinestones in it, and it moves back and forth with Gia's fingertips. "I was thinking if we're getting to know each other, then we should ask deeper questions."

I nod slowly. That makes sense. I keep my flirting light, but I'm sure Hallie will want to talk about the mysteries of the universe or whatever.

Gia continues. "So—so you could ask me something deep. Something other than my favorite color."

So she says, but she's shaking like a greyhound that lost its sweater. "Are you sure?"

"I'm sure," Gia says through clacking teeth. Jordan noses her head into Gia's hands, and as Gia pets her, the trembling seems to slow. I take in the scene, and my curiosity gets the better of me.

"Is Jordan a therapy dog?"

Gia seems surprised and the shaking stops altogether. "Oh yeah, she is."

"Like trained? Or . . ."

"She's trained." Gia sits up a little straighter, rubbing Jordan's ears between her fingers. Jordan closes her eyes like she's in heaven. Gia takes a deep, slightly shaky breath, like she's steeling her resolve. "My anxiety got really bad a year ago. I mean, it's always been bad, but I was stressed more than usual. So Mami got her for me." Gia smiles down at the top of Jordan's head. "Mami complained so much at first. She didn't really like dogs, and Jordan's a rescue, so she already came with her name. But she's really made everything a lot better. Bearable, at least."

I nod, fascinated. I'd suspected the anxiety, but this can't have been easy to admit. Gia looks nervous but determined; she's really serious about my silly little romance plan. Serious enough to open up and share her secret with me. I'm filled with admiration, and though I should let it go (Hallie should know more about her, not me), I can't hold in a follow-up question.

"Does your anxiety have triggers?"

Gia nods. "Talking to strangers. Ordering food at new places. Dates, apparently." She heaves a defeated sigh. "But you know, prepping really helps. Like if I know the menu ahead of time, I can sometimes order by myself. Sometimes."

"So what you're saying is," I say, a playful grin sneaking onto my face, "the romance lessons really help?"

Gia rolls her eyes and sighs again. "Yes, Nav, the romance prep helps."

"See?! I told you I was a doctor, and you were an ass about it."

"You said you were a *romance* doctor. Not a doctor of neurological disorders."

"A girl can have multiple degrees, come on."

We giggle, and there's a pleasant lull in our conversation. This was sort of . . . fun? And we made progress! We laughed, we relaxed, we got Gia to admit a secret. She's scared, but she's doing so well, day after day. Gia Flores, you have my respect.

"Can I ask you a deep question?" Gia asks, breaking me out of my happy thoughts.

I look at Gia, weighing my options. Normally, I have a strict policy on sharing information with new people. I'm vulnerable, but in a fake way; I always go with the story that my dog ran away three years ago and I've never gotten over it (partially true: Cuddles didn't run away, but I am not over it). But Gia shared something big with me, so maybe I can give her something in return. "Okay. Shoot."

Gia looks into my eyes again. Hers are sharp, uncomfortably so. "Why do you want to go to camp so bad? Enough to do all this?"

Whew, Gia does not hold back. I struggle to put into words how I feel about Dad, and the worry about Hallie getting her heart broken where I can't comfort her, and my secret, small feeling that I'm being abandoned. Again. It takes so long that I stuff those feelings right back in their compartmentalization box where they belong. "I'm ignoring that question, and instead I'll tell you my favorite color. It's lavender."

Gia shakes her head like she's disappointed, but doesn't say anything. She just looks at me, like she's waiting for me to say more. Which isn't happening, so I give her a winning smile and stand to go.

"Are you going home?"

"Yep, can't stay forever." I don't want to push Gia too far, and plus, my stomach is making some growly sounds I don't want her to hear.

Gia stands too. She fidgets a little, some of the anxiety creeping back. Jordan keeps her eyes locked on Gia. "You weren't upset by my question, were you?"

"Oh, no way." I laugh, and some of the tension seems to ease from Gia's shoulders. "You can't offend me." I pause, considering my next words. I think Hallie would be fine with that explanation, but the way Gia is looking, she needs more. "I really do have to go. I'm starving, and I have to pick up food for my dad too. So me leaving has nothing to do with your question. Which I'm still not answering, so you can put away the puppy dog eyes."

My elaboration was the right decision, because Gia visibly relaxes. It's like someone unspooled a bunch of thread. "Okay, good. I don't want to hurt your feelings. I like romance lessons."

Something softens in my chest at her words. "Yeah, me too."

I gather my things, and Gia walks me to her door. I give Jordan one more hug and head to my car. Gia waves, and says, "Sorry I didn't think to get snacks. Next time I'll have some. Or . . ." Gia fidgets again, looking at my feet. "You could eat dinner here? If that's not too weird?"

I smile, even though Gia can't see it due to being very interested in my tennis shoes. Now that I think about it, I've never seen anyone besides Gia in this mansion. I bet her mom (and dad?) works late too. Eating dinner alone sucks. I'd know.

"Well, next time I'll cook something for him ahead of time and we can eat dinner together."

Gia finally looks up and matches my smile. "Deal."

I pat her shoulder, practically beaming. We're making progress, finally. Things are looking up. "Great work today. Next time I come here, you better be ready to respect my PhD."

Gia laughs, and I wave, leaving her house to head to Sonic. It's not until I'm buckled and circling her insane driveway that a bit of longing pinches my chest. For some reason, I wish I was eating my greasy Sonic food with Gia. I shake off the weird feeling and point my car in the direction of a burger and Tater Tots with my name on it.

CHAPTER 11

I'm stressed, so I'm baking.

Normally, I make it my policy not to be stressed about anything. School is what it is, and me cramming for a test to get four extra points isn't worth the trouble. I'd rather be asleep. But lately, three particular things have been buzzing anxiously at the back of my mind, and tonight they're combining to be unbearable.

Dad is the first. Despite us silently stalking around each other and not talking, tonight, he's mysteriously absent. He said a terse, "I'll be back" and left. That was an hour ago and he's still gone. Where the heck is he going at eight on a Tuesday night? I shouldn't care, but I do. I've imagined all sorts of dangerous, horrible reasons for him to be out so late on a weeknight. Sadly, it's probably something boring and benign, but we're not close enough for me to know about it. When are his off days now? What's his schedule exactly? I have no clue. It's depressing to think about, so I try not to. But then that leaves room for my two other worries.

Gia. I'm glad she's getting better at talking with me; she sends me texts about Jordan, told me again that she hates spaghetti (for the third time), and when I ask how her game's going, she sends me paragraphs of incomprehensible jargon. I'm honestly pretty proud. But our *Get to Know Them* talk weighs heavily on my mind. I hate that she asked me about camp, and I hate that she knew it would be a sore spot for me. When did I let her get close enough that she'd know that? Or at least be able to make a really good guess? And why am I sad that I couldn't answer?

And that brings me to the biggest one—Hallie. Since our terrible yoga outing, something feels . . . off. When I text her to hang out, half the time she says she's busy or puts me off until later. I'd almost suspect she has another crush, but she always tells me about those right away so we can scheme about how to get their attention (the best one was when she joined the basketball team because Ginger Banks was on the team too, and she's still on it three years later). I don't know what's going on, or why she's acting different. I don't even get why we went to yoga in the first place. Why is everyone around me changing?

So. Anyway. Brownie time. I know I'm depressed because I'm using dear old Betty Crocker, though I have a recipe my aunt gave me that I usually like to experiment with. I dump the mix into a glass bowl and add the water, vegetable oil, and eggs on autopilot. I thought it would be distracting, but I've done this so much that I don't need to think about it. I'm thinking about my people problems instead.

When the brownies are safely in the oven, I unlock my phone. No text notifications. I tap Hallie's name and type out a message.

come over my dad's not home

Three dots pop up immediately. Your dad's never home lol

Normally I'd laugh at her joke, but tonight, it's not funny. But she doesn't know that and I'm too moody to explain, so I type, i made brownies

Hallie sends a distressed emoji. Damn I want to be there! But I'm with the parents.

what're you doing? And can I join because I don't want to be in this empty house by myself.

Three dots pop up and disappear. And . . . again. I narrow my eyes.

???

We're shopping, Hallie texts. Right after, she adds for camp ☹.

I groan and rest my forehead against the cool countertop. Of course. Of course it's the camp! I almost tell her to come pick me up because I'll need camp stuff too since Gia is doing better, but I don't. I grit my teeth and tap out a torturous have fun ☺.

I lie face down on my counter until the air in the kitchen hangs heavy with sugar and chocolate. But I'm not even hungry. I made an entire pan of brownies, and I don't have anyone to share them with.

Wait, yes I do. I sit up and look at my phone again. Hallie sent me one more message apologizing and saying we'll talk later. But I close her chat and tap Gia's name instead.

> do you like brownies?

Gia doesn't answer right away. Probably playing that game. I stare intently at my phone until three dots pop up a minute later.

> Yes

> But not right now

> what does that mean?

She takes forever to answer again.

> Just not a good time

Oh Lord. Gia texts like a cryptic grandma. This is gonna take all day. I tap the phone icon and when she answers, I say, "What's going on?"

Gia clears her throat. "I didn't think you'd call me."

"I got tired of waiting. What do you mean you don't like brownies right now? You're breaking Betty's heart."

"Who?" Gia laughs a little, but I frown. Something's off about Gia's voice. It's wobbly and weak, like she's been crying.

"Hey, you okay?"

"Y-Yeah."

She's definitely not okay. She's lying. "What's wrong? Gia?"

"I don't feel good. I'm sick, I think." Gia sniffles, her voice tight and soft.

Anxiety leaps into my chest like lightning. "How sick?"

"I've been throwing up all day."

"Shit. Food poisoning?"

"M-Maybe." Gia sniffles one more time. "Sorry, Nav, I don't mean to bother you. It's just that Mami isn't home and I feel so bad—"

"Wait, your mom hasn't been home all day?" I glance at the time at the top of my screen. 9:23.

"Yeah." Gia's voice is tiny.

Oh my God. She's all alone in that big house, all by herself. I get a familiar ache in my chest as I look around the kitchen, the humming refrigerator my only company. She doesn't deserve to be by herself when she's ill. Even Dad, who barely notices I'm there, will check in on me when I'm sick. I jump out of my seat and open the oven. I'm hit with a blast of hot air and chocolate, but I ignore it and put on oven mitts. "Give me five minutes and I'll be on my way."

"What?" Surprise colors Gia's tone. "Really?"

"Yeah, just gotta take the brownies out so I don't burn my house down. Have the door unlocked, okay?"

"Nav, you don't have to—"

"I know, I know. But I am, so open the door. I don't need the cops thinking I'm breaking into your mansion."

Gia lets out a small, exhausted laugh. "Okay. See you soon?"

"Real soon," I say, placing the brownies carefully on the stovetop. They're mushy, not all the way cooked, but I'm surprised I don't care I'm wasting food. An urgency pushes me forward, making me hastily turn the oven off, grab my keys, and hop into my car without a second thought.

I drive as quick as I can to Gia's house, with the faint soundtrack of Gia's sniffles coming from the speaker of my phone. I park close to the door and jump out. "I'm here!"

"It's open," Gia says softly.

I keep my phone close as I touch the front door. It creaks open ominously, but I don't see Gia in the dark gloom of the house. Great, this is the perfect setup for one of Hallie's horror movies. I keep my Black ass firmly on the porch. "Where are you?"

"In my bathroom," Gia says. "I unlocked it from my phone."

That gets a smile out of me. Rich people and their fancy doors. Greatly preferable to masked killers, though.

"I'm coming up." I end the phone call, step over the threshold, and close and lock the door behind me. I freeze when I hear a noise but relax when Jordan's excited bark comes from the top of the stairs. "My baby!! Come to me!"

Jordan's nails click on the hardwood floor as she rockets down the stairs. She licks my hands and legs, then runs back to the steps. She does that over and over, like she's trying to lead me to Gia.

"I know, Lassie. Your mom's fallen down the well." I follow Jordan upstairs and into Gia's bedroom, but then see a soft glow peeking out from a different door. Jordan runs toward the light, and I cautiously peek into Gia's illuminated bathroom.

Gia looks pitiful. She's wearing a loose shirt and pajama pants with koalas on them, and she's wrapped around the toilet in a sad semicircle. Her skin is pale, and the air hangs heavy with that unmistakable sick scent. I've definitely been here before. Tequila and weed brownies—never again.

"Hi, Nav," Gia mumbles. She's got tiny dark semicircles under her eyes.

"Hi, Gia." I enter the bathroom, stepping over Jordan, and kneel beside her. I put a hand on her back, and I'm heartbroken when she flinches. "How are you feeling now?"

"Bad." Gia's eyes fill with unshed tears. "My stomach's killing me."

I rub her back gently, like I would Hallie when she's puking. "It's okay. Give me some info. When did this start?"

"Early . . . right after breakfast."

"And when's the last time you puked?"

"Maybe an hour ago?"

Okay, not great. She's been puking for twelve hours. "Have you had anything to eat or drink?"

Gia shakes her head. Her brown eyes are dull and tired. I touch the back of my hand to her forehead—sweat and heat meets my skin.

"All right, slight fever. Probably a stomach virus. But that means it's almost over!"

Gia gives me a tired smile. "When did you get to be a doctor?"

"Got my degree ten minutes ago."

"Boy, they just give those degrees out," Gia mumbles, her eyes half-closed.

I grin, close to laughter. "Didn't I tell you that you better respect my PhD the next time I came over here?"

Gia chuckles weakly and I put my hand on her back again. "I'll be right back, okay? You try to sit up for me."

Gia nods, and I stand. Jordan takes my spot, lying down next to Gia's stomach. At least she wasn't completely alone all day.

I go downstairs, using my phone as a flashlight. God, her kitchen is huge . . . I poke around for a few minutes, peeking into the giant refrigerator. It's mostly empty, which is surprising. Maybe it's getting close to grocery day. I find her pantry and take a box of crackers and a can of ginger ale (and a Milk-Bone for Jordan because, come on, she deserves it), then tote my prizes back upstairs.

Gia's leaned against her tub when I get back. She looks like she might throw up again, but at least she's vertical. I get to my knees beside her and pop open the can of ginger ale. "Try to drink this, okay?"

She takes it, her hands shaking slightly. "I want a cold one."

"Sorry I don't have liquid nitrogen at my disposal, princess." I try to sound stern, but I'm relieved. She can't be feeling too bad if she's complaining.

Gia sips a little of the ginger ale anyway. While she's drinking it, I search under her bathroom sink and find a washcloth. I run some warm water in the sink. "Try to eat some crackers too, if you can."

"I don't wanna," Gia whines. "My stomach hurts."

"Okay, okay, don't cry about it." I wet the washcloth, wring it out, and return to Gia's side. "Look at me."

She does, and I carefully wipe sweat and an orange smudge of what I hope is food from her cheek. Maybe someone else would be grossed out, but Hallie and I go to a *lot* of parties. Nothing I haven't done before.

Gia looks right into my eyes, hers fevered and huge and round. I smile at her as her too-warm face comes away clean.

"What's the matter?"

"Umm." She's still looking right at me, a bemused sort of wonder on her face. "I don't know."

I laugh and swipe her cheek one more time with the washcloth. "That's fine. Just let me handle everything, okay?"

Gia nods wordlessly. I pause for a second. Despite the fever, her eyes are so pretty. Deep and dark, with tiny specks of light brown in the iris. With a jolt, I realize I've never been this close to her before. Suddenly, I'm feeling a bit of the wonder too.

Jordan nudges my hand, her cold nose shocking me back to the present. I can't space out; I need to get Gia settled. I pat Jordan's head and stand.

"Let's get you cleaned up and in bed."

Gia complains, but she staggers to her feet anyway and brushes her teeth. While she's doing that, I kick a path of junk out of the way so she can stagger to bed without tripping over anything and grab some not-puked-on pajamas she has hanging on the side of her bed. She changes in the bathroom, and I inspect the bed for vomit (none, thankfully).

When Gia leaves the bathroom, she pauses at the door and stares at me for a moment. I watch anxiously; I'm scared she's gonna fall over.

"You okay?"

"Yeah. Kinda lightheaded?"

"Okay, bedtime for you." I usher Gia to her bed.

She climbs in clumsily, and Jordan jumps up beside her. She pulls the covers up to her chin, and I finally breathe easier. She's okay now. She'll nap it off and be fine tomorrow. Dr. Nav, over and out.

Gia looks up at me, her eyes half-closed. "Nav?"

"Hmm?"

"Can we do some romance practice before you go?"

"What? No. You're about to pass out."

Gia blinks at me slowly. Her expression is hard to read: sick, but tentative and something else too. "Can we practice holding hands?"

I stare at Gia for a second. Her expression is tired, exhausted even, but also strangely hopeful. And maybe even scared. It hits me then—she's by herself, in this giant house. She doesn't want me to go. An unfamiliar tender feeling blooms in my chest. Gia isn't just some girl I'm using to help me get into Carnegie Camp. Maybe at first, but I can't pretend that's true anymore. When I look at Gia, I feel soft, maybe a little fragile, maybe something I can't put my finger on. I laugh at our messages and when I was stressed, I texted her, hoping she'd help me devour an entire pan of brownies. I came over here, no questions asked, when she said she was sick. That's not something I'd do for just anyone. That's something I do for the people I care about.

I don't really know what to do with that information, now that I have it. I'm really not used to caring about many people. I have Hallie, but . . .

The realization strikes me—Somehow, without me noticing, Gia became my friend. And I guess it makes sense. We've
been working together nonstop, and part of the job is getting
to know her. She's awkward and quiet, but now I know more
than that. She loves video games and is apparently immune to
my flirtation attempts, and by God does she hate spaghetti.
She texts me pictures of her dog, and I actually look forward to
coming over here. Duh! Of course we're friends. I take a calming breath, relieved I figured that out.

"We don't have to pretend to practice for me to hold your
hand," I say, my voice gentle. "You're my friend, Gia. You can
ask me for that any time."

Gia inhales sharply, then gives me a small smile. "Thanks,
Nav."

"No problem. Do you want me to stay over? I have clothes
in my car."

Gia's eyes widen, but she just nods silently. God, she's so
awkward and adorable, I can't stand it.

"All right, be right back. Hang on."

I jog downstairs, grab the bag I always take to Hallie's,
and come back. One quick change in Gia's bathroom later,
I'm standing at the edge of her bed. I almost climb in before I
remember I'm not at Hallie's, and I can't take over her sleeping
space without asking.

"Umm . . . can I sleep in here?"

Gia nods again. Her eyes are huge, bless her. I can't stop a
laugh from bursting out of my chest.

"I'm not gonna bite you!"

"You don't know what you do in your sleep." But nevertheless, Gia scoots over, leaving me a huge amount of space. Man, I have *got* to invest in a king-sized bed.

I climb into Gia's bed, avoiding disturbing the already-snoring Jordan, and cover my shoulders with the comforter. Her sheets feel like a T-shirt softened from repeated use. I'm immediately sleepy, comforted by the familiar texture. Maybe after I get Gia and Hallie together, I can convince her to let me have these sheets. Or I'll just stay here all the time.

I roll to my side and hold my hand out. "Here you go."

Gia tentatively touches her palm to mine. Her skin is soft and cool, surprisingly. Maybe her fever is going down.

"Thank you, Nav," Gia whispers. "For everything."

"No problem. Really. You'd be surprised how much vomit I've cleaned up since I started high school."

We both laugh and then fall silent. As Gia's hand warms in mine, the stress from before and the worry for Gia crashes down on me at once, and before I know it, I'm fast asleep.

CHAPTER 12

When I wake up, I have no idea where I am.

I stare at the high, non-popcorn ceiling in a haze. Cool sheets . . . but something warm is draped over my legs, and someone's head is nestled on my shoulder. Where the hell am I? I don't have a hangover, so I didn't go home with a party guest. I turn my head, and I see Gia, eyes closed, breathing deeply, cuddled up to my side.

Ah—I'm at Gia's house. I blink further awake as new information assaults my brain; Gia is a clingy sleeper, and Jordan is too. The dog sits on my chest, panting happily in my face, while Gia is cuddling me like I'm a giant stuffed animal. I blink again, wide awake now, a little overwhelmed. This is a lot.

Gia sighs in her sleep and hugs me closer. I watch her for a second, warm fondness filling me from the inside out. She's endearing even when she's asleep, her long eyelashes brushing against her cheeks. I carefully extract one arm from under Jordan and touch my hand to her forehead. Cool, no unnatural warmth. Her fever is down. I didn't know I had any tension in my shoulders, but I feel myself relaxing. She's okay, thank goodness.

I lie still for a few minutes, enjoying the moment. It's quiet, ceiling fan humming gently above us. Gia's breathing softly in my ear, her arms wrapped around my arm, one of her legs bumped against mine. Jordan stares into my eyes, tail thumping against my stomach. This . . . is really nice. Even when I stay with Hallie, she's not super clingy like this. But I don't mind it. I don't mind it at all.

My bladder spoils the moment, threatening to ruin the bed if I don't get up *right now*. Carefully, I untangle my limbs from Gia. Well, I try. She groans when I move and hugs me tighter. I'm ready to risk it all and pee on myself.

Jordan jumps to the floor, and I try again. This time, Gia lets my arm go. I ease out of bed, and when both feet are on the floor, I turn to look at her. Still fast asleep, her arms curled around my pillow instead. I cover her shoulders with the comforter and tiptoe to the bathroom.

After I'm done, I wash my hands and return to the bedroom. I squint at the time on Gia's TV—8:20 a.m. I can't go back to sleep now, but I don't want to wake her up either . . . I'm getting unwelcome flashbacks to elementary school sleepovers, when I woke up before everyone else and had to stare at the wall for two hours.

Jordan walks to the door and looks back at me expectantly.

"What?" I whisper.

Jordan comes to me, tail wagging, then goes back to the door.

"Okay, guess I'll go on a dog adventure . . ." I follow Jordan, who trots downstairs, through the kitchen, and waits by the glass door that leads to the pool. She looks at me again and woofs softly. "Gotcha. Bladder emergency for you too."

I open the door for her, and she runs into the backyard, nose to the ground. She stays firmly on the bright green grass surrounded by a tall fence and goes nowhere near the giant pool in the middle. I knew I liked Jordan for a reason. I watch her for a while, but she pounces on a purple monkey toy and doesn't go to the bathroom. Maybe she tricked me into letting her outside to play. I'll leave the door open, and she can come back whenever she's done.

I wander into the kitchen while I wait for her. I was on a mission last night, so I didn't notice, but damn is this kitchen nice. Granite countertops, white sparkly backsplash, brand-new silver and black appliances. I want to be rich so bad. I open the double-door steel fridge, barely registering Jordan's nails clicking on the hardwood floor behind me. Nothing magically appeared while I was sleeping. There's not a lot to look at—something homemade in several glass jars, a haphazard assortment of half-used butter, eggs. Some veggies. But no snacks or anything I can grab first, apologize later. Ugh. Can I DoorDash something? At eight thirty in the morning?

Jordan barks happily behind me and I turn to scold her because she can't demand all my attention while I'm starving, but she's not next to me. She's actually across the room, jumping at the feet of a woman . . . I've never seen before.

She's never seen me before either, because her eyes are bugged out of her head. "Who are you?"

"Uh." My brain catches up with the situation. I'm in a strange house, rifling through a strange fridge for food. And this woman looks so familiar . . . she's Latina, a little taller than me, wearing a sharp navy-blue business suit and long skirt. It dawns on me when I look into familiar brown eyes. She must be Gia's mom.

"What're you doing in my house?" Gia's mom glares at me, the shock gone.

"I'm Gia's friend! My name's Nav." I hold my hands up in surrender. "Not trying to rob you, I swear. I mean, I am hungry, so I was gonna eat something, but that's it."

Gia's mom doesn't look convinced. Her eyes narrow. "Gia hasn't mentioned any Nav."

Well, that's offensive. I've been here like four times. "We're new friends, so—"

"I'm calling the police."

Shit. I really don't need this. They will definitely murder me if they think I'm stealing from this nice ass house. "No, wait! Gia was sick, so I came over to check on her. I swear."

Gia's mom frowns at me, her hand frozen in her jacket. "How did you know she wasn't feeling well?"

"Because I'm her friend, like I said—"

I'm cut off by the stairs creaking. Gia's mom and I wait, and Gia sheepishly peeks into the kitchen.

"Ah! Come here, my baby." Gia's mom embraces her and hugs her tight. Gia seems to melt in her arms as her mom fusses and kisses her hair. She asks her a question in Spanish, and Gia responds in Spanish too. Gia's mom nods and then glances at me. She hugs Gia to her side, like I'm about to attack them. Rough first impression.

"Mija, is this your friend? She says she is."

Gia smiles at me and I breathe a sigh of relief. "Yeah, Mami, this is Nav. She came to visit me."

"But she is your friend?" Gia's mom's voice is tinged with hope.

Gia meets my eyes and the smiles grows. "Yeah, she's my friend."

I grin back, a funny, mushy feeling at the back of my stomach.

Gia's mom finally relaxes. The tension melts from her shoulders and she turns to Gia, hands on her hips. "Gia, why didn't you say you were inviting your friend over? The house is a mess and there's no food. And you didn't even introduce us!" Gia's mom ignores her daughter's sullen expression and comes to me. She puts her hands on mine, shocking me. "It's so nice to meet you, Nav! I'm sorry for my less-than-warm welcome, but I was pretty shocked to see you in my fridge, you know."

"Oh yeah, I know." I laugh a little, feeling awkward. This new friend thing is *very* new. Hallie is my best and only friend, and we've known each other since before we had teeth. Her parents are basically my parents, so I'm not used to meeting new ones.

"You're welcome here any time," Gia's mom says warmly. "Do you want me to make you something to eat? Oh, do you want to go swimming? It's not so hot yet, so perfect timing! Maybe you girls can watch a movie as well? Did Gia show you the media room? Very fancy!"

I just nod, a bit overwhelmed. How can Gia be so shy when her mom is a Chatty Cathy?

"Mami, please," Gia begs. She says something in Spanish, and her mom laughs affectionately.

"Okay, okay. I'll be upstairs. Nice to meet you, Nav!" Gia's mom goes upstairs, and Jordan follows her, tail wagging happily. Gia and I stand in the kitchen for a few seconds, staring at each other.

"Are you feeling better?" I finally say.

Gia looks away, rocking back on her heels. "Yeah. I am."

I stare at her for a few seconds, then laugh. She looks up in alarm, and I close the distance between us to sit at her kitchen island. "Don't be all shy with me now. I cleaned up your puke. We're friends."

Gia relaxes and grins. She sits on the barstool next to me. "I'm embarrassed, okay? I can't believe you did all that."

"All what? Taking care of my friend who was near death?"

"Well," Gia says, kicking her feet. She looks down at her clasped hands. "I guess I was surprised because no one has ever done that for me before."

I wait until she looks at me before smiling back. "Well, you're stuck with me now. Even after you get with Hallie, we can still be friends. I'll just annoy you both."

A strange look passes over Gia's face, but she settles on happiness. "Deal."

"Good! Now that that's settled, are you gonna make me some food or what?"

Gia shakes her head. "That reminds me—you can't stay."

"Wow, okay. *Take care of me and then get out.*"

"No, that's not what I mean. Your dad called. That's what woke me up." Gia gives me my phone . . . which has seven texts from Dad. Shit. I didn't tell him I was staying over. "I answered because he called three times in a row. But I shouldn't have, because I think I made him panic."

"Fuck," I mutter. My ass is grass for real.

"I don't think he's mad," Gia offers. "I tried to explain what happened, but I didn't do a good job. And I called him Mr. Nav."

"Oh God." I can't help but laugh at that image. I'm laughing, but I'm sure Dad isn't. I hop off the island stool, dread in my gut. "Okay, I'll go. I have to work tomorrow, but I can come over the day after and we can practice more."

Gia's eyes shine a little. "Okay. See you later."

"See ya!" I gather all my stuff from Gia's room, and ten minutes later, I'm on the road to face Dad's wrath. And even though I'm not looking forward to it, I don't regret coming over to help. It's weird, but all I can think about is Gia's gentle smile all the way home.

♡ ♡ ♡

When I get home, Dad is waiting on the porch for me.

I put the car in park and hesitate before getting out. I can't sit here and prepare like usual—he's looking right at me. Shit.

I get out and walk slowly up the steps. Dad stands up from the one patio chair we have out here, which I don't think I've ever seen him sit in. I try to give him my best smile.

"Hey, Dad."

Dad glares at me, arms folded over his huge chest. Ah, he's real mad. And this time it really is my fault. I should have texted him about this. I just . . . forgot.

"Let me tell you a story." Dad's voice is an even rumble. "I come back home and my daughter's car isn't in the driveway. After I said I'll be right back."

"Dad, I—"

He holds his hand up to stop me and the protests die in my throat. "And my daughter *still* doesn't come home by eleven. And I think, I'm not going to be upset, because it's summer, and she's probably spending the night with Hallie. But this morning when I get the mail, I see Cathy, and she tells me that my daughter isn't there."

I kick at a piece of gravel. I can't even look at him. "I'm sorry, Dad. This is my bad, I know."

"Yeah, it definitely is your bad." Dad takes a heavy breath in. "Who in the hell is Gia? And why is she answering your phone?"

"She's my friend. She got sick, and I was worried about her, so I went over to her house. I'm sorry."

Dad glares down at me for what I swear is a full minute and then closes his eyes. "Okay. I'm not gonna yell at you. Because obviously that's not working."

All right, well, that's not terrible. But if he's not going to yell—

Dad holds his hand out to me. "Give me the phone."

Dammit. There it is. "Dad, I said I'm sorry—"

"If you don't feel the need to use it for important things, you don't need it at all."

I stare at his open palm. I don't mind giving him my phone, but . . . Galaxy Cat. I can't miss logging in once a day, even if it's just for a minute.

"How long?"

Dad raises his eyebrows. "Excuse me?"

"How long are you gonna keep it?"

"As long as I damn well want, since I paid for it."

I really don't want this to be a fight, but my temper is growing, festering like the beginnings of a wildfire. "Let's negotiate. Take my laptop."

"Naveah." Dad's voice is deadly serious. "Give me that phone right now."

"I can't." I can't explain to him about Galaxy Cat. I can't explain that I need that counter. I need to know the days, how long it's been since Mom left, since our family fell apart, since Dad stopped loving me. I need this stupid cat game.

"What do you mean you can't? You can and you will—"

"It's important!" I'm screaming. I can't help it. I rub my face in my hands. "Please, Dad. Don't do this. Laptop, TV, whatever. Just let me keep the phone."

Dad is silent, so I risk a look at him. He's watching me with a look of pure bewilderment, like I'm a wild animal in an alien zoo. He takes a slow, deep breath. "I'll have the phone when you're home. You can have it at work."

I only need a minute to log in, and I've already done today's while I was in Gia's bathroom. I nod, all the fight rushing out of me. I place the phone in his hand.

"Thanks, Dad."

Dad shakes his head, like he's confused. "I don't know why you got all worked up. It's just a phone, Naveah. You're lucky it's not your keys."

My temper flares again. Jesus, I said I was sorry. Nothing's ever enough for him. "You can't take that. Grandpa and I bought that car, not you."

Dad narrows his eyes at me, the confusion gone, and uneasiness creeps up my spine. But he doesn't yell. He just moves out of the way, revealing the open front door.

"Room," he says, his voice still even. "Now."

"Gladly." I go up to my room, head held high, and I only relax when my door is closed. I immediately get on my laptop to type out a message to Hallie.

> Dad took my phone. KILL ME.

She answers right away. Shit that sucks. What is his problem??

See?! Even Hallie knows he's being weird. I don't know. I wish he'd leave me alone.

I stare at my message, mixed feelings swirling in my gut. I don't know what Dad is thinking anymore. I don't know why he's trying to change things. I can't really say that I don't deserve his wrath this time, but I really didn't think to text him.

And maybe that's the sad part. It didn't cross my mind because I thought he wouldn't care. But, weirdly, it looks like he *does* care. In the most frustrating way possible, but still. And I don't know what to think about that.

Hallie and I move on to talking about *Texas Chainsaw Massacre* (hate it) and *Halloween* (that one is okay, actually), and then what we're doing tomorrow, but I can't shake the glum, confusing feeling of finally having a parent again after three years of losing them both.

CHAPTER 13

Ethan grunts around the break room, lifting papers and clutter from the squat coffee table and dropping them back down again. I glare at him over the top of my magazine, hoping he can feel the daggers coming from my eyes. He's not doing anything wrong, except being a nuisance and a headache, but I don't like him existing near me.

"Can't you go do some work?" he snaps at me.

"Can't you go brush your teeth?"

Ethan flips me off and I roll my eyes. I'm so bored I could die. If I have to spend another second with Ethan, I really might. Death by douchebag. Probably wouldn't be the first time.

The faint sound of the bell on the front door makes me get up. I'd actually rather work than be with him. "Try not to burn down the place while I'm working, yeah?"

Ethan flips me off again but keeps looking for his whatever. I shake my head and leave the break room, tightening my apron as I go.

"Welcome to Sweet—"

I cut myself off, shocked into silence. Gia stands at the counter, glancing around the store nervously. She's wearing the cutest blue dress with a tiny white flower pattern and white sandals. No glasses today. When she sees me, she breaks into a beautiful smile.

"Gia! Came to visit me at work?" I lean on the counter and wink at her. I'm kind of delighted . . . ! Only Hallie visits me at Sweet Teeth. Not even Dad has been here before.

A familiar patchy blush creeps up Gia's neck and her smile turns embarrassed. Finally! The wink finally got to her.

"I'm kidding. What's up?"

"Nothing. I mean, I did come to visit you." Gia smooths down her dress and takes a deep breath. "I want to thank you for what you did for me."

"No, no, stop." I wave my hand in the air. "It was no problem. Think of it as a friend perk."

Gia's expression softens. "I do, but it was still really thoughtful. And, umm, I think it would be nice if we could, umm, hang out again."

I frown in confusion. "I'm coming over tomorrow, right? For practice?"

"Right. But also, maybe we could, umm . . ." Gia takes another deep breath as her face does its best tomato impression. Oh man, this is a real regression. Maybe she gets more nervous when she's outside of her room. I didn't plan for this at all! We have so far to go in just two weeks.

"Take your time," I say gently.

Gia's anxious expression turns into gratitude. "Okay. Hold on. Give me a second." I watch as she walks to the door, turns in a tight circle, then comes back. Miraculously, she does seem calmer. Huh.

Gia looks into my eyes, hers deep and serious. "Okay. I'm ready. Nav, would you like to go to the movies with me sometime?"

I blink in surprise. The answer is yes, of course. Who doesn't love greasy popcorn and making fun of the ugly men hot women choose to make out with? But why did she get so nervous to ask me? Maybe because we're such new friends? Our dynamic is different now, so that's probably it.

"Sure," I say, grinning. "Oh, this'll be great practice for your date with Hallie! You get more nervous when you're out of your element, right?"

Gia stares at me like her brain is short-circuiting for a full ten seconds. But she eventually says, "Right."

"This could be a practice date! A final exam!" I nod to myself, getting worked up at the idea. It'll be our last practice before the Big Event. "We can go two weeks from now. What do you think?"

Gia breathes out a heavy breath. For some reason, she looks kind of disappointed. "Okay. Let's do it."

I frown. Maybe she's not ready? "Don't be nervous, Gia. You can do this. We have plenty of time to practice before this."

Gia laughs a little. She smiles, a real one this time. "Okay. We can do this."

"Good! Now, do you want some ice cream? Or a cupcake? I made the red velvet ones this morning."

Gia raises her eyebrows in surprise. "You make the desserts?"

"Yeah, man. Who the hell else is gonna do it? My manager couldn't bake if his life depended on it."

Gia laughs. "Okay, I'll try one—"

The doorbell tinkles again, and I look up. For the second time, I'm delightfully surprised.

"Hallie!"

Hallie breezes inside, waving cheerfully. She's wearing white leggings, a long pink top, and black-and-pink tennis shoes. The outfit looks suspiciously like yoga wear. "Hiiii, I came to visit!"

"Yeah, you came to eat."

Hallie grins. "Guilty. Oh, hi, Gia!"

I glance at Gia, resisting the urge to grimace. Shit, it's way too soon for this. Gia stares at Hallie, and her skin has dropped the tomato act in exchange for that pale shade of beige she had when she was sick. I wait for a few stressful seconds, but Gia doesn't say anything. Okay, Nav to the rescue.

"I made red velvet cupcakes," I tell Hallie. "I'll get two! Hang on a second." I lean down and grab two cupcakes from the display case, then hand them to Hallie and Gia. Hallie unwraps hers immediately, but Gia is looking down at hers like it'll bite her.

"God, this is so good, Nav," Hallie groans after taking a bite.

Now Gia's looking at Hallie like *she'll* bite her. Pretty sure we should not be afraid of our crushes, so this isn't going well.

"I have to go," Gia blurts. She clears her throat and picks up her cupcake. She holds it delicately in her palm, like it's a rare jewel. "I'll eat this at home. I promise. I will eat it."

"Okay, Gia. I believe you." I can't keep the laugh out of my voice. "See you tomorrow."

She nods stiffly, then nods even more stiffly at Hallie, and wanders out the door. I watch her until she gets into her car to make sure she doesn't pass out in the parking lot. She cranks up and drives away, and I breathe a sigh of relief. Not great, but not a complete disaster. She nodded at Hallie at least. That's something.

Hallie watches Gia go too, then turns to me. Her eyebrows are almost up to her hairline. "All right. You gotta tell me. What's with you and Gia?"

I hesitate but cave. I can't hide that I'm hanging out with Gia after that. I just won't mention what we're doing when we hang out. "Me and Gia are friends."

"Oh." Hallie takes another bite of her cupcake, seemingly thinking. "Since when?"

"Since two weeks ago, I guess."

"Huh." Hallie finishes her cupcake and tosses the wrapper into the trash. But she doesn't say anything else. She just looks at me.

"What?"

Hallie shrugs, one hand under her chin. "Nothing. I think it's kind of nice that you're friends, that's all. She seems really great."

"She is." I blink when that comes out of my mouth. Why did I say that? I mean, it's true. Gia is great. Hallie'll see when she can finally say a few words instead of just nodding. "But she's looking forward to your redo date."

"Yeah." Hallie is looking at me like I told a joke and she's trying not to laugh. "Me too."

Her voice sounds kind of weird, but I let it go. "What's up? You come to bother me again?"

"No, I came to ask if you wanted to hang out this weekend. Unless you're hanging out with Gia . . . ?"

"No, I'll see her tomorrow. What do you have in mind?"

Hallie's eyes sparkle mischievously. "Let's go hiking."

Sharp hurt stabs my chest. No. Yoga is one thing, but hiking is something I can't do. "Hallie . . ."

"I know it's exercise, but it'll be fun!"

I can't. Painful memories try to surface, but I shove them down into the compartmentalization box where they belong. "Anything else. Please."

Hallie's face falls, and I'm filled with guilt. She isn't trying to hurt me, but she probably doesn't remember I used to go hiking with Mom. She doesn't remember how Mom and I would make a whole day of it, hiking in the morning, browsing a bookstore near noon, getting ice cream at Ivan's to end the day. I can't relive this. Not even for Hallie.

"If you don't want to come, that's okay. We can do something else." Hallie traces a circle on the countertop with her finger, not looking at me.

I rub my face with my hands. Like yoga, I'm picking up that this may be important. And since something—I still don't know what—upset her at yoga, I don't think I should refuse. I don't get it, but Hallie's my best friend. I can try to endure thirty painful minutes for her. "Fine. Okay. Pick me up on Saturday."

Hallie looks up, her expression euphoric. "Really?"

"Only for you."

"Yay! Nav you're the best! You'll love it, I swear."

I give her a smile, but it's more like a grimace. I know I used to love hiking. But after ignoring that particular pain for so long, I don't know how I'll feel about reopening old wounds.

CHAPTER 14

I ring Gia's doorbell, and an eruption of barking comes from the other side of the door. After a few seconds, Gia opens it, an anxious smile on her face.

"Hey, Nav—"

She's cut off by Jordan zooming out of the house and leaping into my arms. I grab her and spin her around, laughing.

"Hello, my little cabbage roll! Look at you!!"

Gia watches with amusement as Jordan tries to lick my face off. "I think Jordan likes you more than me."

"I don't think, I *know*." I laugh, squeeze Jordan one more time, and put her down. She pants happily and trots into the house. Gia opens the door wider and I come in too.

"What're we doing today?" Gia asks. She's not wearing her pajamas for once; she's in a cute long top (no animal decals to be seen) and fitted jeans. And no glasses. Usually she's so relaxed, so why is today different? Though I guess it's sort of late; I slept until noon, so I didn't drag myself over here until four. Some civilized people actually get dressed in the summer, I guess.

"I was thinking that you're getting too comfortable in your room. No offense, but you were terrible at Sweet Teeth."

"Full offense taken," Gia mutters, but she's smiling a little. "So where should we go?"

"Let's not get too crazy right off. Is there somewhere you like to go? Somewhere you feel comfortable?"

Gia looks at me blankly. "I just moved here."

"Okay, let me think . . ." Somewhere she can relax, be comfortable, but still be able to talk to me . . .

"What about the park?" Gia suggests. "I haven't gone yet, and it looks really nice when I drive by to go to school."

"No freaking way. It's like a hundred degrees."

Gia rolls her eyes, grinning. "Okay, what about the rec center? I haven't been there either."

Why do all my friends suddenly want to work out? Where can I find some lazy people to hang out with? "Fine, but we're only going to the indoor track. No sports."

Gia laughs. "Okay, deal. Come on, let's tell Mami."

I'm a little taken aback, but I follow her up the stairs anyway. I didn't think to tell Dad anything. He has no clue where I am or where I'm going. It's nice that Gia and her mom are close enough to tell each other where they're headed. I try to ignore the twinge of jealousy that thought brings.

Gia leads me up the steps and down her labyrinth of a hallway until we get to an open door at the end. Gia's mom sits at a wooden desk, typing away at her laptop. She's much more casual than when I saw her last; she's in gray sweatpants and a giant plain T-shirt, and she has a pencil in her mouth. The pencil drops out as she turns to greet us, a brilliant smile on her face.

"Nav! Hello, so good to see you again!"

"Hi, Ms. Flores—"

Gia's mom rockets out of her chair and makes a beeline for me. I'm stunned into silence as she envelopes me in a huge hug. It's over as quick as it began, and she starts straightening my shirt, beaming. "Are you hungry? I can make you and Gia something! Has Gia even offered you anything yet?" She turns to Gia and says something sharp in Spanish. Gia doesn't reply, but she heaves a sigh like she has to singlehandedly solve the world's problems.

A grin tugs at my lips. "I'm good, Ms. Flores, thank you. Me and Gia were going to the gym."

"Oh, you are?" Ms. Flores raises an eyebrow at Gia.

"We were going to ask." Gia shoots a reproachful glare at me, and I grin apologetically. Whoops. Hope I didn't get Gia in trouble.

"It's fine, you can go," Ms. Flores says, smiling now. "But you're going to the gym dressed like that? In front of your friend?"

Gia mutters something in Spanish, and Ms. Flores's grin grows wider.

"I'm going to change," Gia says. "Be right back, Nav." She hurries from the room before I have a chance to say anything.

Ms. Flores doesn't miss a beat. She immediately launches into rapid-fire questions about me: how long I've lived in Mapleton, if I'm excited about the upcoming senior year, if I had any classes with Gia. I answer anything she asks, secretly pleased. No parent has ever taken so much interest in me. Hallie's mom doesn't count, since I've known her my whole life. I should make more friends!

I hear Gia's footsteps returning, and Ms. Flores puts her hands on my shoulders. She smiles fondly at me. "I'm glad you're Gia's friend, Nav."

My face warms, a little flustered, a lot happy. "Me too."

Gia enters the room. She's changed into galaxy leggings, midnight-blue tennis shoes, and a plain blue T-shirt. Still no glasses. She pulls her dark wavy hair back into a ponytail, and I don't know why I'm staring, but she looks so cute in athletic wear. Maybe I'm underdressed? Maybe I should go change too.

Ms. Flores smirks at Gia. "Much better."

A blush creeps up Gia's neck, and she grabs my arm. "All right, time to go. Bye, Mami." Gia practically drags me out of her mom's office. I laugh and wave to Ms. Flores, who follows us to the top of the stairs.

"Bye! Be careful! Drive safe!" Ms. Flores waves back at me, and Gia turns to wave too. I pat Jordan's cute little head, and then we leave Gia's house.

"I love your mom," I say as soon as we're out of earshot.

Gia smiles and rolls her eyes. "I do too. Even when she's teasing me."

I frown. Teasing her about what? I don't get to ask, because Gia says, "Do you want to drive or me?"

I nod to my car. Gia still seems flustered from the conversation with her mom, and I don't want to make her any more anxious. "I'll drive."

115

We both get into my car, I crank up, and soon I'm pulling away from Gia's manor. We don't talk at first, but it's not a bad silence. It's comfortable, like how Hallie and I can sit for hours, lying on her bed and listening to music.

"Thanks for offering to drive," Gia says, looking out her window. "But I really don't mind it. It doesn't make me nervous."

"Well, now you tell me!" I shake my head, laughing. I feel like I learn something new about Gia every day. Speaking of . . . "Your mom doesn't still think I'm a delinquent who steals your food, does she?"

"Not at all." Gia laughs. "The opposite, actually. She's so happy I have a friend now."

I glance at Gia from the corner of my eye. She did seem happy. *Really* happy. I promised myself earlier that I wouldn't get close to Gia, but hell, we're friends now. I'm curious about her life, her mom, and that huge house. "She's worried because of the move?"

"Kind of. I've always, umm, had trouble making friends." Gia still peers out the window, her shoulders tense. "We moved a lot, so I never really had the opportunity. And the anxiety doesn't help."

"Well, we're working on that last part."

Gia looks at me then, a grateful gleam in her eye.

"Did you move for your mom's work?"

"No. It's kind of a long story."

"That's okay," I say, pulling into the rec center parking lot. "We have time."

Gia and I pause the conversation while we walk up to the

massive rec center. We pass through the automatic doors, and Gia looks around, apparently enthralled with the huge lobby. My body is preemptively cramping, remembering the yoga. We check in with the front desk, and the receptionist gives us a free pass for an hour. God, I hope we're not here that long. If I exercise that much, my legs will fall off.

We go to the indoor track, which is on the second floor. It loops around the basketball court, so we have a view of kids and parents shooting hoops. I look for Hallie, but she's nowhere to be seen.

Gia and I walk half a lap before she speaks.

"So, we didn't always live like we do now. I grew up in Texas, and we lived with my abuela, abuelo, and tía. And it was fine, but when I was ten, Mami got an investor in her project, and things really changed."

"What was her project?"

"You know Snuggables?"

I nod. They're stuffed animals meant for calming down kids. They have cute, cartoonish designs, and people at school swear they sleep better when they have them. Recently, they've exploded in popularity. Hallie said she wanted an orange seahorse one, and when I tried to order it for her birthday, every store was sold out. Some maniac on eBay tried to sell it to me for four hundred dollars.

"Yeah, I know them. Why?"

Gia grins. "Mami invented them."

"Holy shit. You're kidding."

"Not kidding. If you want one, let me know. Free Snuggables for life."

"Jesus Christ. No wonder you live in a mansion."

Gia smiles at me. "We didn't always. Mami said when she made it big, she wanted to build a house with everything we ever wanted. But it took three years to build, so we bounced around a lot while she worked on the Snuggables."

"You didn't stay in Texas?"

Gia shakes her head. "Mami and Abuela got into a huge fight, and we left. And it's not like we had my father to depend on." She says *father* like a curse, bitterness heavy in her tone.

I stay quiet, waiting for her to elaborate, but she doesn't. Another half lap later, I say, "It's all right. My mom isn't around either."

Gia looks at me, her expression hard to read. "Divorce?"

"Yeah."

"Same."

We walk in heavy silence for a while. Now I'm thinking about Mom, and how she took me out to celebrate a good grade on a test right before she left. We went hiking (back when I tolerated exercise), we went shopping, we went to Ivan's. I thought it was the best day of my life. And then three days later, she tells me she's going on a trip to "find herself" because she "needs some space." And she takes herself and our dog and one of our cars on said trip, and I haven't heard from her since. Sometimes I think about it and I want to cry. Sometimes I feel so disgusted I want to throw up. But now, even though my eyes sting a little,

I'm grateful that Gia is here. She's gone through the same thing, the absence, and that's something no one else has understood before. Hallie is there for me, and I love her, but she doesn't get it. Her parents are madly in love with each other and with her. She doesn't understand how it feels to be abandoned, or how it feels to cry yourself to sleep and pray that somehow Mom will come to her senses and come home. And even though it sucks, a whole fucking lot, I'm glad I have someone who's been in that dark place with me.

"Anyway," I say, trying to sort out the feelings of despair and anger and gratitude, "it's fine. We're fine without her. Dad is a pain in the ass, but he stayed. I have to at least give him credit for that."

"Was he mad about you staying over?"

"Livid." I shake my head. "I'm grounded."

"What're you doing here with me, then?" Gia jokes.

I laugh too. "I mean, I can get around the grounding. He pisses me off so much. You know what he said? 'You're lucky I don't take your keys.' Can you believe that? I told him he can't take my car because he didn't pay for it—I did. Grandpa helped, but that's irrelevant."

"Ah," Gia says, an amused look on her face. "You're kind of a brat, aren't you?"

I stare at her, speechless. "Are you serious? You're supposed to be on my side!"

Gia shrugs, trying not to laugh. "I would be, but come on. He was worried about you."

"There's a first time for everything," I mutter. Louder, I say, "So what, you think I should just take this?"

"I don't know. But I think it's nice that he's there for you."

I think of Gia's mom not being able to take care of her sick daughter and sigh. She's right, but I don't like it.

"Fine. Whatever. No more talking about Dad, I can't take it."

Gia grins. "Okay. What now?"

"Let's do some romance practice—" I jump when my phone beeps in my pocket. Dad let me have it back for work, and then I just . . . didn't return it. He'll be mad at me, but whatever. I pull it out—wait, it's been an hour already? Gia and I look at each other in surprise. I didn't even notice we'd talked that long. Wait, it's amazing that Gia talked to me this long! We both grin at each other, and I'm full of warm energy, a gentle kind of excitement. Gia is getting better every day, and I'm so glad I get to help.

"Want to do more practice?" I ask.

Gia nods. "Sure. Do we renew our passes?"

I shake my head and wink. "I've got something else in mind."

CHAPTER 15

Gia and I stand in the park, our gazes focused straight ahead. It's getting late, so it's not as hot, and kids are running through the trees, playing tag. But we didn't come here to play games. I'm looking at the ice cream truck parked dead ahead.

"Go get me some ice cream," I tell Gia.

Gia looks at me like she might faint. My strategy is to get Gia used to talking casually to people other than me. And if her pale, about-to-pass-out complexion is something to go on, this is gonna be a challenge.

"I can't," Gia whispers. "I can't even order food at a restaurant. Mami orders for me."

"Well, I'm not doing that, so you gotta."

Gia's eyes widen pleadingly. "Come on, what does this have to do with romance practice? I'm not romancing the ice cream guy. He's not my type."

I snort out a laugh. "This is confidence practice. It counts as communication too—if you can talk to strangers, you can talk to Hallie. And when you go on a date with Hallie, I want you to try ordering food for yourself."

Gia looks like she's gonna swallow her tongue, but suddenly, determination washes over her face. Her eyebrows scrunch together and she takes a deep breath. "Okay. Okay, I can do it. What do you want?"

I beam at her. "There we go! I want one of those red, white, and blue Popsicles."

Gia nods to herself gravely, like she's about to go on a life-and-death mission. "Okay. I'll be right back."

I nod, but Gia doesn't move. I put a hand on her back and nudge her forward. "You've got this. I'm right here."

Gia shoots me a worried glance, but her feet unstick from the ground and she wobbles to the ice cream truck. Two kids jump in front of her, and she flinches but waits patiently. She looks back at me, and I give her a thumbs-up. A kid ahead of her comes away with an oozing vanilla cone. There's one more between her and the truck . . .

And she runs back to me.

Gia is panting like she's run a marathon, even though the truck is ten feet away. "I decided I'm not hungry."

"What about my Popsicle?"

Gia looks at me helplessly. "I have ice cream at home . . . ?"

"I'm lactose intolerant."

Suddenly, Gia grabs at her hair, startling me. She makes a sound that's a cross between a grunt and a soft roar. "Why are you like this? Buy your own Popsicle!"

"This is for your own good!"

Gia closes her hands into fists, like she's trying to ground herself. But her hands are still up by her face from grabbing her hair, so it looks like she's about to fight me.

"What, are we boxing?!" I mimic her position, grinning. "If you wanna fight, let's go."

She blinks at me, and then she starts laughing. All the tension from her shoulders disappears in an instant.

"You're the worst," she says, wiping a tear from her eye. "I'm gonna go buy the Popsicle now."

"Good. You can do this, okay?"

Gia nods, then goes back to the truck. She's only shaking a little, so that's probably a good sign. This time there's no line, so she walks right up to the window. I watch, my shoulders tense too. *Come on, Gia. You can do this.* Gia opens her mouth but takes a fearful step back. Shit. She's folding.

But wait . . . Gia takes a deep breath and walks in a tight circle, like she did at Sweet Teeth. Then, she returns to the truck. She talks to the man, gives him some cash, and waits. And a few seconds later, she's holding a red, white, and blue Popsicle and a strawberry shortcake one.

I run to meet her, giddy with excitement. "You did it!"

"I did!" Gia's smile is euphoric. God, I'm so proud, I could grab her face and kiss her. I haven't felt this worked up since Hallie's basketball team went to the finals. Except they lost and Gia won this battle, so I feel ten times better.

I pat Gia on the back, grinning. "Let's go sit down and eat our prize."

The playground has some pretty good swings, so I lead Gia there. A few children are shrieking on the jungle gym, but thankfully the swings are empty. We sit next to each other, and Gia gives me my Popsicle. I take a bite, shuddering at the cold against my teeth. It tastes like red and childhood and victory.

"I can't believe I did that," Gia says, her voice hushed. She sways in her swing, face upturned to the sky. "Usually it takes me months of going somewhere to get used to it before I can order."

"What was different this time?"

Gia looks at me, her brown eyes shining in the fading sun. "I guess you."

My breath catches in my chest. That's . . . unexpected. And nice. Really, really nice. Warm heat fills my face, and I smile at her. "I got you, Gia. I know you can do it. And if you can't, that's fine. We'll try again tomorrow."

Gia stares at her lap. "Abuela always hated that I was 'weird.' And I know Mami loves me, but even she gave up after getting Jordan for me and I wasn't immediately cured. You're the first person who's stuck with me."

"Well," I say, taking another bite of my Popsicle. I'm suddenly embarrassed, which is a weird feeling. I'm usually shameless, but Gia's sincerity is moving me. "What are friends for?"

Gia smiles at me, and it's like I'm basking in the rapidly setting sun. In the fading light, she's not just cute, but beautiful. I have to look away because that embarrassment is creeping up on me again. I don't know why I'm being so weird! Maybe because I'm not used to having another close friend. And it does feel like that. I do feel close to Gia, closer every time she lets me a little more into her world. And I guess the embarrassment comes from the fact that I'm really happy to be part of it.

We eat in comfortable silence for a while, watching the sun go down. The sky fills with oranges and reds, and I can't help but feel a weird sort of happiness. When's the last time I paid attention to a sunset? When's the last time I was even outside to see one?

"Do you think I'll make it in time?" Gia asks, startling me out of my happy bubble.

"Yeah, of course. Ice cream today, fancy dinner tomorrow."

Gia looks doubtful, so I continue.

"It's a first date, Gia. Dinner, movie, wave good night because we don't kiss on the first one. It's not forever."

Gia licks the remaining ice cream from her wooden stick before answering. "What if I want forever?"

Oh boy. Another bleeding heart like Hallie. I sigh and finish my Popsicle too. I toss it to the ground (don't worry, I'll get it). "You sound just like Hallie. She always falls in love with everyone she dates."

I glance at Gia, and she looks hopeful. I can practically see her thinking, *Me too?*

"And honestly I don't get the appeal. What's wrong with hookups?"

"Nothing," Gia says. "But I don't want a hookup. Don't you want to be with someone you trust?"

"I don't trust anyone."

Gia laughs and shakes her head. "But wouldn't it be nice to?"

I give her a noncommittal shrug and she continues.

"Do you think you'd ever try dating instead?"

I swing for a second, thinking. I don't see the point in it. True love isn't real. It's not a thing that actually exists. Look at Mom and Dad. Hell, Gia's parents. People don't stay together. If I started dating like Hallie, I'd just be disappointed. And I've had enough of that for a lifetime.

"Probably not," I tell Gia. I can't stand the way her face falls so I add, "It would have to be a really special girl."

"I'll take that." Gia's phone chirps, and she pulls it out of her pocket. She makes an exasperated face. "Mami wants to know when we're coming home. And she also wants to know if you can stay for dinner."

"We can go now, if you want. And also *yes*."

Gia looks at me, eyebrows raised. I wait for her to say something, but she doesn't.

"What?"

"Don't you have something to text your dad?"

Oh hell, I forgot again. I sigh and pull out my phone. "You're an asshole, you know that?"

"If it keeps you from fighting with your dad, I'll wear that cape gladly."

I roll my eyes and text Dad.

can i eat dinner at Gia's house?

I wait, and Dad texts back a minute later.

Be home by nine.

126

It's only six thirty, so that's perfect. I show Gia the text. "We good to go, princess?"

Gia stands, and I do too. "We're good. Proud of you, Nav."

I pick up my Popsicle stick, and Gia and I leave the park. We climb into my car, and I glance at my phone while Gia's buckling up. I have one more text from Dad.

Thank you for asking me.

Even though I'm mad at him, a weak part of me softens. I guess I'm proud of me too.

CHAPTER 16

I glare at the trees of Doppler Forest, dread in my gut. This was a mistake.

We're at the entrance, and I already want to go home. The forest is dense, full of deciduous and pine trees flanking some shady trails. There's rumored to be a waterfall somewhere in this mess, but I'm sure not about to go searching for it. There are probably bears in here too. That'd be just my luck—eaten by a bear on a hike I don't even want to be on.

Hallie is excited, chatting up a storm, ignoring the undoubtedly sour expression on my face. "I figure we can take this trail and pause at the top to take pictures."

Sure enough, she has a camera swinging from her neck. It's kind of a nice one too . . . why haven't I seen it before?

"When did you get into photography?"

Hallie shrugs, smiling. "Just trying it out."

Huh. She's never liked hiking before either. Or yoga. We're "just trying out" a lot of things lately.

I don't say anything more, and Hallie leads the way to one of the trails. I'm immediately in a worse mood as we step onto the worn dirt mixed with gravel. This is the same trail Mom and I always took. Sweat drips down my back and pools under my arms, and it's not all from the heat.

"I hate this," I complain. The trees shield us from the sun, but I can't bring myself to be happy about it.

"We just started!" Hallie laughs. She aims her camera at a tree and starts clicking.

"Yeah, and I wish we'd end it quick," I mutter.

She doesn't answer; she keeps pointing her camera at random trees and leaves.

We climb the glorified hill for what feels like forever. The farther we go, the worse my mood gets. "This sucks. Why're we hiking in the middle of summer?"

"It's just June," Hallie says. She takes more pictures, so I can't really see her face.

"Yeah, like I said, hot as hell. Why couldn't we do this in March or something?"

Hallie doesn't answer, and soon all I can hear is my own panting in my ears. I close my eyes against the sun and the memories threatening to flood out of their box.

"Can we go soon? Is it too late to turn around?"

Hallie ignores me and keeps walking, clicking her camera. I stay quiet too, brooding, seething in my head, until we reach the hilltop.

"Oh, look!" Hallie points at a red bird. She takes pictures frantically and then aims the camera to the view atop the hill. It is—or would be—a great view; you can see the entire city of Mapleton from here, and all the buildings look like toys and the people like ants. An unwelcome memory pushes itself to the forefront of my mind; Mom and I eating lunch up here, admiring the view, making up stories about the ant-people down below. It was one of the only things we did together, just us. I take a shaky breath and will myself not to cry. I shouldn't have come here.

"Yeah, bird, cityscape, great." I huff and kick a rock. My feet are throbbing faintly, and I'm refusing to look to my left, where I know a bench sits. A bench with Mom and my initials carved into the seat, plus the date from three years ago. "How much longer?"

Hallie doesn't answer at first. She slowly lowers her camera, then turns around to face me. And she looks . . . upset? Wait, is she angry?

"What's your deal, Nav?"

"What's that supposed to mean?" I'm immediately defensive. What's she mad at me for?

"You're always so negative. Why is it that everything I want to do is stupid?"

"I never said that." Tightness grips my chest. Where is this coming from? Hallie and I hardly ever fight. "I hate exercising, you know that."

"I know, but I invited you because I thought you'd have fun. But you didn't even try. You just complained the whole time."

"This isn't fair. I said I didn't want to go hiking, and you basically begged me to."

Hallie stares at me for a few seconds, her cheeks puffed out a little. Which I would normally think is cute, but right now my alarm bells are going off. Something isn't right. The whole day has felt off, and now Hallie is arguing with me? Why? What's going on?

"Fine," Hallie says finally. "I guess I should have picked something else."

"Yeah." I want to end it there, but she deserves an explanation. "Mom and I used to come here."

All the anger and frustration leave Hallie's face in an instant. "Shit, Nav, I'm sorry."

"No, it's fine. I wanted to go with you, I just . . . it's hard."

"You could have told me." Hallie's voice is heavy with regret.

I know I could have. She would have understood. But I don't know how to bring it up with her. We don't talk about Mom—those are the friend rules I set, and no matter how much it hurts sometimes, I can't bring myself to break them. I want to do dumb shit with Hallie, because that's what we've always done. Even if I hate horror movies and yoga, I've always stuck it out because that's what we do. It's just that this one was too much. I don't know how to say any of that to Hallie, though, so I opt for, "It's fine. I'll go anywhere else, but can we not come here again?"

"Yeah, of course." Hallie hugs me, which would be sweet except we're both sweaty. "God, I feel like such an ass now. You can pick the next place, I swear."

"Which'll be Sarah's party. So I can get shit-faced and forget all the exercise you're making me do."

Hallie laughs. She squeezes me tighter. "Let's go. We'll get Sarah's present and stop for ice cream, okay?"

I smile into her shoulder, thinking about my lactose intolerance lie to Gia. She'd kill me if she saw me eating ice cream after that. "It's cool, Hal. But I will take some AC."

We walk down the hill again, and things feel normal between us. But I'm still uneasy. Hallie and I never fight. Well, not never, but it's rare. Usually it's over her many breakups and broken hearts—

I stop walking. That's it. That's what's different. I've been hanging out with Gia so I didn't notice, but she hasn't talked about her breakup once in two weeks.

"What's wrong?" Hallie asks, looking back at me with raised eyebrows.

I examine her face. She's curious, but not angry. She also doesn't look tired from crying herself to sleep at night. In fact, she seems kind of happy. "So . . . you haven't mentioned Peter lately."

"Oh." Hallie looks away for a second, then returns her gaze to me. "I guess I haven't been thinking about him."

"Really." That can't be right. She was sobbing in my lap two weeks ago. It takes her forever to get over her exes . . . usually, the moping only stops when she finds someone new to obsess over. "So you've moved on?"

Hallie shrugs, and we start walking again. Her car is in sight, thank God.

"Yeah, I think I have. You were right—he was wasting my time. So I shouldn't let him take any more."

When has she ever listened to me about her partners? I don't say anything as we climb into her car. She sets the AC to full blast and fiddles with her rearview mirror but doesn't say anything else.

"Hallie?"

"Yeah?"

"You'd tell me if something was going on, right?"

Hallie looks genuinely surprised. "Yeah, of course. I really am over him, I promise."

I don't think she's lying. But that doesn't make me feel any better. Because Hallie is acting so weird, not like Hallie at all. Even if I'm infinitely glad she's leaving dickheads in the dust, I can't ignore that's something she wouldn't normally do. She wouldn't normally try yoga or hiking or photography. While I'm at Gia's, she is doing something else, something I'm not part of.

And that scares me more than I'd like to admit.

♡♡♡

I sit outside my house for a few minutes, staring into the illuminated front window. Again. This is becoming a pattern.

I hung out with Hallie after the disaster hike, but I left early because I knew Dad would be on the warpath again. I don't feel like cooking after sweating in the horrible heat today, so I stopped by Zaxby's. I'd prefer going straight to bed, but looks like that isn't happening. Dad isn't pacing the living room this time, but his car *is* in the driveway, so no chance of me avoiding him. I shake my head and gather my Zaxby's bags. Might as well get it over with.

I parked close to the house, but it feels like it takes forever to get to the front door. The bags of food are heavy in my hands. I almost want to turn around and go back to Hallie's, and I would except I'm starving and microwaved bread tastes horrible. I take a deep breath and open my door.

Dad is dozing in his armchair, but he starts awake as soon as the door swings open. He blinks at me for a second and I stare warily back.

"Oh, Naveah," he says. He still looks kind of sleepy, which is a good thing. Maybe he'll let me sneak upstairs without us screaming at each other. He glances at my bags and sits up straighter. "You already ate?"

"Umm, no. But I'm about to."

"Oh."

We stare at each other. As the seconds tick by, the awkwardness dials up more and more. What does he want me to say? He can see the bags in my hand. This is awful. I hate this.

Dad clears his throat, which makes me jump. "I didn't know you were picking up food. I should have called you."

"Why?"

Dad wordlessly stands and goes to the microwave. He withdraws . . . a Zaxby's bag.

"I got you a chicken sandwich," he says, staring at me. It's like his mouth wants to smile but isn't sure how. "No mayo. Extra pickles."

I look at Dad, and my mouth is doing the same thing his is. I want to smile, because that's exactly what I ordered tonight.

Somehow, despite the three absent years, he remembered. But even though I want to grin and give him a hug, my brain warns that there's something not quite right with this scene. I'm in a strange reality where everything is just a little off. Dad ignores me. I do the dinner hunting. He doesn't bring me exactly what I wanted after a long day. He doesn't care about me. That's reality. Not . . . this. Whatever this is.

"I'll eat yours tomorrow for lunch," I say, without the smile I wanted to give him.

He nods. His expression remains stoic. "Makes sense. I'll call next time."

"That's okay." I hesitate, then put his bag on the counter. "I got a salad for you."

Surprise crosses Dad's face, and I have to work hard to keep the triumphant grin at bay. "Fried or grilled?"

"Grilled. I know you like fried better, but your doctor said . . ." I trail off. I wasn't supposed to overhear that phone call, but Dad is loud and I was awake watching a cooking show, so . . .

"Oh." Dad looks like he wants to say more, but he doesn't. We stare at each other for another few excruciating seconds before I can't take it anymore.

"I'm going to bed."

"Okay." Dad clears his throat again. "Good night, Naveah."

"Night, Dad."

I go to my room and shut the door. I take a few deep breaths. God that was *weird*. But also weirdly nice? Kind of? It was awkward and tense, but we didn't yell at each other. We didn't even argue. A modern miracle.

I get dressed in my pajamas, thinking of this strange, tentative truce between me and Dad. It almost feels like we're stretching unfamiliar muscles, sore from disuse. It's strange. And uncomfortable. But maybe, like actual sore muscles, it'll be worth it in the end? I load up Netflix on my laptop, dubious. Somehow, I can't imagine us changing that much.

I watch *The Great British Baking Show* for the rest of the night, but I'm distracted. I can't shake the uneasy, yet somehow peaceful, feeling of finally having a normal conversation with Dad again.

CHAPTER 17

Gia opens the door, surprise on her face. She's wearing pajamas with pink cats on them and her glasses, which somehow makes me feel a little better.

"You're early!"

I am. I'm kinda not feeling good. Dad's being so weird, and Hallie is acting weird now too. I lay in bed all night and couldn't sleep. So even though I wasn't supposed to come over to Gia's until 3:00 p.m., here I am at noon because I thought having one person stay the same would make me feel better. And, oddly, it does.

"Is that okay?"

"Sure, you can come over whenever." She opens the door for me, and Jordan comes flying down the top steps. I open my arms to catch her, mood already ten times better.

"My little eggplant!! How are you, fluffy butt?!"

"You change her name every time you see her," Gia says, laughing.

I kiss Jordan's head as she wriggles in delight. "She deserves it! I mean, look at her. She's a perfect dog."

Gia smiles as we climb the steps to her room. The house is dark and eerily quiet, like it was on my first few visits. Maybe Gia's mom is gone again. Off to save the world and rake in a

137

fortune, one stuffed animal at a time. Talk about goals.

"We can't start practice yet," Gia says. She heads to her Snorlax beanbag and sits down. "I have to level up and farm equipment first. We have an event coming up."

"First of all, I didn't understand a single thing you just said." I sit down on the other Pokémon beanbag, which Gia informed me was Gengar.

Gia chuckles and boots up her game. "It's kind of like a tournament. We're doing PVP—player versus player—so the guildies and I need to be ready. It's a lot different than playing against the computer."

"Guildies?!" I laugh as Gia's face turns scarlet.

"Don't make fun of me!" She throws a pillow at me, and I catch it, still laughing. "You'll try the game one day and end up liking it."

"Not a chance. It looks boring as hell and way too complicated—"

Suddenly, I shut up. I'm getting terrible déjà vu about the hike with Hallie. She said I was always negative, and I fought with her about it in the woods, but oh God, am I? Is she right?

"You okay?" Gia asks timidly.

I turn to look at her, full of guilt and horror and shame. "Do you think I'm a negative person?"

"Umm . . ." Gia looks at me for a second, then pauses her game. She takes her headset off and places it on the floor. "No, but what's this about? You seem really upset."

I *am* upset. My heart's beating furiously in my chest, and my palms are damp with sweat. "Hallie said I'm always negative and complaining about the things that she likes. And maybe that's true? I did it just now, with your game. And when Hallie and I went to yoga."

"Okay," Gia says slowly. "That doesn't mean you're a negative person. Maybe you don't like trying new things."

Huh. I have had the same Subway order for ten years. And there's the thousand-plus-day streak of Galaxy Cat. "Yeah, maybe you're right."

"That's not a bad thing," Gia says. "It means you're predictable."

"That definitely sounds like a bad thing."

"Fine, then—consistent?"

I nod slowly. That's sounding a little better. "But I didn't mean to hurt Hallie's feelings with my . . . consistency. Or yours, about your game."

Gia waves her hand lazily in the air. "You don't hurt my feelings. I know it's a tough game to get into, and it probably makes no sense to you. But I love it, so who cares?"

"Wow." I feel like I'm seeing Gia in a brand-new light. "Where's that confidence when Hallie's trying to talk to you?"

"That's different!" Gia protests.

It's really not, but she's not ready to hear that yet. "Okay, well, listen. I'm sorry I've been mean about your game. You love it, and I haven't given it a chance. Do you think you could show me how to play now?"

Gia puts a hand on my shoulder and looks right into my eyes. "Nav, I would normally say yes to this character development, but I have to prepare for the tournament. You're going to have to play some other time."

Wow. I'm so shocked, I burst into laughter.

Gia grins. "Besides, you probably wouldn't like it. You like idle games right? Like Galaxy Cat?"

"How do you know about GC?"

"You play it all the time in art."

Touché. "I don't actually like that game. I just play it because I always have."

"See? Not liking new things," Gia says, poking me in the side. "But if you want to try something new that's not the game I need to grind on, let me think . . ."

Gia leaves my side and rifles around on her bookshelf. She returns with a coral Nintendo Switch and gives it to me. I boot it up, curious. I used to have a hand-me-down 3DS from my older cousin, Ben, but once that broke, I didn't replace it. I've seen Switches in ads, but I haven't had a reason to play one until now.

"The game in there is called *Starlight Seasons*," Gia says. She puts her headset back on but doesn't resume the game yet. "Start a new save file."

A cartoon kid pops up on the loading screen, along with stylized cows, chickens, and donkeys. "What kind of game is it?"

"Farming sim." Gia restarts her game, and the green-haired dwarf runs around a grassy terrain.

"How do I play?"

Gia taps the top of my head with her controller. She gives me an easy grin. "I'm sure you can figure it out."

Well, fine. I grumble a little and set up a new save file under Gia's. She's spent 120 hours on this, so it's gotta be decent. I name my character, and soon I'm lost in meeting townspeople, catching wild animals to tame them, and fixing up my busted ass farm. After a while, I lean on Gia to get comfortable, my head against her thigh, the Switch propped on my belly. I swear I don't move for an hour, completely engrossed.

Something bright flashes on the TV, and I pause to look over at Gia's game. The dwarf frantically swings an axe, but a giant red dragon snaps his swinging arm off like a twig.

"Fuck," Gia mutters under her breath. Are her hands shaking? No, it must be when the controllers vibrate when the health is low. "Nick, heal me!"

"Damn," I say, watching her dodge the dragon's fangs and approach what looks like a little kid in an overgrown robe, "you're playing like shit."

Gia glares at me. I hear faint, tinny laughter from her headset.

"How's the farm going?"

"Great, actually." I grin at her. "Better than your dragon-slaying campaign."

Gia makes a face at me, and I snuggle closer to her. Something about this, the farm game, listening to Gia's muttered curses, Jordan curled up at both our sides, feels better than anything I've felt since summer started.

I play until Gia's Switch is on three percent. I save and put it down, and watch Gia play for a while. I'm suddenly sleepy, like I've eaten a warm bowl of soup and an after-meal itis is threatening to pull me under.

"I can't play while you're watching me," Gia whines. Sure enough, her dwarf trips and falls down a dark mine shaft. Voices groan from the headset.

"Then stop playing." I'm just teasing. I think if I watch for too much longer, I'll fall asleep.

But Gia sighs heavily and saves her game. "I'll be back later, okay? Yep, we'll get the chest tonight, don't worry. Yeah, yeah, Alan, that's cute. Bye." Gia touches her headset, annoyance crossing her face.

"You didn't have to stop for me. I didn't mean to bother you."

"No, no." Gia looks down at me, and for the first time I realize my head is still in her lap. "You never bother me, Nav."

Whoa. My heart's kinda going crazy for some reason. I grin up at her, ignoring my heart rattling around in my rib cage. "That was a really good line. You're learning so much already!"

Gia rolls her eyes, but her neck is turning pink. "Are we doing romance practice today or not?"

I stay quiet, thinking. I don't really want to practice; I want to hang out with Gia today. Which isn't weird, surely, because Gia is my friend.

"Today, let's do Quality Time. It's easy, because we just have to spend time together. We can do practical practice later."

I expect her to argue, but she doesn't. She stands, rotates her beanbag chair, and sits down so that she's slouching like I am, back-to-back. Our heads are lying next to each other. "Okay."

For a second, we lie there, staring up at Gia's ceiling. Jordan snores softly at my feet. It's calm and sweet, and I find myself sleepy again.

"Can I ask you a question?" Gia says after a few silent minutes.

"Yeah, of course."

"So, Hallie likes girls." Gia pauses for a second, adjusting her beanbag chair. "And boys."

"She's bisexual, yes." Hallie is out and proud to everyone, so I feel fine about clarifying for Gia.

"Okay. And you like girls too."

"If you're asking me if I'm a lesbian, the answer is yes."

Gia breathes out, but it's not quite a sigh. Relief? "Me too. I don't really get boys, if I'm honest."

"Yeah, I mean girls are cute and smell good. Why would I want anything else?"

Gia laughs, and I smile at the ceiling.

"Why'd you ask?"

"Well . . ." Gia fidgets again. Jordan lifts her head sleepily and looks at Gia. "I was wondering . . . if Hallie likes girls and you also like girls . . ."

A light bulb turns on in my head. "Oh, no, Gia. There's nothing going on with me and Hallie. Never has, never will."

"Oh." Gia doesn't say anything for a while, so I keep talking.

"Hallie and I have known each other since we were born. Her mom and my mom were really tight, like 'buy houses in the

143

same neighborhood' close, so we were always together. Hallie's pretty much my sister."

"That's really nice," Gia says, and her tone sounds sincere. "It's cool that you have someone that close."

"Yeah. She's my best friend." I nudge Gia with my elbow. "One of the only friends I have."

"Wait, what?" Gia looks back at me, upside down. "You have a ton of friends. You're always talking to someone different when I see you at school."

"Correction: I know a lot of people. That doesn't mean they're my friends. I don't know their last names, or text them, or know anything personal about them. They're the weed hookup, or throw great parties. You know."

"Wow. I didn't know being your friend was such an exclusive club."

"Yep. You, Hallie, my cousin Ben. And Ben probably doesn't count because he's family."

"Do you wish you had more friends?" Gia's voice has a wistful edge to it.

"Nah." I grin at her. "I've got everything I need."

Gia looks away, smiling, and I look away too. My heart is doing that strange, pounding thing again. Man, I'm being so weird today. I blame Hallie. And Dad.

It is true, though. I thought Hallie was all I needed. But I've come to really like Gia. I like that she blushes easily, but unevenly in cute patches. I like her seemingly endless supply of animal-themed pajamas. I like that she isn't scared to call me out on my shit. I like how excited she gets when she orders Popsicles by herself and how she refuses to give up on this deal, no matter how hard it gets. I'm glad we met. I almost don't want to give her away to Hallie! It'll be kind of lonely to be the third wheel. And when I think of them on their official date, all the excitement I felt before is gone.

"Do you think it's still possible?" Gia asks, startling me out of my not-so-fun fantasy. "Getting over my anxiety, I mean."

"You don't have to get over it. Just manage it."

"Is that good enough?"

"Only you can decide that, but for the record, it's good enough for me. And I'm sure it's good enough for Hallie too." I lean farther back, so the top of my head bumps Gia's. "She's your dream girl, after all."

"I think I changed my mind on that." Gia folds her hands over her stomach, staring up at the ceiling again. "Maybe dream girls don't exist."

"Hey, hey, no giving up." I sit up, shaking off my sleepiness. She's obviously getting anxious; Jordan is pawing at her arm. "Let's get some practice in, and then we can mope around."

Gia sits up too and holds Jordan to her chest. She meets my eyes, and I'm surprised to see that her expression is a little sad. "Okay. Let's go. What's the practice for today?"

I stand and put my hands on my hips. "I think it's time for that movie."

CHAPTER 18

Gia looks at me like I said we're about to eat a hamster. "We're going to the movies? Right now?"

"No. Don't panic."

Gia takes a shaky breath. Definitely on the edge of panic. I hurry to explain.

"I know I said the movies should be the final date, but I think we should practice first." The Sweet Teeth behavior weighs heavily on my mind. "You've got that fancy media room, yeah? Let's watch something in there."

The tension melts out of Gia's shoulders like ice cream in an Alabama summer. She smiles at me, a huge one that takes me by surprise. "Okay, we should! You want to watch something right now?"

"Yep, but let's get popcorn first. You do have popcorn, right?"

"Of course." Gia sounds insulted, which pulls a grin out of me. She leads the way out of her room, and I follow her downstairs to the kitchen. I sit at the island while Gia grabs a bag of extra butter popcorn from her pantry, tears off the plastic, and puts it in the microwave. "I actually haven't used the media room much."

"Really? Why not?"

"I don't know. It's boring by myself, I guess." Gia crosses her arms over her chest, frowning at the microwave like she's deep in thought. "I watch movies on my laptop."

"Well, not today! You've gotta put up with me now."

Gia dumps popcorn into a well-worn green bowl and turns to me. She looks like she's ready to go to war, not watch a movie. "What now?"

I grab the popcorn bowl. Its gentle heat warms my palms. "When we go on our Final Exam date, I want you to order our tickets."

Gia's eyebrows pull together. "I don't think—"

"You can," I interrupt her. "Imagine we're at the movies and I'm the ticket guy."

"If we're at the movies, you won't be behind the counter. You don't work there."

Ugh, Gia has no imagination at all. "Fine, okay, let's say I got a part-time job after school, and I work at Cineplex now."

"And Sweet Teeth?"

"Yes. And I work at Sweet Teeth too."

"That's a lot of work," Gia says. She looks faintly anxious and twists her fidget ring between her fingers. "You'll be exhausted after school starts. Are you saving up for something?"

If Gia wasn't so adorable with her concern for my fake well-being, I'd scream.

"All right. This isn't working. Hang on." I abandon the popcorn and pick up Jordan, who'd been hovering at my feet hoping I'd drop some food. I put her in my chair and then walk around the island and stand next to Gia. "There, now Jordan is the ticket guy. I'm here with you, like I'll be on the Final Exam."

Gia smiles at me, and then at Jordan, whose eyes are bugged out of her head as she stares at the popcorn. But she doesn't lunge for it, like Cuddles would have done. Such a good girl!

"Dogs can't work at Cineplex either." But it's working, because Gia stops fidgeting with her ring. She looks at me, only slightly nervous. "What movie are we seeing?"

"You can pick," I say. "Though Hallie will probably want to see a horror."

A dark look crosses Gia's face, but she turns to Jordan and says, "Two tickets to *Fangs and Fury*, please."

Jordan barks, startling me, and Gia and I start laughing. "She's the perfect employee! Is there anything this Yule log can't do?!"

"She's really bad at math," Gia says, grinning. "But other than that, perfect."

We play with Jordan for a few minutes, rewarding her hard work with popcorn, and then I follow Gia to the fancy media room.

I was expecting a small movie theater, but it's a lot simpler than that. There are three rows of couches, each higher than the one in front of it, and there's a giant TV that covers one wall. The couches are surprisingly not new; the one in the front row looks worn and broken in, and it's covered in comfortable blankets. I sit down on that one, pleased when I sink into the middle. That's what I like most about Gia's house; it's obviously new, but it has small touches like an old popcorn bowl or a couch that's seen better days. It's nice. Gia fiddles with the remote and boots up Netflix. She scrolls through until she settles on *Fangs and Fury*, a straight-to-streaming vampire action flick that's allegedly gory. I hold in a shudder. Not at all what I would have picked, but this is Gia's show now.

"Ready?" she calls, hand on the light switch.

"Ready." I jump when she flips it off. Now the only light is from a cute cat-shaped lamp on the end table next to the couch. Gia settles into the seat next to me and turns off the lamp. We're plunged into stunning darkness, and for a second, I almost reach for her hand to find her in the dark. My eyes adjust after a few seconds and find her anyway, where she's frowning in concentration at the remote. She pushes a button and the movie begins.

I'm immediately bored. I'm not a movie person on the best day, and action ones, supernatural or otherwise, put me to sleep. I pull out my phone and scroll lazily through Instagram before the ugly vampire guy can even explain what kind of model his car is or whatever.

"Are you on your phone?" Gia whispers, startling me.

"Yeah," I whisper back. But then I remember I'm at Gia's house and not at the actual movies and smile.

Gia isn't smiling. She looks annoyed. "This is bad movie etiquette."

"Okay, movie snob."

"I'm not a movie snob," Gia says, keeping her voice hushed. Her tone is haughty, just like a movie snob's would be. "Everyone knows you can't be on your phone at the movies."

"Movie police, then."

Gia sighs heavily, and I try to pay attention, but I'm so bored. I keep glancing at Gia, how her illuminated face is serious with rapt attention. When the vampire makes a cringey joke, I catch the exact moment Gia wrinkles her nose like an adorable rabbit. She glances at me too, as if asking *Can you believe this?*, and I burst out laughing. She matches my laugh and nudges me playfully with her knee.

"Don't distract me," she whispers, still giggling.

"Don't blame me! The grease in his hair is distracting enough."

Gia laughs again, and I turn my attention to the movie, still grinning. Somehow, watching movies with Gia is bearable. After that, I end up doing a running commentary through the entire film, and Gia giggles along with me. When it's over, we have an empty bowl of popcorn and my phone's nearly at full battery.

"That was fun," Gia says, then seems surprised she said that out loud.

"Yeah, it was." Which is weird, because I mean it. The movie sucked, but hanging out with Gia really didn't. I stand, shaking off the strange feeling. "Okay, next! Now, we'll go to dinner."

"Do you want real dinner?" Gia asks.

I raise my eyebrows. "You're willing to go out? And order by yourself?"

"God, no," Gia snorts. "We're using DoorDash."

I roll my eyes, but I'm laughing too. I kind of adore Gia.

She's so funny, and I'm always surprised by what she's going to say next. "All right then, let's do it."

I find out Gia is just as much a food snob as she is a movie snob. No french fries (too greasy), no quesadillas (compared to Texas, the Mexican food here is a crime), no Burger King (apparently, it is the most inferior of all the fast-food chains). We bicker for twenty gleeful minutes on what to order, and finally settle on Chinese food. But it's going to take forty-five minutes for them to make Gia's highly complicated order, so we settle in the living room to wait.

"Am I doing okay so far?" Gia asks suddenly.

"You're doing great." I sit up a little straighter. "Though now is a good time to practice some Communication."

"Okay." Gia rubs Jordan's ears between her thumb and forefinger, but she doesn't seem as tense as before. She looks at me (a little over my head, anyway). "What do we do?"

"You probably won't agree with Hallie on everything. God knows her taste in movies is horrible. But you can't be scared to tell her how you really feel." I smile at Gia when she starts fidgeting. "You can practice with me, because we're friends. I won't be offended by what you say, so you don't have to be scared."

"What should I say?"

"Whatever you want."

Gia frowns at me. She's looking into my eyes for once. "You shouldn't be on your phone at the movies. Because you didn't pay attention, and now we can't discuss the movie over dinner."

151

Wow! That's really good, actually. I'd expected her to be timid, but she's going for it. "Ah, man, you and Hallie are always on my case about that. I don't even like movies." I stare into Gia's eyes so she'll remember this next part. "But I hear you, and it won't happen again. Phone away during movie time. Promise."

Gia seems surprised by my response, so I grin.

"Easy, right?"

"Yeah, but . . ." Gia seems troubled. "Why didn't you tell me you don't like movies? We could have done something else."

"Eh, I'm more of a reality TV fan." You don't have to pay attention during cooking shows, and I can draw or play the cursed Galaxy Cat at the same time. "But I don't mind watching a movie if you want to. I like spending time with you."

I stop, a little stunned by my honesty. It's true, though, isn't it? I like coming here. I like hanging out with Gia and scheming up ridiculous romance lessons. She's doing great, honestly, but selfishly, I get a lot out of our practices too. It's almost as if Gia means as much to me as Hallie does.

For some reason, my face is hot. And Gia's eyes are wide, and we haven't spoken for a good thirty seconds. Shit, I made things awkward.

"That was good communication," Gia finally says, a tentative smile on her face.

Thank God she's bailing me out. I clear my throat and will my face to go back to a normal temperature. "I'm the professor, remember?"

"Right," Gia says, rolling her eyes. "You have a communication PhD too?"

"Absolutely! One day you'll respect me and my four hundred degrees."

We laugh, and Gia hugs Jordan to her chest. "Can we practice something else?"

Oh, that's new. I raise my eyebrows, already curious. "Yeah, of course. What's up?"

"I'm not good at small talk," Gia admits. "Takara always says I'm like a bull crashing into a conversation."

"Who's Takara again?"

Gia twists her fingers in the hem of her shirt. "One of the guildies. They always try to give me advice."

I nod and consider this for a second. Gia is frank and asks some hard questions sometimes, but I don't think it's a bad thing. "That's fine. The way you talk, I mean."

"Yeah?"

"Yeah. Here, let me ask you something right now."

Gia nods, eyes wide, and I point to Jordan.

"You told me Jordan is a therapy dog."

"Right."

"So that means you've been to therapy before."

Gia nods slowly, and I continue.

"Are you going to therapy for your anxiety now?"

Gia struggles for a few seconds. Jordan looks up at her, but Gia takes a deep breath before answering. "I used to go. But I've never found the right person. And honestly, I don't think Mami believes in therapy."

"Same for my family. They think it's a scam."

My cousin Ben told my aunt that he was feeling depressed,

and she told him to eat and go lay down. And don't get me started on Dad. We probably should have seen someone after Mom left. But we just shut down and stopped talking, and now I have two ruined parental relationships instead of one. I'm an emotional orphan. That makes *me* depressed, so I focus on Gia again.

"You should go if you want to, though."

Gia shrugs. She looks at my feet, and her expression is vaguely unhappy. "My cousin always says I should go back, but . . . I don't know."

Maybe it's time for a topic change. "You talk to me about it when you're ready, okay?" I nudge her leg with my foot, causing her to look up. "Now, your turn. What deep, bull-in-china-shop question do you have to ask me?"

Gia doesn't hesitate. "Why do you want to go to Carnegie Camp?"

My instinct is to groan and deflect, like I did last time. I hate thinking about that fucking camp. I hate having to open up the compartmentalization box I put it in and rifle through my feelings. But this time, I hesitate. It hurts, but maybe I could answer. For Gia, I think I could. Maybe take a peek into the box, at least.

I rub my face with my hands. Maybe this will be easier with my eyes closed. "Hallie's going."

"Right." Gia's voice is gentle.

I'm sure she can relate to this teeth pulling I'm about to do. "Because Hallie's smart."

"Yeah." Gia's already prying the box open, because now I'm thinking that Hallie earned that spot at camp. She studies for hours while I doodle and watch *Worth It*. She's fantastic at math and science, and watches videos on obscure facts in her spare time. Hallie prepped her application for weeks, and I turned mine in last minute. She deserves to go to Carnegie Camp, and I don't. But even though I know that, I can't let her go. A harsh, sour feeling burns in my gut, and I wish I hadn't ordered anything to eat.

"She's my best friend, and I worry about her." I hesitate but add, "And me."

"Why?" Gia's voice is soft, soothing. I still can't look at her.

"She's my only friend. She was my only friend, before you, I mean." I take another breath. "And honestly, I don't want to be alone."

Saying it out loud sucks. Even though I know it's true, deep in my spirit, it sucks to admit that I'm a pathetic girl who can't be without her best friend for six weeks. But I'm desperate here. With Dad acting so weird, facing down six weeks alone is unbearable. I need this. I need to get out of this town and preserve what little I have so I don't lose something precious to me again.

"I get that," Gia says.

I finally look up, and Gia's expression is serious.

"I'm really grateful for the guildies, but it's not the same as having real-life connections, you know? I'm the youngest in the group. Kenny and Camilla talk about their kids and Takara and

Alan talk about college, and it's just . . ." Gia blows out a breath. She looks annoyed, but sad too. "Last summer, I didn't talk to a single person face-to-face except Mami. I sat inside and watched YouTube and Twitch, and played games. I watched the days go by, and I couldn't move. I wanted to move, to meet someone or make friends, but I couldn't do it. It was horrible. I felt like if I didn't do something, I was going to be a recluse forever."

"So that's why talking to Hallie is so important?"

Gia nods gravely. "Even if it's hard. Even if I throw up after romance lessons."

"Wait, what—"

"Anyway," Gia talks over me. "I decided to change. And it worked."

I mean, that's a generous assessment. She hasn't talked to Hallie yet, though the stiff nod at Sweet Teeth was progress. "How so?"

Gia looks right into my eyes and smiles. "I met you."

"Oh." Involuntary heat fills my face, and my heart kicks up its rhythm. Why am I so frazzled? And flattered? And feeling some secret joy, a thrill of understanding and connection, and, God, am I blushing?!

I'm thankful when the doorbell rings and Gia flinches, shocked out of our moment. She jumps to her feet but doesn't move, so I shake my head and collect the food for her. But the feeling from before lingers. Even as Gia washes her hands and distributes our Chinese boxes, I'm warm and fuzzy and feeling weirdly like cotton candy or something. What is *wrong* with me today? I'm almost not surprised when I say, "Do you want to go to a party with me on Saturday?"

"Absolutely not."

We both laugh at her immediate refusal. Some of the strangeness fades, and I'm heading back to normal land. Gia is my friend, my goofy, antisocial friend. That's all. "Does 'let me down easy' mean nothing to you?"

"Sorry," Gia says. She takes a bite of her food—some complicated version of orange chicken—and I remember her anxiety around eating with Hallie. She doesn't seem the least bit scared right now. "I really can't go. We have a tournament coming up and it's PVP, so I can't miss."

"I get it," I say, though I don't. And though I'm weirdly disappointed. I don't even know why I asked. Sarah's party would be *way* too much for Gia. But . . . I guess I wanted to hang out with her more.

I stay for another hour, laughing at her jokes, playing with Jordan and complaining about her game, but that strangeness from earlier lingers all day long.

CHAPTER 19

Hallie runs a curling iron through her hair, tongue sticking out in concentration. I fluff the curly part of my hair, frowning at the sides. I need to shave them when I have a minute; I'm starting to look less "cool lesbian" and more "woolly mammoth." While Hallie carefully puts on eyeliner, I straighten my shirt, which is a loose white T-shirt that says "HBIC." I don't know who it belongs to (I woke up wearing it one day after a party), but it's mine now and I love it. I bet Gia would get a kick out of it.

"What's the plan?" I ask Hallie as she finishes her makeup. I never wear any—too much effort.

"Sarah's is right down the road, so we can walk there and back."

Oh hell yeah, no DD? I could sing right now. "Curfew?"

"Midnight."

"Got your present?"

Hallie pauses with the iron and holds up a pink bag with white tissue paper sticking out of the top. "Got it!"

"All right, let's get this rollin'." I have my present too, which is some generic Bath & Body Works relaxation pack. But hey, who doesn't need lotion and fuzzy socks? I'm mainly concerned about the three hours we've got to have some fun. I'd like longer, but I've made do with less.

Hallie and I finish getting ready, and then we trek downstairs to face her parents. Hallie's mom (Aunt Cathy to me) is peering into the fridge, but I don't see her dad. Aunt Cathy straightens when we get to the kitchen, already smiling. She's tall, always wears her hair in an ornate bun, and always has on some sort of silver jewelry. I've never seen her in pajamas or sweatpants; it's luxury dresses and tasteful makeup only. Her cheekbones are sharp and defined, and she has really intense brown eyes. Hallie is a perfect mix of her parents (she has her dad's rounder face and her mom's sharp eyes), but the main difference is that Hallie is a light brown, borderline tan, and Aunt Cathy has a rich brown skin tone. When I was little, I was convinced Aunt Cathy used to be a model. Now she winks at me when I bring it up.

"Sarah's birthday?" Aunt Cathy asks.

I hold up my present. "Yes, ma'am."

Aunt Cathy nods to me and turns her sharp gaze to Hallie. "You'll be safe?"

"Promise," Hallie says, miming a cross over her heart for emphasis. That's another difference; Aunt Cathy is a serious, straitlaced person. She'd die if she knew we've even tasted alcohol. Hallie's a lot more fun.

"Home by midnight," Aunt Cathy says, sending a warning glance at Hallie. Then she turns to me, smiling, and gives me a hug.

I hug her back, but it's awkward. I hate that it's awkward. Before Mom left, Aunt Cathy was just my mom's best friend and my pseudo–second mother, and that was it. But since then, I've been thinking. She and Mom were an inseparable duo, true ride-or-dies. So when Mom left, I was surprised that Aunt Cathy picked us. She chose me and Dad over Mom, her best friend, her platonic soulmate as they liked to say. But that doesn't make me feel better. It makes me think that one day, Hallie and I might split up. It makes me think that nothing is permanent— not motherhood, not friendship, certainly not my cozy family life I had before Mom decided we were too much trouble.

Honestly, it makes me sick.

But hey, that's nothing some cheap beer can't fix. So I hug Aunt Cathy back, smile through her lengthy warnings to Hallie, and I don't breathe easily until we're out of the house and into the warm night.

Hallie stretches her arms to the sky. "God, I'm so ready for this party."

I put my dark thoughts away as we arrive at Sarah's house. The yard is choked with cars, and bass is already leaking from the windows. Beautiful. "Me too."

Hallie and I grin at each other before we walk into Sarah's house. A sea of familiar faces greets me. Stephanie smoking on the stairs. Eric bobbing his head to the music near the fireplace. Jet chatting with Katie in the corner. And everyone is holding a red SOLO cup. This is probably what heaven looks like.

"Kitchen?" Hallie says, her voice loud over the music.

"You know it."

We weave through the crowd to get there. Sarah has taste,

so the music is a mix of pop and hip-hop, all songs accompanied by heavy bass. I feel vibrations in my shoes as it shakes the house. Several people shout at me, waving happily. I wave back, grinning. Acquaintances, like I told Gia. But happy acquaintances give free drinks and free weed, so I'll keep smiling until the night is over.

Jeremy approaches us and slaps his palm with mine. "What's up, Nav?"

"Here to party," I say, grinning.

Jeremy cheats off me in math. And in return . . .

He presses something cool into my palm. "For my best friend. Got a seventy-six on my exam."

I open my hand to take a peek. One slightly squished pack of gummy bears. And they're not just full of congealed sugar. My grin gets wider. "Congratulations, my man."

Jeremy wanders off, chatting with Mike, so I follow Hallie to the kitchen. We finally spy Sarah, enthusiastically chatting with someone else on Hallie's basketball team.

"Happy birthday!" Hallie sings.

I join in, and we both hold out our gift bags to Sarah. Her eyes get as big as dinner plates, and she squeals.

"Hal! Nav! You shouldn't have!" She takes our gifts anyway, holding them to her chest.

"I hope you like it," I say, smiling. I didn't know she'd be so happy with the junk I picked out. Now I'm really feeling bad I didn't give her a gift last year.

"I do!" Sarah leans close to us and we lean in too, so we can hear. "Want to help me put these up? I have party favors."

Oh yeah? I glance at Hallie, curious, and she shrugs. "Lead the way," Hallie says.

We follow Sarah, weaving through the bodies of sweaty teenagers choking her house. She leads us to the garage, somewhere I've never been. Near the door, there's a card table by a squat fridge with a lock on the outside. There are red cups down here too, but only a few, and three sad-looking two liters of Sprite sit next to the fridge. The table has four gifts on it. Sarah places ours next to the other four.

She's quiet for a second, then says, "You see all those people upstairs? Only six people brought me anything. Like, not even a card."

"Oh, Sarah." Hallie gives her a hug, and I feel extra rotten. "I'm sorry."

"Don't be. I don't mind using my house, and I want everyone to have a good time. But . . ." Sarah breaks Hallie's hug and takes off her necklace. Which I'm now seeing is a small key on a delicate gold chain. She bends and unlocks the fridge with the key-necklace. "I want my real friends to have extra fun." Sarah opens the fridge and pulls out a bottle of vodka. She gives Hallie and me a mischievous grin. "Beer for the freeloaders, but only the finest for my real friends."

I could kiss Sarah. And Hallie, for giving me the heads-up about the gift. Hallie grins at me, and I pick up a red SOLO cup from the table. "Thanks, Sarah. You're awesome, you know that?"

"I know." Sarah pours me half a cup of clear vodka and tops

it off with Sprite. She does this for Hallie too. "Come to me when you want a refill. I hope y'all have a good time."

Oh, I *know* we will. We troop back inside, and Sarah quickly disappears to mingle with her guests. Hallie and I mill around in the kitchen, trying not to look too excited about our secret liquor. Heavy bass throbs through the room, and people are already dancing, laughing too loud, and sloshing their drinks. Sarah went all out this year. Hallie takes a sip from her cup and winces. "God, this is strong."

"Sounds like you can't keep up!" I sip mine too and barely hold in a shudder. Liquid fire burns my throat as the vodka goes down, extra painful because of the Sprite's carbonation. I'm not used to this. Usually it's beer, watered down to make it last longer. This is something else altogether.

Hallie starts talking to a teammate, babbling enthusiastically about basketball. I tune them out and sweep the room while I take ginger sips from my drink. It's a fairly big party—good job, Sarah. Plenty of people I don't know. A tall guy with a scruffy beard talking to Jeremy, someone who looks a lot like Sarah chatting to Ivan, and . . . a dark-skinned girl with a diamond nose ring standing by herself, observing the party with a beer in one hand.

Oh, hello.

"Hallie," I say, not taking my eyes off the girl. "I'm gonna be right back."

"Stay safe!" Hallie chirps. She elbows me mockingly. "Make good decisions."

163

"I always do."

I approach the girl, an easy grin on my face. I'm not nervous, but my heart rate does kick up a little when she meets my eyes.

"Haven't seen you around before."

The girl studies my face for a second before answering. Her eyes are a deep, dark brown, and she has intricate braids curled into a bun on top of her head. One has a distinct purple streak woven through it. "I'm in town for the party."

"Did you bring a present?" I ask.

"Yep. It's a birthday, after all."

"Then why're you drinking beer?"

The girl finally smiles. It's a half smile, only the right side of her lip pulling up. She doesn't show her teeth, but her eyes are intrigued. I can work with that. "I know better than to drink Sarah's alcohol."

I put my hand over my heart. "I'll try to be careful. What's your name?"

"Julia." She nods at my shirt, the half grin still on her face. "I'm guessing you're Head Bitch?"

"In Charge. Gotta address me by my full title."

Julia and I stare at each other for a moment. I'm feeling pleasantly buzzed already, the bass thrumming in my veins, in my bones. Julia is cute, especially with the purple braid. She's wearing a plain black tee with some sort of Japanese writing on it and a cartoon character. My mind wanders to Gia for a second—she would maybe like Julia too. They have a nerd thing going on. I wonder how her tournament's going.

"How do you know Sarah?" Julia asks, bringing me back to the present.

"She's on the basketball team. My best friend is on the team too, so, you know."

"Tagging along for free booze?"

I wink at her. "You got it."

"Your secret's safe with me." Julia takes a swig of her beer. "Just be careful. I'm staying with Sarah for a while, so I have to help her clean up. I'd rather avoid the puke."

"All summer?" I ask automatically, but I'm not super interested in her answer. Which is . . . weird? If she's here all summer and we hit it off, we can have a lot more meetings like this. Normally I'd be giddy with my good fortune. But I'm feeling buzzy, and my mind keeps slipping to Gia's dwarf getting taken out by that virtual dragon. She's so fucked in that tournament.

"Only a few weeks. I'm going to Carnegie Camp soon."

My lip curls involuntarily. I can't have a single second of peace from that camp, even at a party. I must be in some kind of sick purgatory. Julia regards my expression with amusement.

"Not a fan?"

"At the moment, no." I don't add that if the stars align, I might see her there, and we can meet up like this at the nerd parties I've heard so much about. I also don't add that I'm kind of looking at the camp with a vague sort of dread.

We chat pleasantly for a few minutes about anything else, talking about school and that she's related to Sarah by some weird second cousin thing. Soon, I'm taking my last swig of vodka and

I'm surprised it's gone so quickly. How'd that happen?

"Need more?" Julia asks. She gives me a smirk. "If you're not poisoned yet."

"I'm telling Sarah you said that!" I'm not, but it gets a chuckle out of us both. I try to tell her I'll be right back, but she steps to my side and playfully hooks her finger through the belt loop of my shorts.

"Let me escort you, Miss Head Bitch. Can't have you tumbling down the stairs."

Oh, this night is gonna be great.

We find Sarah, and soon I'm a cup of mixed drink richer. Hallie catches my eye in the kitchen and starts to approach, but I shoot daggers at her and send her a mental message. *Do not bother me right now.* Hallie pauses, then laughs and gives me a thumbs-up. God, I love Hallie.

God, I love parties. I think I tell Julia this, because she says, "I love them too. You couldn't tell from looking at her, but Sarah throws real ragers."

"That's not why I like them," I say, my words slightly slurred. Already? I'm a drink and a half deep.

"Then why?"

"Because I get to meet cute girls like you."

Julia meets my eyes, hers sparkling in the low lighting. "Can't say I mind that part either."

After that, it's wonderful. I drink, and drink more, and I snag a beer out of the kitchen so I don't keep bothering Sarah and drink some more. And a song I love comes on, so I dance, and Julia dances too, and the bass is in my whole body. I'm laughing, something close to euphoria pouring from my mouth, liquid fire pouring in. The world has beautiful, fuzzy edges and for a second, all my worries about Dad and Hallie and that fucking camp disappear.

Julia says something to me, and I nod, and she leans close and whispers in my ear, her breath hot but sending goose bumps down my arms. And then she kisses my ear, then my cheek, and I turn to meet her and she tastes like cherry lip gloss and my tongue skims the edge of her teeth. I reach up to pull her closer, hungrily, and she comes to meet me. Her skin is so soft, but not as soft as Gia's when I touched her cheek when she was sick. Julia tastes like cherries, but what does Gia taste like?

Wait a minute.

I come up for air, suddenly very close to sober. Why am I thinking about Gia? I'm kissing a hot girl under Sarah's stairs, the party muted and distant behind us. And even though it's dark, I can see how Julia's eyes shine with that same hunger I know mine do. Though hers aren't nearly as pretty as Gia's. And her eyelashes aren't as long.

"You okay?" Julia asks, her head tilted curiously.

"Y-Yeah," I say, even though my alarm bells are going off. This is *not* how parties go. I meet a Julia, or a Rebecca, or a Sadie, we hang out, we kiss, we beg Sarah to please let us use the guest room, thank you, love you, owe you my life. Why the hell is Gia in my head right now? She's not even here. She's playing that dumbass game. And she'd probably be miserable here anyway. But, even so, I kind of wish she was with me.

I pick up my empty cup and smile at Julia, trying to push down the rising panic. "Need to re-up. Be right back."

Julia grins and leans against the stairs, her arms crossed. "Don't take too long. I'm thinking maybe I'll go upstairs soon."

"Am I invited?" I ask, because that's what I'm supposed to say. She gives me a conspiratorial look. Usually, my stomach would swoop with desire and victory, but right now, it just feels nauseous. I am not hooking up with Julia tonight, and I don't know why.

I wade through the partiers, waving at everyone who waves at me first, and end up back in the kitchen. I have to find Sarah. Sarah has the vodka.

"Looks like you're having a good time," Jeremy says, smirking at me. I give him a thumbs-up, combing the crowd for Sarah.

"I always have a good time. You seen Sarah?"

He points to the living room, where I find her talking happily with Mario. I join their conversation—bio exam, ugh—and ten minutes later, my SOLO cup is full of clear liquid again. I sip it at first, but between the dancing and laughing and trying to remember where the hell the stairs are, it's empty again before I know it.

I go back to the kitchen to complain about my empty cup, but Hallie is in here now. We see each other, and Hallie grins and stumbles to me. She wraps her arms around me, and I hug her back.

"Nav!" she sings in my ear. I hold her close, pleasant buzzing in my body. Hallie is here and we're drunk and this is fun. This is how it's supposed to be. "Listen to me. I'm drunk."

"Oh yeah, me too." We laugh together, still hugging.

She lets me go and steps back, swaying a little. "I still love parties. I'm so glad. I was worried."

Still? What does that mean? I open my mouth to ask, but Hallie tackles me in a hug again.

"And I love you! That'll never change. Never ever."

I smile against her shoulder, my body humming with happiness. "I love you forever and ever too."

I told Gia I didn't believe in forever, but I want to believe in this. I believe in Hallie, and that we'll get into that camp and we'll be friends until we're old grandmas and everything will be fine. Nothing has to change. But . . . if I go to camp with Hallie, Gia will give up her spot for me. And that means she won't go. We can't go together. My head is full of duos, me and Hallie, how it's always been, forever and ever. But a third person is crowding in, and I want her to, I want her close to me. That isn't how it should be, but it's how I *want* it to be. What changed? What's wrong with me?

"You okay?" Hallie asks, her grin turning into a frown. I didn't realize she'd stopped hugging me. "You look sick. Are you gonna throw up?"

"No way," I say, but maybe I am. I'm so confused. Why do I care so much about Gia? We're business friends. She said so in the beginning of our deal, and I agreed. But now we're real friends, friends who watch movies together, share painful family secrets, hang out for endless, wonderful hours. And yet something is *still* wrong. I don't think about kissing Hallie. I don't think about how Hallie tastes or how smooth her skin is. Hallie is my friend, but Gia is . . .

I'm distracted by a tall white dude lumbering up to us. His face is pink, and he's sweaty—I recognize him as Greg from the boys' basketball team.

"Hey, Hallie," he says. He's fidgeting a little, which is so annoying. Stand up straight, man. Gia would do better than this. "Wanna dance some more?"

"No, thanks," Hallie says. She drapes an arm around me, grinning. "My friend's about to puke."

"Stop slandering me," I complain, but my words are slurred. I'm not even sure if I said them out loud or if they're knocking around in my head, where Gia has been hanging out all night. I can't stop thinking about her cute smile and her awkwardness and just everything. And that damn game. Is she winning? Did she beat the other team or guild or whatever? I should text her. That would be polite and not at all weird.

I'd tuned out Hallie and Greg's conversation, but I snap back into it when he says, "Maybe we should get out of here?"

I glance at Hallie, who frowns.

"No, Greg. I mean I had fun tonight, but I'm taking a break. Working on myself, you know?"

Greg hovers awkwardly, looking like he doesn't comprehend her words. "Maybe a goodbye kiss, then?"

"Hey, fuck face," I spit, wedging myself between them. "She said beat it."

Greg's face twists in annoyance. "I wasn't talking to you."

"Well, *I'm* talking to *you*. She said she's not interested, so go try to convince someone else to fuck you."

"Nav," Hallie hisses in my ear, but I ignore her.

All the frustration and confusion from tonight crash together, and I'm mad. Why is it that Hallie attracts all these horrible dudes with boundary issues? Why can't anyone take a fucking hint? Why are all the options so horrible in this town? Gia unhelpfully pops into my brain again, which just makes me madder.

"Didn't know you let your watchdog do all the talking for you," Greg says, looking over my head at Hallie. I'm grinding my teeth so hard, I think I'll chip a tooth.

"My 'watchdog' is my best friend, and you better watch how you talk to her." Hallie's voice is pure venom, and my chest swells with pride. Forever and ever, me and Hallie, like she said.

Greg falters, like he didn't actually expect Hallie to stand with me. Then he gets a surly look and says, "Fine, I don't want a frigid bitch anyway—"

It just happens. The seething anger and confusion and way too much alcohol convince me to curl my hand into a fist and swing at his stupid stomach. But somehow, my aim is off, and my knuckles connect with his chin. He yelps in pain, and I do too, tears springing into my eyes. What in the shit is this guy doing, chin exercises?! My hand is killing me.

Hallie gasps in horror and Greg narrows his eyes at me and balls his fist up too. I swallow down the pain and get ready to fight a guy who outweighs me by at least a hundred pounds.

It started out great, but this has quickly become the worst party I've ever been to.

CHAPTER 20

I sit sullenly on Sarah's couch, Hallie next to me, Greg on her other side. The party is still going on, but Sarah's standing in front of us, arms folded.

"At my birthday party? Really? Come on, guys."

"He started it," I mutter. My head is throbbing, and not just from the alcohol. Greg has a mean right hook. Thought I was gonna pass out. My lip is pulsing in time with my heart, and my right eye doesn't seem to be working so great. But he's worse, so I don't feel too bad.

"I don't care who started it," Sarah snaps.

It's kind of funny—we're all in party jail. Kangaroo court, and Sarah's the judge. Actually, it's really funny. I almost laugh, but Hallie is shooting daggers at me, so I manage to keep it in.

"Okay. I know you're both drunk, but I told y'all there's no fighting at my house. Do you know how hard it is to get blood out of carpet? My parents are coming back tomorrow."

I mutter a half-assed apology, but Greg doesn't look sorry at all, the bastard.

"She attacked *me*," Greg argues.

"And you hit her back? Like gender equality is great, but you're six-foot, man, come on."

Greg sighs but stays quiet.

Hallie finally breaks the tense silence. "Can you forgive them, Sarah? Nav's sorry. Greg is probably sorry. I'll keep Nav with me so there's no more fighting."

Sarah shakes her head. "Y'all know the rules: fighters have to go home. I already called an Uber for you, Greg."

Greg starts swearing, and Hallie groans. I don't feel anything. I'm ready to go home anyway. My face hurts and so does my stomach.

I stand up, swaying dangerously to one side. Sarah catches my arm, and I grin, embarrassed.

"I'm sorry, Sarah, I really am. I hope you have a good birthday anyway." I'm surprised that I mean it. I feel bad no one brought Sarah a gift. And she's really so nice, letting us use her house and drink her beer all the time.

Sarah's expression softens. "It's okay, Nav. Get home safe, all right? You want an Uber too?"

"No, I'll walk." I look back at Hallie, who sighs and gets up too.

"Bye, Sarah." She hugs Sarah, and we head to the door.

I wave bye to everyone, and despite leaving a good hour early, I'm feeling pretty good.

Fresh air hits my face, and I laugh, twirling around with my arms out. "Fuck you, Greg!" I yell to the night sky. When I look down, the world is spinning like a carousel, so much that I fall on my butt. Dew gets on my jeans, and I crack up again.

"Jesus, Nav, get up." Hallie appears in front of me. I grab her outstretched hand, and I'm on my feet again, swaying happily.

The alcohol is hitting me for real now, making my bones feel like warm ooze. I feel invincible. I feel like crying because my face hurts. I feel like hugging Sarah and buying her another birthday gift.

"This is the best," I tell Hallie. I start to tell her about the gummy bears I haven't even touched yet, but she talks over my thoughts.

"This is *not* the best, Nav! Why're you fighting guys?" Hallie's face is puffed up and red. Is she . . . angry?

"He was being an asshole." My words are slow and slurred.

"So what? You can't fight every asshole you meet."

"I should!" I'm so loud for some reason. I take a deep breath to lower my voice. "You always pick the worst guys, you know that? And it's so frustrating. Like you deserve so much better." Gia's face pops into my mind, and my heart does a painful squeeze, a pitiful flutter. "You know you're someone's dream girl, right? Like Gia is here, working so hard for you, and she's so cute and awkward, but not in a bad way. And that Greg asshole barely says a sentence to you and is trying to shove his tongue down your throat. Do you get how frustrated I am?"

Hallie stares at me, her eyes unfocused and confused. "What does Gia have to do with this?"

"I don't know!" Suddenly, my eyes are full of tears. I don't know what Gia has to do with me fighting Greg. I don't know what she has to do with me kissing Julia either. It's just that she *does*, that she's the most important thing.

"I don't—" Hallie groans in frustration. "This is—ugh.

175

Why'd you have to ruin this for me?! I was having fun! This is exactly like yoga."

Hurt lances through me. "This is different. And why're you so interested in yoga all of a sudden anyway? You like basketball and horror movies."

"Well, maybe I want to like more than that!" Hallie's yelling at me, actually yelling. I almost can't believe it. "Maybe I wanna try new things!"

My brain is swimming with the pain of trying to think. I don't get why we're yelling. All I did was protect her. "But why? I don't get it. Why do you want to be so different now? What's wrong with the way things were?"

"Nothing!" Hallie groans again. "I need some space, okay?"

The buzzing in my head stills. She needs space. That's what Mom told me three years ago, and I haven't seen her since. "Oh."

"No, don't do that," Hallie says. She scrubs her hands over her face. "I'm too fucking drunk to explain—I don't mean it like that, I just—"

"If you want space," I say, unable to keep the wobble from my voice, "you can have it. I'm going home."

"Nav," Hallie whines. "Come on, I'm sorry—"

"Fuck you!" I yell, even though I don't mean it. "Go home and get your space!"

"Fine!" Hallie yells back. I cross my arms and wait, and she stumbles down the road to her front door. She looks back several times, and she pauses when she gets to her porch. "Are you coming?" she calls, her voice faint.

"No!"

Hallie flips me off, and I raise my middle finger right back. She yanks open her door and disappears inside.

As soon as I'm alone, the tears start. I don't know why she's doing this. All I wanted to do was help. And now I have to go home and deal with Dad, because I told him I was staying at Hallie's tonight. He'll probably wake up and catch me drunk, and that'll be a whole thing. I'm sick of people yelling at me. I want to go home—but that's not with Dad, and it isn't with Hallie either, not right now. I sniffle, and Gia pops into my head once again. But this time it's the day we played video games together, her playing that needlessly complicated thing and me on my farm, her fan and the faint comments from her headset the only noise, Jordan curled up at our feet.

That's what I want. That's where I should be.

I fumble with my phone, the screen hazy and dim. I touch Gia's name in my texts, but my thumbs won't work. I type out a message and send it, but even I can't read that. Shit.

Gia sends me a reply.

Nav? Are you okay?

I take a deep breath. I can do this.

I'm some. Need rude. Can I one over

Okay, not bad! I send that, and Gia starts typing. But the

dots disappear and a second later, she's calling me.

"Are you having a stroke?" Gia says as soon as I answer.

A laugh pours out of me. A gooey, warm feeling replaces the earlier tears. "No! My thumbs don't work right now, but it's fine. How are you?"

Gia doesn't say anything for a second. "Are you drunk?"

"Yeah, I'm very drunk." I laugh again. "Did you win your tournament?"

"No, but we got second place. Lots of cool gear and skins." Gia sounds genuinely happy, and I'm happy too. "Are you having fun at the party?"

I'm still happy for her, but the tears start again. "No, I got kicked out. And I got in a fight with Hallie."

Gia gasps in my ear. "Are you okay? Like a fist fight or a verbal fight?"

"Umm, both?" I look up at the dark sky, tears making me feel like I'm underwater. "And I don't wanna go home. Can I come over?"

"Yeah, of course." I hear a slight squeak and rustling. "Where are you?"

"Do you know where Sarah's house is?"

"Who?" I hear more noise and a snuffling sound. "Stop, Jordie, I'm fine. Nav? Give me an address."

"Umm . . ." Where does Sarah live again? I look around me, lost. My house is two streets over. Hallie's is between me and Sarah. "Do you know where my house is?"

"Nav," Gia begs. "An address. Give me an address."

"I live on Short Street, but I don't . . ." My head is killing me.

"And you're close to your house?"

"Yeah. Two streets over."

"Got it. Give me like five minutes, okay?"

I nod. "Okay. Oh, can we get food? I'm starving."

"We have food at home," Gia says. I hear a car door opening and closing. "Mami made fajitas before she left, so we can eat those."

"Oh God, that sounds so good." I talk about how much I love fajitas, and before I know it, headlights light up the end of Sarah's street. "Is that you?" My heart races a little with panic. "Am I getting kidnapped?!"

"Stop, it's me." Gia pulls over a few feet from me and gets out of her very nice car. She runs to me, worry all over her face. She's wearing her glasses! I love her glasses. "Are you okay?"

"Gia!" I meet her halfway and wrap my arms around her. She freezes in surprise, and I snuggle her closer. She's so soft. And she smells so good. Like strawberries and lavender and my favorite smell in the world. "You smell great, did you know that? And I love your glasses. Have I ever said that? They're so cute."

"I just took a shower," Gia admits. She hesitates but hugs me back.

My body feels like singing and so do I. Gia gives great hugs.

"What was that about my glasses?"

"They're cute! I love them. Why do you wear contacts sometimes?"

Gia is still hugging me. My mind wanders to her pressing

179

her cheek to the top of my head. That would be amazing. "I don't know. I guess I thought they looked better? My abuela says glasses are sloppy."

"Sorry to your grandma, but she has no sense of style."

Gia chuckles and breaks our hug. Disappointment hangs heavy above my uncuddled head.

"Anyway, are you okay? Are you hurt?"

"Not really. Just a little." I take two wobbly steps back so she can see. But Gia's expression fills with panic.

"Nav! Oh my God, your eye, your lip—" She touches my cheek with her thumb, and I feel like melting. Her touch is so gentle and soft, and her eyelashes are so long.

"You're really pretty," I blurt out, and Gia blinks at me, her eyes huge and wide, like the cutest owl in the world. Then she smiles, and my legs get even wobblier than they already are.

"And you are very drunk. Come on, let's go home."

"I am drunk, but it's true." Still, I manage to convince my legs to wander to her car and get into the passenger seat. Her car is so cool, what the fuck? I touch a ton of buttons on her dashboard, and a blast of cool air hits my face.

Gia gets in too and gently pushes my hand away from the dashboard. "Don't do that."

I think I protest, but I'm not sure. And then we're driving, so I look out of the window. I gasp when I see the moon, which is perfectly round and bright yellow. "Gia, the moon!"

"I know," she says, laughing. "Don't fall out of the window, please."

"Let's go. Let's go to the moon." I stare up at it, strange excitement stirring in my chest. When has the moon been so big? When's the last time I even looked at it?

"We're not going to the moon. We're going to my house."

I laugh, and Gia does too. And I think if we could go to the moon, I'd go with her. If I could, I'd grab the moon right out of the sky and give it to her, if that would make her happy.

I sit back down, and then I remember it's late, maybe midnight, and Gia came out of her gaming den to get me. And she was talking to Jordan. "Are you okay, Gia?"

"What do you mean?"

"You sounded worried on the phone. Are you anxious?" I hold out my hand to her, palm up. "Here, hold my hand."

Gia laughs, then places her right hand in my left. "Thanks, Nav. But I'm not anxious now. I like driving, even when you're destroying my car."

I grin at her, but I don't let go of her hand. It's warm and soft, and I never want to let go. And we don't, even when we pull up at Gia's house. I hold her hand tighter as she parks, and for a while we just sit there, in the dark of the night and the coolness of her garage.

"Is your mom home?" I ask.

Gia shakes her head. Her palm is kind of sweaty now. "No. She won't be back for a few days."

"That's good, 'cause I don't think I can be quiet."

Gia grins and squeezes my hand one more time before letting go. "Come on, let's get inside."

I follow Gia into her house and squeal when Jordan greets us. I want to pick her up, but when I bend down, I lose my balance and fall to my side. Gia gasps, but Jordan goes nuts and licks my face, turning the sudden pain into laughter.

"My potato!! My angel baby nugget!!" I kiss Jordan's cute little nose and she wags her whole body in response.

"At least you're okay," Gia says. "Come to the kitchen."

"Fajita time?"

"Yep. And 'put some ice on your black eye' time."

Everything is fuzzy and wonderful. Jordan sits in my lap, and I'm eating fajitas and fistfuls of popcorn, and Gia's pressing a cool compress to my eye. We talk about *Briar's Blaze* and my farm game, and the moon, and how cute Jordan is every day of her little stubby-legged life. And Gia gives me pajamas to borrow, and a toothbrush to scrub the taste of vodka and Julia's lip gloss from my tongue. I stand in the bathroom, holding my clothes, and I'm overwhelmed by how good this feels, how *right*, how wonderful and sweet and good it is to be with Gia. And it's these small moments, fajitas and games and tossing a tennis ball for a therapy dog at two a.m., not lavish parties or smooth pickup lines, that make everything so perfect. I look in the mirror at myself, at the purple bruise over one eye and fat bottom lip, and I think maybe, just maybe, this is what it means to want forever.

"Nav?" Gia calls. She taps on the door, her touch light. "You okay?"

"I'm okay." I come out of the bathroom, and Gia smiles at

me, and a low swooping sensation blooms in my stomach. I come to her side, and she ushers me to the bed.

"Let's go to sleep, okay?"

"I can stay in here?"

Gia seems surprised. "You stayed with me last time, when I was sick. Do you not want to—"

"No! I do." I do, and I'm so happy that she trusts me enough to stay with her even when she's not sick.

I sit on the bed first, and Jordan crawls to me, tail wagging. I hold the dog close, laughing as she licks my chin. Gia turns off the light and a few seconds later, I feel her weight settle next to me.

I snuggle close to her, Jordan panting happily between us. "Good night, Gia."

"Good night, Nav." Her breath is warm on my face, and I'm so happy and lulled by her and Jordan's breathing that I fall asleep right away.

CHAPTER 21

When I wake up, my head is pounding, my mouth is full of grit, and I'm wearing someone else's shirt and sleeping in someone else's bed.

Must have been a good party.

But wait a minute . . . something's under the covers. I lift the comforter, and Jordan looks up at me, wagging her tail sleepily. I'm at Gia's house? How did I get here?

Slowly, it comes back to me. Sarah's party, Julia, fighting with Greg. The black eye he gave me, the absolute shithead. My eye starts throbbing then, and I groan. Fighting with Hallie. That one sends pain and regret through my chest. But then calling Gia, her picking me up in the middle of the night, spending the night with her. And then there was the soft, mushy feeling I felt, thinking of Gia all night, even when kissing Julia, and thinking that if I could, I'd make sure Gia was happy for the rest of her life.

I stare at my hands, stunned into oblivion. If I didn't know any better, I'd say that I like Gia.

No. No way. I shake my head, as if I can shake that cursed thought right out of my ears. That can't be right. I don't like anyone. I have hookups when I need them, do my own thing when I don't. But, an annoying voice reminds me, I couldn't hook up with Julia. She invited me, and I turned her down to fistfight Greg. Shit. Oh shit, this is bad.

The bedroom door opens, and Gia pokes her head into her room. She's wearing her glasses and light blue pajamas, which have tiny dogs on them. She smiles when she sees me, and my stomach does a funny little swoop.

"Hey, you're awake! You okay?"

I nod dumbly. This can't be happening. But I think it is? Gia is so cute, in a way I didn't think of before. No, I always thought she was cute, from the first day she nervously sat next to me in the school's gym. But until last night, until I couldn't think of anything or anyone else, I couldn't admit it. Shit. Shit shit shit.

Gia comes into her room and Jordan pops up beside me, leaning on my leg. I pet her automatically, and somehow, that calms the panic rising in my chest.

"Are you feeling okay?" Gia asks.

I hold a hand to my temple, smiling sheepishly. "My head's killing me."

"You were hammered, so that checks out." Gia sits at the foot of her bed, smiling gently at me, and she's so cute I could die. I pull the comforter up to my chest, confusion clouding my thoughts. This is so different. With Julia, I felt like kissing her, doing a little more if she was down. But with Gia, I want to sit next to her, and eat breakfast together, and if it's okay with her, hold her undoubtedly sweaty hand. This is too different. This is too much.

185

"Maybe some breakfast will help?" Gia suggests while I silently freak out. "Though it's past noon."

"You can eat breakfast at any time," I say, my voice weak.

Gia frowns at me. "You sure you're okay? You don't feel sick, do you?"

I take a breath to steady myself. I can't think about this right now; I'm being super weird. And I don't even know if I like Gia for sure. This could just be a post-drunk haze thing. I roll out of bed, wincing at my apparently sore arms, and stand. Gia stands too, and Jordan hops off the bed, stretching and yawning.

"I'm okay. What're we eating?"

"I was gonna order something." Gia shrugs, still smiling. "I can't cook."

I heave an exaggerated sigh. "Let the hungover one cook, sure, sure."

"I picked the hungover one up," Gia teases back.

I can't keep a grin off my face. Gia used to be so shy and nervous around me, but now she's not afraid to tease me. Does that mean she thinks of us as more than friends too . . . ?

No. No, bad Nav. No thinking about that. We head to the kitchen, and I poke around in Gia's huge fridge, which is miraculously full now. I select eggs, bell peppers, cheese, and some deli ham.

"How about an omelet?"

Gia nods, and we fall into comfortable silence while I rummage around her kitchen for utensils. I thought they'd be brand-new, but most are old and well loved, like the green popcorn bowl. Maybe Gia's mom likes to cook?

"So," Gia says while I dice bell peppers, "you said you got into a fight with Hallie?"

I don't say anything at first. The fight is raw and ragged in my head. I remember screaming and the deep hurt. But I don't really remember what we were fighting about. "It's whatever."

"Are you sure?" Gia hesitates as I finish the peppers and start cracking the eggs. "You were crying."

I wince. I wish she hadn't seen that. I'm an ugly crier. "I got into that fight with Greg to protect her. Okay, kind of. He was really pissing me off, so it was for me too. But she got so mad at me."

"She was probably upset you got hurt," Gia says. "Your eye looked so bad last night."

"Okay, fine. I can see that. But it's also . . ." I trail off. I don't know how to tell her about how Hallie is changing, and maybe our friendship is too.

"It's okay," Gia says after a moment of silence. She gives me a reassuring smile. "You and Hallie are best friends. You'll make up."

"Yeah, maybe." I poke at the eggs in the skillet, feeling low. "Sometimes I feel like things are changing. Hallie's changing."

"That's normal, right?" Gia says, leaning her head on one hand. "Nothing can stay the same forever."

I focus on our omelets for a few seconds. "I thought we would."

Gia doesn't say anything but makes a sympathetic face. We don't speak until both our omelets are done and we're sitting next to each other at the bar.

"If it helps," Gia says, bringing me a fork and knife, "I'm still your friend. And I'm not going anywhere."

I look at Gia, and all the affection in the world surges up to my face, which is heated like I've been sunburned. "Thanks, Gia. But I know you just want the free omelets."

"No way! I haven't even tasted it yet." She does, and her eyes widen. "Okay, yeah, it's the omelets. Holy shit, this is so good."

I smile at my plate and dig in too. It *is* really good, but I'm also really hungover, so I'm biased. Every bite makes my headache lessen but my eye hurt a little worse. Thank God it's summertime. I'd be mortified going to school with a shiner.

"Are we doing some practice today?" Gia asks after a minute. I look over and her omelet is already gone.

I take another bite of my food. If we do practice, when I'm feeling like this . . . No, no, I need time. "Umm, maybe tomorrow. I feel like shit."

Gia grins, and my heart does a pitiful flutter. "Okay. But this is your own fault, you know."

"Don't do that. I was only planning on beer. I didn't even eat the gummies." Wait, where are my gummies? I check my pockets, but I'm wearing shorts I don't recognize. "Did I have some gummy bears with me?"

Gia shakes her head. "Just your phone."

I let out a groan and collapse on the bar. "Worst party ever. I fight with Hallie, a big dude punches me in the face, and I lose my bears!"

"The after-party was fun at least," Gia says, still grinning. "I ate so much popcorn and fajitas I wanted to puke."

Flashes of our night play through my aching brain. It was fun. I had more fun here than at the parties I normally love. Maybe it's not that the party was so terrible. Maybe it's that I like hanging out with Gia so much more.

Gia's phone lets out a merry tune that sounds suspiciously like an anime opening. She mutes it without looking at the screen. "Hate spam calls."

But it rings again. She frowns and mutes it a second time. And then it dings with a text tone. She glances at her phone and freezes.

"What's wrong?"

"I-It's from Hallie." Gia looks at me, and I swear she's actually trembling. "What do I do?!"

"Calm down, what does it say?"

"I don't know. I haven't opened it."

"Oh God." I shake my head, laughing. "Open it! Maybe she's wondering how you are."

Gia makes a pitiful face at me, and I almost want to look for her. But I can't. This is part of her training. We have to be able to look at our crush's texts before meeting them face-to-face.

"Okay. Here I go." Gia takes a deep breath, then another. She opens her texts and reads it quickly. But she doesn't seem happy. The more she reads, the wider her eyes get in alarm. "Nav, shit."

"What? What's wrong?"

Gia shows me the text.

> Hey Gia, so sorry to bother you but is Nav with you? I've been calling her all morning but I can't find her and she's not at home. I'm really worried.

"Fuck," I mutter. "I think my phone's dead. Can I call her?"

Gia nods and gives me her phone. I call Hallie and she picks up right away.

"Gia? Hi, sorry again, but—"

"Hey, it's me."

Hallie is quiet for a few seconds. Then she says, "Nav, what the fuck is wrong with you?"

Okay, not a great start. "I'm sorry, I was really drunk and—"

"You're such an asshole, you know that?" Hallie's voice is shaking, probably with rage. "Why didn't you go home? Or at least text me you were with Gia?"

"Well, sorry I don't tell you my every move." I really am being an asshole now, but I can't stop. The hurt from our fight is back and raw, and I want her to feel a fraction of what I do. "You're the one who said you needed space, so that's what you got."

I can practically hear Hallie seething on the phone. "We can talk later. You're clearly fine. But call your dad, okay? He's about to have a heart attack."

I wince. That's not gonna be fun at all. "Okay. I will. Bye."

"Bye." She hangs up.

I give Gia her phone back, dread and hurt replacing all the earlier happiness. "Will you drive me home?"

Gia makes a sympathetic face. "Yeah. Let's go."

I gather my clothes from last night and dead phone (and not my gummy bears), and join Gia in her car. We drive to my house in silence, except for me to tell her my house number.

"You'll be okay?" Gia asks. She looks deeply serious, like she'd drive away right now if I said the word. Which makes that gentle affection grow deeper in my chest.

"I'll be okay." I offer Gia a grin. "I'll text you later. If Dad doesn't murder me." I laugh, but Gia doesn't.

"Call me if you need me, Nav." Gia's voice is steady, and there's no hint of a joke in her tone. "I'll be right there. I promise."

I look in Gia's deep brown eyes, and a mean little devil in my head dares me to lean in and . . . I don't know. I scramble out of the car before I do anything stupid. "I will."

"Oh, hang on." Gia rummages in her glove compartment and gives me a Walmart bag. I look in it and find her Nintendo Switch and its charger. "Since you'll probably be grounded, you can farm for a while."

As I smile at Gia, what I was denying all day comes to the forefront. I do like Gia. I like her in a way I've never experienced before; I want to be near her, I want to hear all about that stupid game. I want to make her food in her kitchen and lean against her shoulder. I want to kiss her until we're both dizzy and then laugh because we'll both be embarrassed but into it.

I like Gia in a romantic way, something I haven't felt since my short-lived middle school crushes. Since life got so hard.

And I want to tell her all of this, I want to hold her face in my hands and never let go, but I can't. Because Gia likes Hallie. And even though that thought brings a cavernous hurt deep in my chest, I know it's true. This is why I'm even close to Gia at all. Gia doesn't like me, and that's one thing that won't change.

"Thanks, Gia" is what emerges from my mess of thoughts. "See you later."

I wave and go to my front porch. She waves back, and I take a deep breath to put the liking-Gia problem to the back of my mind and focus on the Dad-is-going-to-kill-me one. I steady myself and take another breath. Here we go.

CHAPTER 22

Dad leaps to his feet as soon as I open the door. He's wearing basketball shorts, a white, loose tank top, and has bags under his eyes like he hasn't slept all night.

I'm in trouble.

"Naveah Danielle Hampton, get in here." His voice is a low growl.

I close the door reluctantly and step closer. The middle name? I'm dead. I'm never seeing Gia or Hallie again.

"Umm, hi, Dad. So, really, it's a funny story—"

Dad stares at my face, his mouth open. "What happened to your eye?"

Shit. I forgot about this. The situation is rapidly deteriorating, and I haven't said a full sentence yet. "I-It's not a big deal. It doesn't even hurt."

"Who— What—" Dad looks like he's struggling for words. And getting madder and madder by the second. "Who did this to you? Was it that Gia person?"

"No! No, she would never. I got into a fight at the party, that's all."

"Why are you fighting? With who? No, we'll deal with that later. Why did you lie to me? You said you were spending the night with Hallie."

"That was the plan, but—"

"But what?" Dad raises his voice to a dull roar. "Do you know how worried I was when you didn't answer your phone? And Cathy hadn't seen you since the night before?"

"I'm trying to tell you what happened—"

"I don't care what happened!" Dad is full-on yelling now. "You don't just disappear for half a day where no one can find you!"

"I'm *trying* to say that I got into a fight with Hallie!"

I'm yelling now too. Anger is burning me from the inside out, threatening to swallow me whole. He's always such an asshole, and he never listens to me. I'm so tired of this, I could scream.

"I went to Gia's instead, and my phone was dead!"

Dad shakes his head, like he's bewildered. "That was incredibly selfish, Naveah. Why didn't you come home?"

"This is why!" I'm screaming at him, tears in my eyes. "This is why, Dad. I'm so sick of you yelling at me! You act like you're so concerned all of a sudden but just stop! You don't care about me, and that's fine, but stop pretending that you do!"

"Naveah, you better watch your mouth."

Dad takes a step toward me, and I flinch, thinking of Greg's drunken right hook coming at my face. I don't even know why I do it. Dad's never hit me before, not even when I was little and getting into everything. Mom was always the discipline one. But maybe he's had enough of me yelling at him too.

I wait, eyes half-closed, but Dad doesn't move. I open my eyes all the way, and my stomach plummets to my toes. Dad doesn't look angry anymore—

He's devastated.

Dad looks at me, his eyebrows pulled together like he's about to cry. Then, he takes a step back, and two more. He rubs his face with his palms, and when his hands fall away, his expression is calm and cool again.

"We're gonna talk about this later. But for now, you're grounded. Your keys are mine. Your TV and laptop are mine. You can have your phone while I'm at the plant, but as soon as I get back, that's mine too."

I try to muster up some indignation, but his almost-tears rattle me. All I feel is confused. "What about work?"

"You're not leaving this house until further notice."

I should protest about my job, my only source of income, but now really doesn't seem like the time. "Fine."

Dad nods to the stairs. "Go to your room and don't come out until I say so."

I go upstairs without another word. I don't know how to feel. I can't ever tell what he's thinking. He screams at me and then acts like he's gonna cry? Does he love me or hate me? And how do I feel about him? I don't know. I don't know anything anymore.

I change out of Gia's borrowed pajamas and into my actual ones. Then I burrow under my covers, close my eyes, and cry until I have no tears left.

♡♡♡

I wake up to a tapping sound.

I sit up, groggy. What time is it? I reach for Jordan before I realize I'm at home, in Dad's version of jail. Great. He came and literally ripped my TV off the wall and took my phone and laptop (thank goodness I played Galaxy Cat before I fell asleep), but we haven't spoken since the disaster of a conversation. I heard him order pizza, but I didn't go downstairs, and he didn't come up to get me. I ignored the hunger pangs and willed myself to sleep.

Another tap. My window? I stay in bed, a little afraid. Shit, what if someone is breaking in? Do I even have a weapon? Not a lot I can do with a lamp.

"Nav," a faint voice hisses. "It's me. Are you asleep?"

I sit up then. Hallie? I get out of my bed and sure enough, Hallie is sitting outside my window, perched precariously on a branch of the large oak tree.

I fly to the window and open it, heart pounding. "What are you doing?! You're gonna fall and break your neck, and then there'll be blood all over my house."

Hallie laughs, then covers her mouth with one hand. "Stop, I'm trying not to get caught. Help me in."

I grab her hand, and Hallie scrambles into my room. We haven't done this since we were in elementary school, so it's a lot more complicated than I remember. When she's safely in my room, we just stare at each other. Heavy, awkward silence fills the space between us. This sucks. When have things been awkward with Hallie? I can't remember the last time we had a fight this big.

Hallie takes a deep breath. Then she punches me in the shoulder.

"Oww!" I hiss, but it's mostly out of reflex. It didn't hurt. "What was that for?"

"That's for being an asshole and disappearing off the face of the earth all day." Hallie's expression is scolding, severe. "I thought you got abducted by aliens or something."

"I did. They brought me back because I was annoying."

Hallie rolls her eyes, the hint of a smile on her lips. "Are you gonna apologize, or am I gonna have to punch you again?"

"I'm sorry." I look into her eyes so she can tell I mean it. "I didn't mean to scare you. I was so wasted, I didn't think to text anyone. And then my phone died and I slept until noon."

Hallie's expression softens. "I know."

"Are we good?" I ask. I want to be good. I want all of this to go away, go back to normal.

Hallie pulls me into a hug. "We're good. You're an asshole, but you're my asshole."

I hug her tight as all the anger and awkwardness disappears, and I'm whole again.

We sit on my bed, huddled close together. There's another silence, but this one is comfortable, easy. My mind wanders to Gia, and the way we can play games together for hours without saying a word.

"How bad was it?" Hallie asks. She doesn't elaborate, but I know what she means.

"Bad. I thought he was gonna kill me." I think back to the hurt on his face and wince. "No car, laptop, or TV. I get the phone sometimes, but not at night."

"Woof," Hallie says. "I get it, though. I've never seen Uncle David like that. I thought we were going to have to take him to the hospital."

I look down at my bare feet. I don't get Dad. This means he has to care, right? I can't pretend that he doesn't, not after that. But then why did he ignore me for so long? I thought we had an unspoken agreement: as long as I don't bother him, I can do whatever I want. But all of a sudden, in the last few weeks, he broke that agreement. I just don't know why.

Thinking about Dad is depressing me, so I change the subject. "Do you want to talk about our fight?"

Hallie breathes a heavy breath. "Yeah. I'm sorry for what I said, Nav. I couldn't explain because I was so drunk. I'm never drinking vodka again."

"I doubt it," I joke. "But explain now. Because I did feel a little abandoned."

"I didn't mean it like that at all." Hallie sighs. "When I said I needed space, I meant I want to try some new things. I feel kind of stifled, if that makes sense?"

It doesn't. I don't get it at all. "But why? Do you even like hiking? Or yoga?"

"I don't know yet. That's the point! Actually, you're the one who convinced me."

I frown. I don't remember telling Hallie to do more exercise and drag me along with her. "What do you mean?"

"Remember when we were studying for finals? And I was sad about Peter, and you said I was a whole person by myself?

And I don't have to fill a void because it doesn't exist?"

Oh yeah, I did say that. "Yeah. And that's still true, you know."

Hallie nods. "I know. I'd never thought about it like that. But it made me realize that if I am a whole person, I want to figure out who that person is, you know? I've just chased crushes forever. But is that all there is to me? I joined the basketball team for a girl, and I like horror movies because of an ex. I feel like my whole personality came from other people. So I wanted to test out a few different things, to get to know the real me."

I stay quiet for a second. I kind of get it now. I hate change, but Hallie doesn't. She wants to do other things than what we've always done. She wants space to grow. Even if that space takes her away from me.

But if I'm honest, deep down, I'm happy for her. Because I haven't seen her crying over some stupid guy in weeks. I haven't had to pick up the pieces of her heart when a girl dumps her for being "boring." Hallie is straying out of our cozy, familiar bubble, but if she's happy, if she finally feels good enough to not take second best from everyone she dates, I have to let her go. Because I love her so much, I'd rather her be happy without me than unhappy with me.

But it still hurts. I don't want her to leave me behind, not with my confusing dad and debilitating loneliness. That's why going to camp together is crucial. My summer, maybe my future, hinges on this. So even though I like Gia, and even though Hallie is moving beyond my reach, I have to stick to the plan. I have to keep this one thing the same.

"I get it," I tell Hallie. I smile at her, and she smiles back. "Go do your yoga and shit."

"Ah, Nav, I love you." She hugs me, and I know she means it.

Which is why I feel awful when I say, "So, if someone asked you out, you'd say no?"

Hallie searches my face, frowning. "If it was a person I liked, I wouldn't say no. But why?"

"Just asking," I say quickly. "I really am happy for you, Hallie. If you wanna go digging for fossils or whatever, let me know."

Hallie laughs. "I would, but you're probably grounded forever."

Yeah, probably. I shrug, smiling. "I'll have to do it over Zoom, then."

Hallie stays for a few more minutes, but soon she's climbing out my window again. I watch anxiously until she's safe on the ground.

"Bye, Nav!" Hallie whispers. "Text me when you can."

I wave, smiling. "See ya, babe," I say, but I don't think she hears me.

CHAPTER 23

"How do I kill the dark chickens?" I ask Gia. My left thumb toggles the joystick on her Switch, and my character darts around freshly grown pumpkins.

"You don't kill them," Gia says, her voice loud in my ear. She must be wearing her headset. "You have to befriend them. And then take care of them until the curse is lifted."

"Sounds like a lot of fucking work," I mutter, but nevertheless head to the mine to befriend a dumb chicken.

It's been three days since Dad grounded me, and also three days since I've left the house. Or spoken to Dad. I've been locked in my room, where I am now, going nuts. I migrate from the bed to the desk chair to the floor and back to the bed again. It's a nightmare. I'm bored out of my mind, but Gia's game has kept me sane. Sunflower Farm is now three acres and has five cows, two donkeys, and a ton of chickens. And hopefully a cursed one coming soon.

The sounds of *Briar's Blaze* leak into my earbuds, along with Gia's inelegant swearing. I'm glad she can't see me, because I've got a big, goofy grin on my face. When I first met her, I wouldn't have believed that Gia could do anything more than tremble when she tried to talk to me. But now I know Gia as sort of a goof, enthusiastic when it comes to that weird game, sharp-tongued when she wants to be, observant . . . Sometimes I feel like I know Gia Flores as well as I know Hallie. With the huge disadvantage that I don't want to kiss Hallie and with Gia, I really, really do.

I clear my throat, hoping that'll clear my useless brain too. No thinking about kissing Gia! She doesn't like me anyway. I ignore the sting that thought brings. "Quit playing that game and concentrate. We're supposed to be practicing."

"You're playing a game too," Gia whines. I hear the dull roar of a dragon and more swearing, followed by a cheer. "FUCK YEAH, I killed the dragon! Give me that sweet loot."

"You're ridiculous, you know that?" Still, I'm grinning. "Why can't you play a nice quiet game like me?"

"That's my game too?" Gia sounds indignant, and the image of her puffing out her chest makes me laugh out loud. "Why are you laughing? And what are we practicing anyway? There's not a lot we can do over the phone."

Yeah . . . she's right. I thought just talking would be good practice, but after a little bit of awkwardness the first day, she was fine. Maybe the phone doesn't make her nearly as nervous? "Okay, do you have any ideas?"

Gia hums absently. "What about love languages? That seems important."

"Love what?"

"Love languages?" Gia's voice has a lilt at the end, like I'm the moron for not knowing what she's talking about. "How people like to be loved?"

"Yeah, I'm pretty sure that's fake."

"It's not. Google it."

I do and Google confirms my suspicions. "It's about as real as astrology, which means not at all."

"Typical Leo response."

I roll my eyes so much I'm scared they'll get stuck at the top of my head. I never took Gia for an astrology girlie! This is a deal-breaker. (Who am I kidding? I'm looking up Leo characteristics as we speak.)

Gia chuckles in the silence and speaks over the sound of a slot machine or whatever she's doing on that game. "Even if it is fake, it's still fun! We should prepare for it, in case it comes up."

I go back to the love languages tab and scan the options. "I'm skeptical. I can't tell what mine is."

"Physical touch," Gia says immediately.

"How do you know?"

"Trust me, I know."

I don't like the way she said that. Her voice is full of certainty and amusement, and if I didn't know better, she also sounds nervous? Maybe because she's making fun of me.

"We'll see about that." I text Hallie right away.

> what's my love language?

Hallie responds in two seconds.

> Physical touch. Obv lol

"Why does everyone say mine is touch?" I complain out loud.

"You like to be close to people," Gia says. "That's not a bad thing."

"No, I . . ." I trail off, thinking of when I spend the night with Hallie and I cuddle with her all night long. And when I'm with Gia, I snuggle close, as close as I can, and we play our respective games in cozy silence. But I don't do this with everyone. Usually, I avoid people. But with Hallie, and I guess now Gia, I don't mind being close to them. My face warms when I remember what this is called—love language.

"Nav? You still there?" Gia asks.

"Yeah." My brain scrambles to come up with a response that won't betray my red-hot face and thudding heartbeat. "If we're pretending love languages are real, I guess it might be true."

"It is!" Gia laughs, and I feel myself melting. She sounds so happy. And she's so happy with *me*, talking to *me*. My emotions waffle between extreme pride and goofy giddiness and dark despair because I really should *not* be feeling like this.

"If you're done making fun of me, we should discuss yours."

"Hmm . . . I don't know," Gia says.

I scan the options again. "What about words of affirmation?"

Gia is quiet for a second, like she's thinking. Then she says, "I think you're right. Can I tell you something personal?"

My heart does a funny little leap, which I try to stamp down. "Yeah, of course."

"I don't make friends easily. But since I've been hanging out with you, I don't know, I feel more confident?"

"Good! That means I'm doing my job."

Gia laughs again. "No, listen. You always believe in me. And you tell me I can do the things I'm scared to do. Like when I tried to order the ice cream. I got lightheaded and wanted to quit, but you wouldn't let me. And now I can order at that truck anytime." Gia takes a small breath. "I guess I'm saying thank you, Nav. For everything."

I smile at my ceiling, starry-eyed and mushy and incredibly happy. "You're welcome, Gia."

I stiffen when I hear a car door slam outside. I check the time—five forty-five. Dad's home. Ugh.

"Your dad's home?" Gia asks.

How'd she know? I didn't even say anything.

"Yeah. Gotta go."

"Okay. Talk to you tomorrow?"

"You got it, babe."

I almost swallow my tongue. *Fuck,* I shouldn't have said that! Gia doesn't know that inside joke between me and Hallie, and my gay ass doesn't mean it as a joke with Gia. I hate myself. Gia's apparently stunned into silence, so I quickly hang up, grab my pillow, and scream into it. Fucking hell, I have got to get this crush under control.

By the time I calm down, Dad's knocking on my door. End of phone time. I get up and open the door, my hand already outstretched to drop my phone into his palm.

But this time, he's not holding his hand out. Today he's holding a paper plate with a slice of pizza on it. He clears his throat and offers it to me. "You haven't eaten dinner in a while."

False. I just wait until he goes to bed. Does he really think I haven't eaten in three days? Some of my caution melts, and I take the plate.

"Thanks, Dad."

"You're welcome."

I wait for Dad to leave, but he doesn't. He clears his throat again. "Let's talk about your grounding."

"Umm, okay."

Dad backs away from my door and gestures downstairs. "At the table?"

Is he asking me or telling me? He's so confusing. I want to snap at him, but I rein in the irritation and nod. I follow him downstairs, where I'm met with the sight of two big Papa Johns pizza boxes and a smaller box containing a brownie. I love those greasy, pizza-joint brownies. Did he remember . . . ?

Dad sits at the table first, and I follow. We eat in awkward silence for a while. I'm determined not to speak first. Even if I did, what would I say? I stayed in the house like he asked. I'm even missing work. What more does he want?

Dad finishes his second slice of pizza and looks at me. He's making me nervous, so I stop eating too. Dad fidgets with the empty plate in front of him but doesn't look away.

"Let's talk now."

"Okay."

"First, Naveah . . . thank you."

I blink at him in surprise. I was not expecting that. "For what?"

"For listening to me. You stayed put, you didn't try to run away, and you let me have a few days to cool off and think. So, thank you."

"Umm . . ." I'm not sure what to say. This is really weird. I don't know if I've ever heard Dad thank me for following his instructions. "You're welcome?"

Dad's mouth twitches, like he wants to smile. He remains stoic, though. "Secondly . . . I'm sorry."

I'm shocked into silence for a second time. Dad is apologizing . . . to me? Am I dreaming? Is this some kind of alternate universe?

Dad continues when I don't say anything. "I'm sorry that I didn't make you feel welcome in your own home. And I'm really sorry that I made you think I'd hurt you." Dad's eyes shine with unshed tears. "When you flinched from me, Naveah, it broke my heart. I never wanted to be the parent whose child is afraid of them. But somehow along the way, I messed up. And that kills me."

I stare at Dad, trying to comprehend what he's saying. "I'm not scared of you, Dad. I mean, I am a little, but not like that. I flinched because I got punched by Greg the night before and my eye was hurting. It's not you, I promise."

Dad doesn't look happy about my reassurances. He still looks incredibly sad. "That's another thing. I don't know who Greg is. Or why you're fighting with him. I don't know who Gia is either, or why you'd argue with Hallie. Last I heard, you were joined at the hip. There's so much I don't know about my own daughter, and that's purely on me. Part of the reason I was so upset with you is because when Hallie's mother told me you were missing, I didn't have the slightest clue where to start looking. And that scared me."

"Dad . . ." I can't say much else. My eyes sting a little now too. What he says makes sense. I didn't introduce him to Gia, and I lied about going to that party. He had to be scared. "I'm sorry too."

"It's okay. The party was a symptom of a larger problem." Dad takes a shaky breath. "Which is, at least for me, your mother."

My muscles lock up at the mention of her. We haven't talked about this in three years. Not once since the day she left. "Dad, I—"

"No, listen. Please listen."

I nod, but something like panic creeps into my chest. I don't want to talk about her. I don't even want to think about her. I've kept it together for three years by pushing her out, and now he wants to talk? I don't know if I can handle it.

Dad looks equally wrecked. He stares down at the table like it's going to jump up and swallow him in one bite. "You're old enough to know the details now. But I think you'll be upset because really, there aren't any. I'm going to be honest, Naveah, when your mother left, it broke me. I was completely blindsided. I thought everything was fine. I went to work, I came home to you two, we spent time together with all three of us. I thought we were happy. So when Nicole told me she wasn't, and she was leaving, I couldn't cope. For years I hoped she would come home and everything would pick back up where we left off. But she didn't. And one day, I woke up and realized I'd wasted three years, praying for a miracle that would never happen."

Dad and I sit in heavy silence. I'm near tears, the table blurring into a mess of brown wood and grease-stained white plates. I knew Dad was hurting, but this is too much. It's too much emotion, too much heartbreak. I had to deal with my own, and now I'm taking in his too. Mom really fucked up this family, and for what? For that "space" Hallie's going on about? I feel so sick I want to puke up all my pizza.

"All that said, grief isn't a good excuse for me being absent." Dad clears his throat and wipes his eyes until they're free of water. "Logistically, it was difficult. Going from a two-income household to one is rough. I had to work more to keep the lights on. A lot of days, I was just surviving. But that's not an excuse either. I should have been there for you. I should have been a good father and not gotten so wrapped up in my own grief that I didn't notice you were hurting too." Dad takes a nervous breath. "I've started therapy. And it's really helping."

Surprise knocks some of the tears from my eyes. Dad, going to therapy? "Seriously?"

Dad's face is intense and focused. "Seriously. So, all of this is to say that I'm trying. I'm trying to be your dad again, not some stranger who lives in your house. I want to know about Gia, if you want to tell me. And I want to know who Greg is, so I can kill him."

I smile a little. Greg would shit his pants if he saw Dad coming.

"And I want to know you, not the thirteen-year-old you that I remember. But now. I want to be Dad again, if you're ready to forgive me. And if not, that's okay too. It's up to you."

I look at Dad, uncertain. I know what he's saying, and honestly it makes me all warm and fuzzy inside that he wants to try again. And he really is trying. Therapy is not an easy step, especially for a family that doesn't believe in it. But I don't know if I can ignore the way he ignored me. I don't know if I can forgive him for abandoning me, just like Mom did.

"Can I think about it?"

Dad's face falls, which kills me. "Of course."

I hesitate, wanting to say more but not knowing how. Finally, I settle on "Am I still grounded?"

Dad chuckles, which makes me feel better. "Yes. But only until tomorrow."

I nod and give him my phone. He takes it, and we stare at each other for a long moment. A small part of me wants to throw my arms around him and cry and be the little kid who can run to her dad about everything. But I'm not there. Not yet.

"Good night, Dad. And . . . thanks for telling me all that stuff."

Dad nods. "You're welcome. Good night."

CHAPTER 24

Hallie shows up on my doorstep, looking innocent and doe-eyed.

"Uncle David," she says, doing her best pleading-puppy impression, "can Nav come over while you're at work today? I heard she isn't grounded anymore."

Dad sighs like he's a thousand years old. I'm sure he's tired of our scheming. But when Hallie texted and said Be at your door in five minutes, how can I say no?

"Yes, Hallie." He turns to me, his eyes sharp, but cautious. "I would like you to be home by ten, Naveah. You have work tomorrow."

I would like you to be home, huh? It's not an order, but a suggestion. He meant what he said about not forcing me.

I try to smile at Dad, but I'm sure it's tense and anxious. I need more time with this new change. "Be back later, Dad."

He nods, and Hallie waves at him as she loops her arm in mine. "Thanks, Uncle David! We'll be good, I promise."

Dad doesn't say anything, so I follow Hallie as she trots down my driveway.

"Why didn't you bring your car to pick me up?" I complain as soon as we're out of earshot. "It's a thousand degrees out here."

"There she is." Hallie laughs. She bumps my hip with hers playfully. "You were starting to go crazy in that house."

She's not kidding. I'm so relieved to be in the sunlight again, I could faint. Or it could be the hot as hell sun beaming down my back. "Thanks for saving me, knight in shining gym shorts."

Hallie gives me a mock salute as her house comes into view. "Anytime. Though you're more of a dragon than a princess."

I roll my eyes and laugh. God, I'm so glad everything's back to normal.

And for a while, it is. Hallie forces me to watch a new horror movie, so I counter with *Hotel Hell* (she hates reality TV, so it's good revenge). Hallie paints her nails, and I play Galaxy Cat on my phone. It's so normal I want to cry.

But then, I notice Hallie's room has changed. I didn't notice at first because it was dark for the movies, but gone are the tacky posters of K-pop bands I've teased her about for years. Now, she has a few terrible photographs in their place, strung together on a string with leaves on the ends. I squint at them and can barely make out a red bird, a sunlit path, and a bench I know well. The pictures from our hike.

A sour taste wells up in my mouth. Things feel the same, but they're not. Hallie is changing. But . . . I watch Hallie coat her midnight-blue nails with clear polish, concentrating, and the bad taste recedes. I could be nasty about the changes if I wanted. But I don't want to.

"So, did photography stick?" I ask Hallie.

She glances at me. She has a complicated expression on her face. "Sort of. Maybe."

"Real promising."

"Shut up." Hallie chuckles and blows gently on her fingernails. She lets them get long in the summer because they have to be short for basketball, so I'm sure she's enjoying the extra canvas space. "I don't think I like it. I put up the pictures I took today to see how I feel about them."

"And?"

"God, they're fucking awful, aren't they?"

A snort-laugh escapes my throat. Hallie groans and whacks me with her pillow.

"Glad you said it and not me!" I sit up, still grinning, but I want her to know I'm serious when I say this. "Listen, if you like taking pictures, it doesn't matter if they're good."

Hallie smiles at me. "Yeah, I know. But I don't think photography is for me."

"Well, what did you decide on?"

"I like yoga," Hallie says. "And I kind of started getting into art. Not doing it but like . . . looking at it. Does that make sense?"

"No," I say, laughing. "But if you like it, I say do it."

Hallie beams at me. "Thanks, Nav. Now, what about you?"

"What about me?"

Hallie looks away, at something behind me. "I was wondering how you were feeling about camp. There's only a week left."

Ugh. *Ugh.* I cannot escape that freaking camp. I want to throw up so someone can talk about anything else. Hallie doesn't know that if all goes to plan, I'll be right there with her. She also doesn't know about my annoying crush on Gia and that the thought of leaving her here alone in that big empty house, in this big empty town, also makes me want to puke.

Hallie meets my eyes and her eyebrows pull together. "That bad, huh?"

"No, it's just . . ." I trail off, sighing. "It's nothing."

"If it makes you feel better, it's mostly SAT prep and math. Not like, canoeing and shit."

"Like I'd be interested in canoeing anyway. I wanna go to the *parties*."

Hallie grins. "Yeah. I am pretty hyped about that."

"Don't rub it in," I complain.

Hallie laughs. "Maybe it won't be a bad thing."

My stomach turns when I think of Hallie and her "space." "Why?"

"Because," Hallie says, her grin growing slowly, "you'll get to spend a lot of time with Gia. It's good that you've made a new friend."

Not if I can help it. Which bums me out even further. "Speaking of Gia, we should nail down the day for your redo date. She's really excited."

Hallie smiles at her fingernails. They're dry now, so she's probably going to move on to the toes. "Oh, really?"

"Yeah. I know she messed up the first time, but don't worry, she can definitely talk now."

Hallie gets off the bed and goes to her vanity, where she looks through her nail polish options. "Actually, can you tell me more about Gia?"

I frown at her back. I'm getting an ominous feeling . . . but maybe this is Hallie being interested in Gia. This is a good thing. That's what I tell my nauseous stomach, anyway. "What do you want to know?"

"You think she's cute?"

"Oh, she's so cute. Like, Hallie, you wouldn't believe. She has this stupidly complicated game she plays all the time, and she's so nerdy about it, it's adorable. And when she gets nervous, she turns bright red, but not all at once! It's so cute I could die."

Hallie makes a hmm-ing sound in her throat. "When you hang out, what do you guys do?"

"Usually, we play games."

Hallie turns to look at me. She has one eyebrow raised. "You play video games now?"

"I play *one* game. And listen to her nerd out about the complicated one."

"Right, right." Hallie turns back to her vanity.

She's taking forever to pick a color. I always pick the same one—soft pink, which isn't too much different from my natural nail color.

"And what else?"

"I mean, I don't know. We eat together and talk." And practice romance, but Hallie doesn't have to know that.

"Sounds like you have fun," Hallie says.

At first, I'm worried she's jealous, but she doesn't sound upset. She almost sounds . . . amused. Weird. But I better clarify so there's no misunderstanding (ignoring my annoying feelings,

215

of course, because I am *not* going to ruin this for all three of us, so help me).

"Yeah. But I'm not making moves on your girl, I promise."

Hallie chuckles. She finally picks a color—looks like yellow. She picks up another one and trots to me. "Wouldn't dream of it, Nav."

I search her face for a clue to how to respond to this weird conversation, but she just looks entertained. "Anyway, enough about me and Gia—you want to go on the redo date on Saturday? Right before you leave on Monday?"

Hallie grins. "Sure." She puts a nail polish color in my palm—bright green. Ugh. "Saturday it is."

"Great!" That's what I say, but God, I'm miserable. Hallie will be having fun with Gia on Saturday. That's so soon. I have to shut down this crush before then or I'll be at risk of breaking my own heart. I clear my throat and take the polish. "You better cut your nails before you go on a date with my friend."

Hallie bursts into laughter, and I smile, but I can't bring myself to laugh with her.

CHAPTER 25

I step into Sweet Teeth at eight a.m., and I almost want to kiss the sticky counters. Freedom at last! And money! Ten dollars an hour, but hey, better than minimum wage. And I'm out of my cursed room. Things are looking up.

"Hey!" Ethan yells from the break room as soon as I step foot through the back door. "What took you so long? Get in here and get to work."

All right, good mood is gone.

"A 'hey, Nav' would be nice. Expected, even." I round the corner to peek into the break room.

Ethan is lounging in "his" chair, a plush red armchair he loves. He threatens me with death if I ever sit in it, which is why I do as often as possible.

Ethan glares at me. "Where've you been? I should write you up for no-showing three days in a row."

"First of all, I was only on the schedule for two of those days, and second, I texted you and said I couldn't come." I roll my eyes. "Besides, you can handle me taking a few days off."

Ethan is quiet. Too quiet. I narrow my eyes at him.

"You *can* handle the store when I'm not here, right?"

"Get to work," Ethan barks.

I have a real bad feeling about this. I hurry to the front,

where the shelves should be full of baked goods. And they are . . . empty. Just two lone blueberry muffins that look drier than the Sahara, and a sad, squished bonbon.

"Ethan, what the fuck?"

"Start baking," he grunts.

"How the hell am I supposed to bake *everything*?" I glance at the clock wildly—8:10. I have three hours before the lunch crowd. Fuck.

I curse Ethan's name, family, and everything I can think of while I throw on an apron and get to work. I have to start the dough-based stuff first because it has to proof, then the cakes, then the chocolate work. Oh my God, I'm gonna kill him. How the fuck has he been running this shop for days with no food?! He's gonna give his sweet old grandma a heart attack. And me too for good measure.

I'm so busy baking that I barely hear the bell tinkle above the front door. I groan, covered in sweat and flour and chocolate. "Can you get that?" I yell to Ethan.

He doesn't answer, because of course he doesn't. I groan again and take off my apron. Nav, the one-man show, once again. I run to the front, a plastic smile pasted on my face. "Welcome to Sweet Teeth—"

I choke on my words, because a customer doesn't wait at the counter—it's Shirley. The owner and my boss. I would normally be happy to see her, but I've only replenished the chocolate chip cookies and one flavor of cupcakes. And the sad, crumbly muffins are front and center. Shit.

"Hi, Naveah," Shirley says. She smiles, her eyes crinkled, but her shoulders are tense. Ah, fuck. We're dead.

"Hey! How are you?" I glance frantically at the vacant shelves before me. Even the ice cream is half-empty.

"Good. Just came to check on everything." Shirley's smile slowly slips off her face. "I see that we're out of a lot of sweets. I'm assuming we had a big order this morning?"

I debate on lying, but if I'm caught, I'll definitely be fired. "No, ma'am. But I'm working on it, I promise. We still have an hour until lunch."

I expect Shirley to give me a tongue lashing, but she looks confused. "What do you mean you're working on it? Are you baking?"

"What?"

"Why are you baking?" Shirley asks. "Ethan should be taking care of that."

Shit. I was not supposed to say that. This whole time she's been thinking Ethan has been baking and I'm running support. This day could not get any worse. I glance behind me, where Ethan is probably picking his nose in the break room. I should rat him out, but I'm a girl of integrity. He's bribed my silence with many Egg McMuffins. "I, umm, I'm helping! It's been hard since I wasn't here for a few days."

Again, Shirley looks confused. "I didn't know you weren't here?"

Oh, Ethan, you are in trouble. There's only so much damage control I can do. A moment of silence for the future Ethan. "I told Ethan I couldn't make it, but maybe he forgot to tell you?"

Shirley starts to say something, but the bell on the door rings merrily again. I look up, and I'm shocked senseless.

It's Dad.

He's in his work jumpsuit, a gray one smeared with oil. He waves at me awkwardly, and I just want to drop dead. What the hell is he doing here? And why now?! He's never visited me at work before, not once in a year, and he picks the day when I'm about to get chewed out by my boss. Amazing.

Shirley steps to the side, smiling at Dad. "Welcome! Sorry, I'm in the way."

"No," Dad says. He looks so awkward and out of place against the bright yellow walls and cartoon decorations. "I'm here to see my daughter. If it's not a bad time."

It is! It's a terrible time! My lemon cupcakes are gonna be ruined if they stay in the oven much longer. But I can't check on them because Shirley will see me and grill me about why I'm even touching the oven. Hell. I'm in hell.

"Oh, you're Naveah's father?" Shirley's whole face lights up. "I'm the owner! She is *such* a great employee. I'm not here much anymore—bad back—but whenever I come by, she's always hard at work."

Dad seems pleased. He even has a rare small smile on his face. "I'm so happy to hear that. She really enjoys cooking, so this job is perfect for her."

Shirley frowns slightly and looks at me. "You don't bake, though, right? You just run the register."

And then, Ethan picks the perfect time to yell, "Nav, your cupcakes are burning!"

I close my eyes and take a deep breath. I haven't seen a disaster this bad since my after-party stunt. "Can you get them?" I yell back. "I'm busy up here."

"Why're you always fucking around?" Ethan complains.

I practically see the color drain from Shirley's face. And all of that color goes into Dad's, because he suddenly looks like he's gonna murder my manager.

"He's kidding," I say, trying to smooth things over. "Ethan, now really isn't—"

"Get your own cupcakes," Ethan yells. "Hurry up, I need to smoke and if the case is empty when I get back, I'm taking it out of your check."

The fuck he is. And I would say that if I wasn't watching a horror movie go down in front of me. Dad turns to Shirley, slowly, and she looks like she's about to faint.

"You said you're the owner?" Dad's voice is deadly calm.

"Y-Yes," Shirley squeaks.

"Then you need to do something about how that man talked to my daughter. You better handle it before I do."

My eyes widen in shock. I've never heard Dad so serious in my life. Shirley practically leaps behind the counter and disappears into the back. I hear Ethan yelp in surprise, and then the closing of the break room door.

Rest in pieces, Ethan.

Dad takes a deep breath, probably to calm himself. He looks

right at me, his expression grave. "Does he treat you like that all the time?"

"I mean, yeah. But he's harmless." I wave my hand lazily in the air. "He can't do anything to me because he can't bake. Don't tell Shirley, though. I'm not supposed to."

"You shouldn't be disrespected like that." Dad's voice is so serious it surprises me. "I'll talk to him."

"No! No, I'm good. It's fine. Anyway, what can I get you?" I look down at the nearly empty shelves. "Don't say the muffins. They're terrible."

Dad doesn't laugh, but he doesn't look like he'll strangle Ethan anymore either. "I don't want anything. I wanted to make sure you had something to eat for lunch."

I stare at him, confused. "Why?"

Dad looks a little awkward again. He rubs his arm, not meeting my eyes. "I know you missed some shifts while you were grounded." Dad reaches into his pocket and withdraws an oil-smudged twenty-dollar bill. He gives it to me, and I take it, speechless. "Just wanted to make sure you ate."

I stare down at the twenty, disbelief robbing me of all thoughts. This is . . . really nice of him. I have enough for lunch, but he wanted to be certain I wasn't starving to death. He came all this way, on his lunch break probably, to make sure I was okay. He really is trying. I look up at him and smile. "You know I work in a bakery, right?"

Dad finally smiles, a tiny, half one, and I almost forgive him for everything on the spot.

Shirley scares me by popping out of the back. She looks a

hundred years older, which is bad because she's already sixty-five. She takes my hands, and I jump.

"Naveah, I'm so sorry for how my grandson has treated you." She looks right into my eyes, and she seems sincere. "He won't bother you anymore, I promise."

"It's no big deal." As nice as Shirley is being (probably because Dad is glowering at her), it's an empty promise; as soon as she's not looking, it'll be open season on me.

"It is a big deal," Dad says. "How can you be sure he won't bother her?"

"Because I fired him."

I'm shocked into silence. She . . . what? Ethan, her golden boy? Ethan, who can do no wrong? Even Dad looks stunned.

"He told me everything," Shirley continues. "How he's made you do his job and yours, how you've been baking everything in the store for months. I am so ashamed, Naveah. I never dreamed he'd do this. Let me make it up to you."

"Uh . . . okay." I'm still getting over the fact that Ethan was *fired*. Revenge tastes so freaking good. I'll miss the Mickey D's runs, though.

Shirley regards me warmly. "How do you feel about being Sweet Teeth's new manager this summer?"

I gasp. "Seriously?"

"If you want! You'll have to cut back your hours once school starts, of course, but I'm happy to offer you Ethan's wage. That's a permanent change. And also, I'd love to work with you on my own personal recipes. I've tasted your baking, Naveah, and it's incredible. I thought it was Ethan's work this whole time, but he told me he can't even make a cupcake. You have real talent, and I'd love to help you however you need."

A raise? And baking lessons from Shirley? It's too good to be true. But it is true, because Dad is beaming and Shirley is too.

"Congrats, Naveah," Dad says.

"Thank you." I'm so shocked, my voice comes out high and squeaky. I clear my throat and smile at Shirley. "I guess I'm the new manager at Sweet Teeth."

Shirley gives me a huge hug, and I'm too stunned to hug her back. A manager. I'm a manager! This is what I wanted from the beginning . . . isn't it? Worry leaps into me immediately. This will mean longer hours, surely. And what if I'm not as good of a baker as Shirley thinks? And wait, if I'm a manager, then that means I can't go to camp. Or rather, I'll have to make a decision. I love baking; learning directly from Shirley is a dream come true. But I planned on going to camp with Hallie. That was the plan. Can I really change it now, even if this is something I want?

These thoughts are making my stomach hurt, so I put it away for now. I can think about this later, when I'm calmer. I try to focus on Shirley and Dad, both smiling like I won the lottery. Maybe it won't be a disaster. After all, miracles happen; I never dreamed Shirley would fire Ethan. I try to stay positive as Dad waves goodbye and Shirley takes me to the back to show me how to make her famous red velvet cake, but all I can focus on is the undercurrent of fear and dread.

CHAPTER 26

When I ring Gia's doorbell, amid a chorus of happy barking, Gia's mom answers the door.

"Oh, hi, Ms. Flores." I try to cover my shock. I never know when she's gonna pop up. She's like a friendly ghost.

"Hello, Nav!" Gia's mom says. She pulls me inside and gives me a big hug, squeaking a little in my ear. She lets me go and holds me at arm's length, still grinning. "How are you? Are you hungry? Are we officially ungrounded? Gia told me what happened. I'm glad you called her to pick you up, and I'm really glad you didn't try to drive while drunk, but please call your father too! Though you're welcome here any time. Have you tried the pool yet?"

"Uhhh . . ." I stall to try and process her rapid-fire questions. "I'm good. And I'm not grounded anymore. And I haven't tried the pool. I didn't bring a swimsuit."

"Next time!" Gia's mom laughs. She fussily fixes my shirt, smoothing down the shoulders. "You're packed awful light! Did Gia forget to ask you?"

"Ask me what?"

"I'm going out of town until Monday, and you girls get along so well that I suggested you can stay with Gia! She's such a good girl, but I worry, you know?"

225

Oh. Gia didn't mention anything, but I was only ungrounded two days ago, so she probably wouldn't. Though I think she's used to her mom disappearing for days at a time by now. "I'll ask her. I don't mind."

"That's what I told her you'd say! She's so silly, saying she didn't want to bother you." Gia's mom gives me another quick hug, and then she breezes past me. "Gia's upstairs in the shower, but I have to go! Food is in the fridge, but you girls can order whatever you want for dinner. No drinking! Go get your swimsuit and try the pool! Really, I'm serious, it's amazing. Hot tub and everything! Okay, bye, love you, see you later!"

And the friendly ghost is gone, disappearing into her Mercedes and driving away.

I watch her go, a little stunned. Then I pull the door closed and pat Jordan's sweet little head.

"Hello, babycakes!" She leaps into my arms, squirming with joy. I kiss her wet nose. "God, I love you so much. I'm gonna steal you and take you home with me." I tuck her under my arm like a football and climb the stairs to Gia's room.

Gia's door is cracked, but I don't hear the sound of the shower. I knock, a little embarrassed. Before I figured out this annoying crush, I would have just barged in. But now, the thought of accidentally seeing Gia in her underwear makes me want to combust and also die.

"Mami?" Gia calls.

"No, it's Nav."

I hear rapid footsteps, and Gia opens her door. Her hair is

soaking wet and she's wearing blue rabbit-patterned pajama bottoms but a weirdly nice shirt. She's wearing her glasses today.

"You're early!"

"I hope that's okay." I hold up Jordan, grinning. "Your guard dog is useless, by the way."

Gia laughs and takes Jordan from my arms. "She only attacks criminals, so you're safe."

"I don't think licking someone to death counts." I step into Gia's room, which is slowly creeping back to its messy status. She has a bunch of wadded up clothes around her bed and two bags of chips at her gaming station. The middle is free of debris, though.

"Oh, I almost forgot—congrats!" Gia says, her face lighting up. For a second, I'm confused, but then I remember. I told Gia all about my promotion in a rushed text last night, even before I told Hallie.

"Thanks." I rub the back of my neck, looking down at my feet. I didn't tell her how nervous I feel.

"Not excited?" Gia asks.

I shrug, and Gia laughs. That makes me look up, and she's smiling at me.

"The 'not liking new stuff' thing, huh?"

"I hate it when you do that," I complain, but I hope she can't tell how my heart doubled its speed. Who else knows me like this? Hallie, of course, but Gia too, apparently. It's embarrassing how happy her observation makes me.

Gia pokes me playfully, oblivious to how I'm about to melt

into a useless puddle. "Don't worry, it'll be great. Change isn't bad, remember?"

"Yeah, that's what you say." I shuffle my feet, my anxiety from yesterday surging back. "I was thinking about turning it down."

"What? No, you can't!" Gia's passionate tone makes me jump. She stares intently at me, eyebrows scrunched together. "You love baking, right? Why would you turn it down?"

"What if I'm not good enough?" My voice comes out soft and afraid, which I hate.

Gia's expression softens too. "You will be. We can do manager practice, if you want."

"Yeah, yeah, you just want some free food." Weirdly, I do feel better. I don't know what I'll do about camp now, but Gia's gentle reassurances make me feel like I can do anything. I step into the middle of her room, eager to put some distance between us so I can calm my heart down to a normal rate. "Enough about me. Your mom said you were supposed to ask me something?"

Gia mutters under her breath. "She wasn't supposed to say anything."

I grin at her. "I don't mind staying over while she's gone. You know that."

"Ugh and she told you already?" Gia huffs angrily, and I want to squeeze her into a cute little ball and hug her forever. "I don't want to bother you all the time."

"You're not bothering me. And hey, that's plenty of time for romance practice!"

I expect Gia to be happy, but her face falls. "I don't know if we should keep doing romance practice."

My chest tightens with sudden apprehension. "What? Why not?"

Gia fidgets, twisting the black ring around her finger over and over. She won't look at me. "I was thinking maybe I shouldn't date Hallie."

"Oh no, no, ma'am. We are not doing that."

Even though my heart races, I close the gap between us and put my hands on her shoulders. She starts in alarm, looking dead at me now.

"This is your anxiety talking. You *are* going on that date, and you're gonna crush it, and you'll get your happily ever after."

Gia's eyes are so, so pretty up close. She blinks slowly, staring right into mine. "I don't think the anxiety is the problem."

Why is my heart beating triple-time? We're so close, I could easily step forward and press my lips against hers. Which I will *not* do, because Gia likes Hallie, and I'm not ruining both my friendships over my stupid feelings.

I take a weak, shuddery breath. "It is the anxiety, and we'll work through it. Let's do a little bit today, okay?"

Gia makes a face that's almost tortured, but she's smiling. "Okay."

I step away, trying to discreetly calm my heartbeat. "What's got you spooked? You're doing so well."

Gia fiddles with the bottom of her shirt. Jordan sits next to her leg, focused and ready to comfort her if needed. "The date.

You confirmed it with Hallie. I guess it's kind of . . . getting real now?"

Ah, makes sense. But these are normal, pre-date jitters. "It's just Tuesday. Saturday is practically a week away. Plenty of time for prep. Including our Final Exam on Thursday, remember?"

Gia nods, but still looks like she's on the edge of fainting, and her breath comes out in tight wheezes. Not good.

"Okay, let's calm down for a minute. Twenty-minute break. No romance talk allowed until we're breathing normally again."

I steer Gia to her favorite Snorlax beanbag. I still have her Switch, so I get it out, sit on the Gengar bag, and boot up the farm game. Gia stares at me for a second, and I nudge her with my foot.

"Hello, I have pumpkins to harvest. You gonna look at me or are you gonna steal gems from the cave of wonders or whatever?"

Gia finally smiles, and some of the redness creeps back to her normal skin tone. "The Cave of Wonders is from *Aladdin*."

"Whatever! You know what I mean."

Gia makes a big show of explaining the differences between the Cave of Wonders (movie) and the Cave of Adornment (game). Trust me, I do not care, but I find myself listening anyway. Well, I'm not so much listening as watching Gia's very cute face fill with excitement and passion, and wishing I could kiss it.

Our break ends up taking a lot longer than twenty minutes. Gia's team gets trapped in quicksand, and the guildies and I scream encouragement as Gia struggles her way through a ton of enemies by herself. Then, after defeating no less than fifty rabid snakes and clearing the horde, Gia's dwarf keels over dead from residual poison. Gia stares at her TV with blank disbelief, and I laugh so hard snot bubbles out of my nose. And then Gia starts laughing at that, and before we know it, it's been two hours.

"One more thing and I swear we can get started," Gia promises, gaze focused on the TV.

She's collecting ingredients for some kind of stew. How the fuck do you play this thing? I still haven't seen the first-person shooter part.

"Yeah, yeah," I tease. "Just tell me when you're ready."

We play our games in cozy silence, and I'm so focused on farming that I almost miss when the noise of the game dies down around us. Gia says goodbye to her team (I say bye too, and they almost deafen her while screaming, "Bye, business person!") and powers it down. Her grin is sheepish. "Sorry that took so long."

"Nah." I'm glad she's relaxed and not nervous. I almost don't want to bring up romance practice now. For my sake and hers. "This was a great idea. You should listen to your mom more."

Gia rolls her eyes. "She'd love to hear that."

"Don't disrespect Ms. Flores! She's the coolest lady I know." I pause, thinking back to our rapid-fire interaction. "She's weirdly obsessed with the pool, though."

Gia laughs. "She'll make you swim in it soon."

"No way. I can't swim."

Gia's eyes widen. "Please don't say that to her. She's got this huge hang-up on kids having life skills before college. She'll force you into swimming lessons."

"Swimming isn't a life skill. It's recreational at best."

"What happens if you fall into water and start drowning?"

"I'll keep my Black ass away from the ocean, like any reasonable person."

Gia's grin turns mischievous. "You're not scared of the water, are you, Nav?"

Oh God, what have I done? I shrug, playing it cool. "I'm just a sensible human being. People belong on land, that's all."

Gia startles me when she stands up from her beanbag. "Let's go to the pool."

Oh shit. I'm losing control over the situation and quick. It's not that I'm afraid of water. (I just don't like it; is that a crime?) But if I see Gia in a swimsuit, I don't know what I'll do. Pass out, probably. "I don't—I'm suddenly ill. Pool water would definitely make it worse."

Gia's halfway to the door. She looks back at me and grins, the happiest I've seen her in a while. "Come on, it's exposure therapy. Like romance practice."

I groan, but my traitorous body is already up and moving. Because if Gia wants me to do something, goddammit, I'm gonna do it.

I complain the whole way down the steps, into the kitchen, and out into the backyard. I freeze when I see it; a gaping maw of still, clear water. I admired it before, but Gia can't really expect me to get in it, right?

Gia tugs on the hem of my shirt, snapping me back to the present. Her expression is kind now. "Baby steps, like romance lessons. Today we'll just stick our feet in."

Oh, thank God. I breathe a sigh of relief and kick off my shoes. I'm wary while Gia sits on the edge, but I take a deep breath and sit beside her. She dunks her feet into the pool unceremoniously, but I hesitate.

"If I fall in, can you save me?"

"You never go in after a drowning person." Gia is deeply serious. "But I'll throw you a pool noodle."

"My hero." The image of me being saved by an orange Styrofoam noodle makes me laugh, and I decide to be brave. I stick both feet in before I can back out. The water is weirdly warmer than I thought it'd be, and my unease calms to easy confidence. What was I afraid of?

"See?" Gia teases. "Not so bad, huh?"

"Yeah, yeah, rub it in."

Gia chuckles but doesn't say anything else. We sit together for a few minutes, listening to the gurgling water and Jordan attacking her chew toy behind us. I look up at the sky, and I'm surprised at the first notes of pink. Sunset, already? I watch it for a minute, and a previous conversation pops into my mind.

"Gia, look." I point to the sky when she looks up. "It's your favorite color. Flamingo pink."

Gia brightens, pure delight on her face as she gazes up at the sunset. Then she turns that radiance to me, and it's like staring into the sun. "You remembered."

Of course I remember. I remember everything from our romance practices, even the ones where I swore up and down to myself that I didn't like Gia. I remember her disgust for spaghetti, her worry over Hallie watching her eat, that her love language is words of affirmation. I remember the curve of her lip when she smiles, the way her breathing is quick but determined when we're trying something new, her intense glare as she battles sentient rock goblins or whatever the hell she does on that game. I shouldn't know Gia Flores as well as I do, because I made a rule for myself long ago: hookups only. Don't get attached. Disappointment and pain are all that can come from this. But for Gia, I'm starting to think that may be worth it.

But that's an admission wild horses couldn't drag out of me, so I shrug and say, "Yeah, I know, because I like to paint sunsets."

"Will you make one for me sometime?" Gia asks, and it's all I can do not to run home and slap some paint on a canvas right now.

"Yeah. Think of it as a prize when you come back from your date with Hallie." Some of the earlier joy dims, so I hurry to change the subject. "I can see the appeal of the pool now. Your mom continues to be correct about all things."

Gia groans, but it's playful. "She'll love you more than she already does if you tell her that. She adores this thing. I don't even like swimming that much, but she was obsessed with getting a pool. Probably why it took four years to build this stupid house."

"Stupid" house, huh? I'm hyperaware of Gia next to me. Her posture is a little more tense now, but she doesn't seem anxious. She seems like she wants to talk.

"Why'd your mom decide to build here?"

"She said she wanted to live in a small town in the South, but not in Texas. This whole house is her dream come true." Gia pauses, staring into the deepening sunset. "She told me I could have anything I wanted in this house. The media room was my idea. And she got a pool, which she really wanted as a kid, and the circle driveway like the super expensive houses on HGTV. And I mean, it's fine. It's a good house. But she's never here to enjoy it."

I don't say anything at first. I get it, I think. Dad's the same way. He works and works and works, just so he can crash and do it all over again the next day. But he had to. I didn't even think about what Mom leaving meant for us financially. I didn't even think that Dad was grieving, like me, but he had to drag himself to work so we wouldn't be homeless. I didn't want to think about it a couple of days ago, but now I feel like I have to.

"Your mom is probably trying to keep up with everything."

"Yeah," Gia says, her voice soft. "And I don't blame her. She's worked so hard. And she still has so much to deal with because of me."

I frown at her. "What do you mean because of you?"

Gia is quiet. She circles her feet in the water, fidgets with her ring, looks everywhere but at me. But I wait, because I think she's about to tell me something important, and if I press her, I'll never hear it.

"Family is important to us," Gia finally says. Her voice is strange—soft, but with an undercurrent of anger. "Normally, we wouldn't have built here at all. Our family is in Texas. It's where I was born, where Mami grew up. But I ruined it. Before me, Abuela and Mami got along, and everything was fine. But Abuela hated that I had anxiety. She *really* hated that I was queer. She's always treated me differently from my cousins."

God, I hate Gia's grandma so much. I'm seething, but I stay silent. I don't think Gia's done.

"It was little things, mostly. Even if I wanted to be alone, she'd force me to play with my cousins until I got too overwhelmed and had a meltdown. She threw away my video games because she thought they'd isolate me more. If I ever talked about a crush I had on a girl, she'd shut that down real quick. It wasn't all bad; I used to love when she'd braid my hair and tell me stories about her family in Mexico. And she made this great cake I still dream about. Whenever she made it, she'd let me lick the bowl after. I know she was afraid for me, and was trying to get me to be more outgoing, but I don't know. It just made me feel like I was never good enough."

Gia shudders and shifts closer to me, like she's afraid that her demon grandma will pop out of the woods and start lecturing her. "Mami noticed how she treated me, and they got into a ton of fights over it. She'd treat me better for a few days, but while Mami was at work, it would be the same all over again.

236

And one day, Abuela punished me for not being able to talk at a party she hosted. It wasn't that bad; she just ignored me for a week. But that week was Christmas, and all my cousins got gifts from Abuela and I didn't."

Gia closes her eyes, a painful expression on her face. Jordan appears like a fuzzy superhero, a mauled purple monkey dangling from her mouth. She tucks her nose into Gia's elbow, and Gia pats her head. I wait, but when she doesn't speak, I say, "God, you've got a shitty grandma."

Gia laughs a little and opens her eyes. She still won't look at me. "Yeah. That was the last straw. Mami packed up and we moved out the next day. We haven't been back since." Gia takes a deep breath. "I know it's hard for Mami, though. She left her whole family behind to protect me. And I'm grateful, but I miss my cousins and the big family we had. And now Mami's gone a lot, and it's so lonely." Gia's voice breaks on the word *lonely*, and my heart threatens to break right along with it. "I didn't have to have a pool. Or a stupid media room. I just don't want to be by myself all the time."

"I'm sorry about your grandma. She sucks, and your mom was right to get you away from her. Otherwise, we'd both be fighting grannies." Gia laughs, so I continue. "I know you miss your family. But if it helps, now you have me. For as long as you want."

Gia doesn't say anything, so I risk a look. I end up meeting her gaze, which is soft and wonderful and all for me.

"Nav," she says, her voice a whisper. "You know just what to say."

"I'm not just saying it." I can barely focus on the words coming out of my mouth. My gaze is locked with Gia's, and my heart is so full of emotion that it's struggling to beat, and if she leaned close to me right now, I swear I'd kiss her until we were both dizzy. "I know how it feels to be lonely."

The spell is broken when Gia frowns. "But you have Hallie. And your dad seems cool, even if he freaks out a lot."

I look back at the sunset. The sky is deep purple now, and soon stars will pop out like little spots of flour on a dark table. "Yeah, well. It's still hard when your mom decides to dip out and your dad ignores you for three years."

Gia winces. "That's also shitty."

"Yeah, you're telling me. You know she even took the fucking dog? Like who does that? Leaving her family of thirteen years, doesn't call or tell us where she is, and she can't even leave us the dog." The sky turns watery, like I'm looking up from the bottom of the pool. Paws claw up my legs, and when I blink away tears, Jordan's head rests on my chest. I stroke her ears, some of the misery easing. I see why Gia has her now. I really do feel better.

"I'm sorry." Gia scoots closer, so our thighs touch. I get a pleasant little thrill through my whole body, but only half of it is because my body finally realized how much I like Gia. I'm full of a deeper, emotional connection I never thought possible. And even though I'm unmoored, confused about how Dad is acting, overcome with looming grief over Mom, afraid of my new responsibilities at Sweet Teeth, I have Gia. Gia is here with me, sitting next to me because I'm sad, and I'm afraid of her giant pool. It's like we're the only two girls in the world. Two lonely girls not so lonely anymore, because we're together.

I tuck the swelling emotion away and dry my eyes with the sleeve of my shirt. "Thanks, Gia. Anyway, forget it. It's fine."

"It's not fine, but okay." Gia pauses, then says, "What was your dog's name?"

"Cuddles." I see her face in my mind, and I want to cry again. "She was a white miniature poodle. Mean as a snake. She'd rip up my stuff if I pissed her off. But she was mine. She was all of ours."

Gia meets my eyes. "Let's go to a pet store."

I laugh, and some of the pain fades. I snuggle closer to Gia, my head on her shoulder, and Jordan must think we're fine now because she flounces off my lap and attacks that poor monkey again.

"Sorry we didn't do any practice," I say after a minute.

"We did," Gia says. "This was pretty Open and Honest, right?"

I almost want to laugh. It is, isn't it? But that wasn't practice. Not for me, anyway. When I think about Gia having this same moment with Hallie, I want to throw up. Instead, I clear my throat. "No practical practice, then."

Gia stiffens under my cheek, and I look up at her. She seems nervous again, but why? Before I can ask, Gia, carefully, deliberately, holds my hand. I'm so shocked, I can't move. We've held hands before, but in this vulnerable moment, this has to mean something. I want it to mean something, anyway.

"Hand holding is practical, right?" Gia's voice is in a much higher register than it should be, and for some reason, that bursts my bubble of shock. I laugh and hold her hand back, focusing on the way her (very sweaty) hand fits perfectly in mine. I can have this, right? It's selfish, it's greedy, but now, watching the day fade to night, I can have this moment and wish it was forever.

"Right," I say, my voice soft. "You're doing great."

My phone buzzes and ruins the perfect moment. I glare down at a text from Dad.

Are you with Gia?

yes, I text back. Boy, he has no idea. My cheek is still pressed against Gia's shoulder, my hand linked with hers, and my heart sings with pitiful joy from being so close.

Okay, Dad texts back. He adds another one right after. Do you need money for food?

I stare at my phone, a confusing and infuriating amount of affection swirling in my heart. Dad said he loves me, and I'm trying hard to believe him. This kinda makes it easier.

"You okay?" Gia asks. Her voice is gentle, kind. How can she know me well enough to sense when I'm feeling sad, or happy, or a strange mix of the two?

"Yeah. Just Dad being Dad."

"Is that a good thing or a bad thing?"

"It used to be a bad thing, but now I'm not so sure." Weirdly, I kind of want to thank him. I know he worries, and even though I was stuck at home jail, we didn't really talk while I was grounded. Maybe I can make this easier on him. Maybe he deserves some grace, like Ms. Flores working hard to protect her tiny family. Like he did for me, even if he botched it.

"Gia," I say, sitting up from her shoulder. I meet her eyes, hers wide and curious and mine full of determination. "Do you want to go to my house?"

CHAPTER 27

Dad looks at me with blank confusion when I open my front door.

"Hey, Dad. Nothing's wrong, we just wanted to hang out here for a change."

"We?"

I look back and realize Gia hasn't followed me inside. She's waiting nervously on the porch, Jordan dangling from her arms.

"Come on, it's okay."

For a second, I think Gia's gonna have to do her pep talk circle. But when I reach my hand out to her, her shoulders ease down from her ears, and she takes it. She steps into my house, and attempts a smile. "H-Hi."

Dad raises his eyebrows while I explain. "This is my friend, Gia."

He stares at her for a second. "You're the Mr. Nav one, huh?"

Gia's face turns a patchy red, and Dad cracks a rare smile. "Nice to meet you, Gia. Do you want me to order pizza for you both?"

I beam at him. "Yeah, that'd be cool."

Dad nods. "I'll order. You can go ahead and go upstairs. Also . . . is that a dog?"

"Her name is Jordan," I say. "She's housebroken, promise."

242

Dad frowns deeply. "Can I pet her?"

Gia seems surprised. "Umm, y-yeah, she's really nice." Dad pats Jordan's head, and she licks his hand. A small, genuine smile blooms on his face. This was definitely the right decision.

We end up hanging out with Dad while we wait for the pizza. I watch Gia answer Dad's questions about where she's from and who her parents are (Dad has no idea what a Snuggable is, which Gia seems to take delight in). And even though Gia is awkward and nervous at first, she eventually calms down and is able to talk to him normally. She's holding my hand under the table the whole time, though, so she's cheating a little. Not that I'm complaining. If she has to hold my hand forever, I won't care.

When the pizza comes, I expect Gia to want to go upstairs. But she doesn't; she chats happily to Dad about her media room while we eat, then chats to me about the farm game. We end up in a heated debate about befriending the dark chickens (apparently, I'm doing it wrong? Which is whatever, she's clearly jealous of my farming skills). And when I look over at Dad, he's passed out in his armchair, snoring softly . . . with Jordan belly up in his lap, who is also snoring.

"Oh my God," Gia whispers. "This is the cutest thing I've ever seen in my life."

I take a picture of Dad, grinning. "He's always saying we can't get another dog. Now look at him."

Gia and I tiptoe up to my room. I leave the door ajar, so Jordan can come up whenever she decides to stop using Dad as a pillow. I sit on my bed and open my arms wide. "Welcome to my humble abode!"

Gia looks around, smiling. "It's so clean."

"It's not. I just put away all my shit, unlike someone I know." I elbow her teasingly, and Gia giggles. She sits next to me, shoulder to shoulder, and again, I'm met with overwhelming peace. I'm indifferent to my room, but it's cozy and warm, and even though it's much smaller than Gia's, right now it feels like the perfect size.

"Thanks for coming," I tell Gia. "My dad wanted to meet you."

"Probably because he thinks I kidnapped you."

I laugh. That probably wasn't funny at the time, but now it's hilarious. "No, but that's a fantastic reason." I hesitate for a second. The drama with Dad is so confusing. But Gia is here, next to me, lending me her strength. I take a breath to steady myself. "Dad and I kind of fell apart after Mom left. He ignored me after she was gone. And I know he was grieving, but . . ." I trail off, emotion trying to strangle the words from me. Gia puts her hand over mine, and the gentle encouragement pushes the rest of the words out. "I was too, you know? I needed him. And he wasn't there."

"But he's here now?" Gia asks.

"Yeah. He's here now. Annoyingly here. That's why he's been breathing down my neck lately—he's guilty he missed the past three years and wants to make up for it."

Gia nods, her expression thoughtful. "What do you think? Will you forgive him?"

"I don't know. I don't know if he deserves it."

"But you're trying anyway," Gia says. "He wanted to meet me, right?"

When I nod, she continues.

"You didn't have to ask me to come over. And we could have come up here a while ago."

"You're really annoying when you're right."

Gia laughs. "It doesn't have to be all at once, you know. You can take your time. And you already took the first step by introducing me."

I don't say anything, turning her words over in my head. He's trying now. He's trying really, really hard. He's even going to therapy. I should forgive him, right? But a small, stubborn part of me can't let go. The same part that wants this deal to work out, so I go to camp and I can avoid having to think about our confusing new relationship.

"What should we do now?" Gia asks after I'm silent.

I blink and look around my little room. I don't have anything in here for two people to do. Dad hasn't even put my TV back up yet. The only thing I can think of . . . "What about a movie?"

Gia nods, and I grab my laptop from my desk. But there's nowhere for both of us to watch, except . . . the bed. Where we'll be sitting close, probably squished together because it's not nearly as big as Gia's. I take a breath to calm myself and sit the laptop on the end of the bed. I sit as close to the wall as possible. "Come on up."

Gia climbs onto my bed wordlessly. For some reason, her face is beginning to get that blotchy pink color I love. My face is on fire too, but at least Gia can't see it. She hesitates, but after a moment, she closes the distance between us. Our thighs touch, her smooth skin against mine.

I'm definitely gonna have a heart attack tonight.

"What're we watching?" Gia asks as I try not to go into cardiac arrest. "Not horror, please. Or romance. Or anything with sad animals."

"You know, I almost forgot you're a movie snob." I'm starting to relax too, because Gia is being Gia, and really, what's there to be nervous about? She doesn't like me, and she was probably just anxious earlier because she's in a new place. Which hurts, but at least I can function again.

I make a few suggestions, but Gia vetoes each one. We finally settle on a TV show, *Kitchen Nightmares*. I've seen every episode four times, but I don't mind a fifth round, especially with Gia at my side. We watch six episodes back-to-back (and I keep my phone carefully tucked under my thigh the whole time). Gia's never seen it before, so she gets a kick out of Gordon Ramsay's screaming and the disgusting kitchens. The seventh one starts to autoplay, and Gia yawns. I yawn too, even though I'm not super tired.

"Sleepy?" Gia asks me, like she's not the one who started this.

"Only if you are."

Gia nods reluctantly. "I stayed up late last night. But we can watch more tomorrow?"

She phrases it as a question, even though by now she should know I'll always say yes.

"For you? Absolutely."

Gia gives me a soft smile, and butterflies dance against my ribs. I close my laptop and jump off my bed so I don't do anything I regret.

We chat to each other through my bathroom door as we change into pajamas, and soon we're both standing side by side, staring at the bed. I didn't think about it, but we'll have to share. I don't have a sleeping bag. And my bed's smaller than Gia's, so we'll be right next to each other. Oh God.

Jordan pokes her head into my room, jaws stretched wide into a yawn. She looks at us like we're idiots and hops onto my bed, wriggling her cute little butt under my comforter. Somehow, that makes it easier to move. Can't keep Queen Jordan waiting.

"What side do you want?" I ask Gia.

"Umm, it doesn't matter." So she says, but she quickly scrambles into the bed first. I switch off the light and, before I lose my nerve, climb into bed beside Gia.

I know I'm in trouble the second I cover myself with the comforter. She is *right here*, her breathing the opposite of soft and even. I'm rigid, hyperaware of my body and hers and how far apart we are, which is not that far at all. I feel like my heart is gonna hammer right out of my chest. I've never been like this with anyone. All the girls I hooked up with didn't come close to this.

"Are you still awake?" Gia whispers.

Like I could ever fall asleep. "Yeah."

Gia doesn't say anything at first. Then she says, "Do you think your dad likes me?"

"What? Of course he does. Did you see how much he was smiling? That man never smiles."

"I think that was for Jordan."

I laugh as Jordan licks my arm. "Probably her too. But yeah, he likes you, I'm positive." I hesitate for a second, dangerous hope blooming in my chest. "Why?"

"No reason," Gia says quickly. For a tiny, pathetic moment, I want to read too much into that. I want to let myself believe that she's asking because it's important to her that Dad likes her, because she likes me. And I want so badly for that to be true, it hurts.

Jordan nudges my elbow, bullying her way into my arms. I sigh. "Come get your dog, Gia. She's crowding me."

"You must be anxious," Gia says, a laugh at the edge of her words. "For once it's not me."

"Yeah, yeah," I grumble. Jordan licks my chin happily, and I roll my eyes, even though no one can see me. My terrible crush outed by a dog. Humiliating.

"Are you still worried about Sweet Teeth?" Gia asks.

I'm more worried about how Gia's leg brushes mine as she gets comfortable, but I'll ignore that. "Kinda. What if I'm a terrible manager and it ends up as *Kitchen Nightmare* status?"

"Then I'll come help you get it back on track," Gia says immediately. "I can do the remodel stuff. Jordan can catch all the rats in the kitchen."

"I doubt Jordan could catch a tennis ball if you threw it right at her face."

We laugh, and Jordan wriggles from my grip. She lies between us, and a wave of warm sleepiness hits me. Even though I was in a gay panic, it's all slipping away to contentment, to lazy trust and happiness that Gia is here beside me. We don't even have to do anything for me to feel at ease, relaxed. Enough.

"If you open your own bakery," Gia murmurs, her voice heavy with drowsiness, "can I help?"

"No. You can't cook." We both laugh, soft and sleepy. Jordan snores between us. "Why am I opening a bakery again?"

"Because that cupcake you made for me? Best thing I've ever had in my life. Except for maybe the omelet."

I close my eyes, smiling, and somewhere between the joy that she likes my cooking, the warmth of Jordan and Gia beside me, and daydreams of a bakery with Gia working by my side, I fall asleep.

♡ ♡ ♡

When I wake up, my mouth tastes like garlic and pizza. And someone's breathing softly next to my ear.

I freeze, confused and terrified for half a second before I remember Gia slept over. Awareness comes quickly then; Gia's limbs are tangled with mine, and she's pressed against my back, snuggling me like a stuffed animal. I try to ignore how much this makes my heart glow with happiness.

"Thought you didn't like being the big spoon," I murmur out loud. She doesn't stir, so I bask in her warmth for a second. Her breathing is even and slow, and she has one arm hooked around my waist. It's not the first time I've woken up like this. Hell, it's not even the first time I've woken up like this with Gia. But it is the first time I feel safe and wanted, like in another universe we could always cuddle like this. That this clingy sleeping could mean something, that Gia wants me to be this close to her all the time. I close my eyes for a few minutes, listening to her breathing, my own thudding heartbeat, and let myself get lost in pretending.

But my bladder doesn't care what fuzzy, romantic haze my brain is in. I lie still until it's threatening to burst, and then I carefully disentangle us until I'm free. Gia frowns in her sleep, but Jordan takes my place, and her expression smooths as she hugs Jordan close. I cover them with my comforter, battling the urge to kiss them both on the tops of their heads.

After I go to the bathroom, I head downstairs. There's no way I'm crawling back in there without waking her up. I'm hungry anyway, so I might as well make us something. I yawn while I rifle through the fridge. Bacon and eggs? Ooh, maybe cinnamon rolls—

Someone clears their throat behind me and I spin around in surprise. Dad is watching me from the table, a cup of coffee in one hand. No breakfast.

"Hey, Dad."

"Hey, Naveah." He sips his coffee, which is probably black. Gross. "You're up early."

Am I? I glance at the clock above the sink—it's barely seven.

"I had to pee, but now Jordan and Gia are hogging the bed. So I just got up."

Dad stares at me, his expression unreadable, and I fidget. What? Does he want breakfast too? I guess I don't mind. And plain black coffee can't be good for you every single day. Does he even eat breakfast on the days I don't go to school—

"Naveah," Dad says suddenly, startling me. "Are you umm . . ." Dad coughs and looks away. Is he . . . embarrassed? "Are you being safe?"

"What?"

Dad fidgets in his chair. He still won't look at me. "Are you being careful? Like using protection?"

I stare at Dad, shock robbing me of all thoughts. My ears are on fire and faintly ringing. This is not happening. This is not happening! "Dad!"

"I don't want to ask either," Dad says unhappily. "But we didn't exactly talk about the birds and bees, and I'm not sure how it works for the queer community. Am I saying that right?"

"Stop! Please stop." I pinch the bridge of my nose, sorting out this horror of a conversation in my brain. "I don't need the talk, I figured it out by myself. Also why do you think I'm fucking my friend?"

Dad winces. "Language, please. I'm sorry for assuming, but I thought Gia was your girlfriend? You are queer, right?"

"The word you're looking for is lesbian and yes, I am. But how do *you* know that?"

Dad finally meets my eyes, frowning deeply. "Because I'm

251

your father. I've known since you were three."

Oh. That's not what I expected. At all. I haven't come out to Dad; it didn't cross my mind, to be honest. I'm out to Hallie and Gia, and I thought that's all who mattered. But now, suddenly, I'm anxious that he knows. "And that's okay with you . . . ?"

"Yes, of course. You're my daughter, and nothing will change that."

"Oh." Inexplicable warmth fills me from my head to my toes.

Dad rubs the back of his neck. "I thought your mom would be here for this, but you just have me. I hope that's okay."

I smile at him. "It's okay." My happy bubble pops when I realize we haven't addressed the problem. "But listen, Gia isn't my girlfriend."

"She's not?" Dad frowns in confusion. "But you both looked so happy last night. It seemed like you really like her."

Curse me and my weirdly perceptive dad. "That's beside the point. We're just friends. So the birds-and-bees talk is irrelevant."

"Oh. Okay." Dad doesn't look like he believes me. Which is fair, because I don't believe me either.

"But . . ." I hesitate, then smile at Dad. "If we were dating, I'm glad that it would be okay with you."

Dad smiles back. "I like anyone who makes you happy, Naveah. Friend or otherwise. Gia is welcome here at any time."

We grin at each other for a second, and then I turn away, embarrassed. I'm supposed to be mad at him, and now look at me. He's making it so hard to not forgive him. A small, ever-growing part of me wants to, but not yet. I can't forget that he left me alone to fend for myself for three years. One nice conversation can't fix that. But, still . . .

"I'm making me and Gia breakfast," I tell Dad, my back still turned to him. "Do you want some before you go to work?"

I hear Dad laugh a little behind me. "Yes, thank you. I'd love that."

CHAPTER 28

i'm outside!

I stare at my text, a little nervous. Today is Thursday, the Final Exam, the day Gia and I go on a date. A fake one, but still. I'm nervous for her, but I'm also nervous for *me*. I've been in a sleepless frenzy since our hangout on Tuesday. I can't stop thinking about her hand in mine, how our fingers laced together perfectly. I researched *Briar's Blaze* (for all of twenty minutes, admittedly, because I got overwhelmed) so I could understand what the hell she's talking about sometimes. I've sketched three sunsets, taking care to use flamingo pink in each one. I'm down bad.

I'm 100 percent not over this crush, and 1,000 percent not ready to pretend I don't like her, so today might be brutal. But even if it is, I have to do this for Gia. I can't falter at the finish line. More than anything, I want her to be happy. Even if that happiness isn't with me.

On my way!

Gia texts back. She also sends me a picture.

I open it and grin. Jordan's wearing sunglasses and a pink dress. The caption says Can I come too?

254

I text back, but add two crying emojis.

That's another issue—the movies. That's where we planned to go from the beginning, but the more I thought about it, the worse that felt. Gia is a movie snob; she'd probably be miserable if I picked and indecisive to the point of panic if I let her pick. Plus, movie dates are boring, clichéd. They're for strangers meeting for the first time. Anyone I cracked my rib cage open for and spilled my guts to is not a stranger. So I decided to change the date. I know I'm being selfish again, but we already practiced for a movie; she's prepared for that. So, for a few hours, I decided to take her somewhere she'll love.

I have to wait a few minutes, but soon, Gia opens the front door. And when she does, all the air is sucked right out of my lungs. She's wearing the sundress with strawberries on it, from the first time we met. She's also wearing red Converse with white symbols from *Briar's Blaze* on them, which is so nerdy and also so Gia. She has her hair in a single long braid, a white ribbon looped between the strands of her hair. And she's wearing her glasses.

Gia smiles nervously at me. "Do I look okay?"

I blink a few times, trying to recalibrate my brain. Okay? She looks gorgeous. And incredible. And a little nervous, but I don't mind because right now she's so perfectly Gia. And I want to tell her all these things, but I don't want her to think I'm a freak who's crushing on her (which I am, of course). It has to mean something that she's wearing the same dress she wore

255

when we first met, right? And she's wearing her glasses. I told her I loved her glasses.

This can't be a coincidence. She has to have done this on purpose.

My brain is doubtful, but my heart aches for it to be so. My heart wants this to be part of a confession, Gia's shy way of telling me she likes me just as much as I like her. My brain is telling me to get over myself.

But I shove my embarrassing, complicated feelings away and focus on Gia again; she's waiting for my answer. I swallow my dry spit and attempt to fix my face. "You look beautiful."

Gia blushes a little, and I thank the big man upstairs that she can't see mine.

"You do too," Gia says. "I like your shirt."

I look down at myself. I'm wearing dark jeans and tennis shoes, which were easy, but I agonized over the shirt. I finally settled on a blue short-sleeve button-down, but nothing I have felt fancy enough for a date. It's kind of sad now that I think about it, but this is my first date too. I don't usually wine and dine the girls I hook up with.

"It's not that great," I say, sighing.

"Yeah, you're right." Gia grins at me, her eyes twinkling with mischief. "Nothing beats Head Bitch in Charge."

"Shut up," I say, laughing. I offer my hand to her. "Let's go."

Gia takes my hand, hers warm and familiar in mine, and we walk to my car together.

"So on your real date, you can make small talk in the car," I tell Gia when we're both buckled up. "But I'll give you a hint. If you mention basketball to Hallie, she'll never shut up."

Gia laughs. "Okay, let me take notes." She taps on her phone, smiling. "What's yours?"

"My what?"

"The topic that you won't shut up about."

"*Cutthroat Kitchen* is not a good cooking show. It's a farce and an exercise in gambling, and there's no amount of skill involved."

Gia whistles, grinning. "I like that show, though."

"Get outta my car."

Gia laughs again, and I smile at the road ahead. Somehow, I think I'm about to have a really good time.

I glance at Gia out of the corner of my eye. She's not texting or playing a game like I'd be; she's staring out of the passenger-side window, phone face down in her lap. She looks happy, a simple, benign happiness I don't get to see often. She doesn't seem nervous at all. On one hand, I'm so proud I could burst. All the practice, all the drives and hangouts and spending time together has paid off. It's our big day, and the only thing I see on her face is contentment. On the other hand, that makes me extra worried about where I'm actually taking her. I hope I'm making the right decision and she's not disappointed.

Gia blinks when I drive by the turnoff to the movie theater. "Nav, you missed it."

"I know." I grip the steering wheel nervously. My palms are slick against the cracked leather.

"Oh no." Gia frowns at me. "Am I being kidnapped?"

And just like that, my nerves are gone. I laugh, which turns into a gross snort. "It's payback for last time."

"*You* called *me* to pick you up!" Gia sounds indignant, which makes me laugh harder. "But seriously, we're not going to the movies?"

"No, I figured we can try something else."

Gia fidgets with her ring, but there's no blotchy blush, no heavy breathing of terror. "Okay. I trust you."

I'm so overcome with emotion that *my* breath gets short. She's struggled with her anxiety her whole life, and surprises aren't high on her list. But because she trusts me, something that would have been a meltdown four weeks ago is just a small fidget ring experience. Gia can't do this to me. She can't make me fall in love with her two days before she starts dating my best friend. But she is, and it's happening, and there's nothing I can do about it.

"You look upset," Gia says. Her brow furrows, and now she's anxious. "It's not a haunted corn maze, is it? I hate those."

"Why would I be taking you to a corn maze in June?" I shake my head, laughing at the image. "It's insulting you'd think I'd take you to exercise at all. Come on, Gia, you know me better than that."

"I don't think you exercise in corn mazes." Gia looks thoughtful now. "Maybe the running in terror counts as cardio? But I don't run, I freeze. The one time I went, I passed out. I woke up in the hospital."

"What?!" Her matter-of-fact delivery makes me laugh harder. I mentally make a note to never take Gia to anything remotely haunted in October. But then, a second later, I realize I'm not taking Gia anywhere after this. I swallow the bitter lump in my throat before I respond. "Stop catastrophizing. No corn maze, no passing out."

I expect Gia to laugh, but she doesn't. I sneak a glance out of the corner of my eye, and Gia's frowning at her lap.

"What's on your mind?"

"Can I ask you a deep question?"

"Yeah, always."

"Do you think I need therapy?"

I tap my fingertip on the wheel, thinking. That's a loaded question if I've ever heard one. My instinct is to lie to soothe her anxiety. But I've never lied to Gia (except about my crush on her, which hardly counts), and now doesn't seem like the time to start.

"Yeah. I think it'd be good for you."

Gia breathes out, a haggard sigh. "What happened to sparing my feelings?"

"When have you ever spared mine?" I drop my joking tone and glance at her, so she knows I'm serious. "Listen, therapy isn't a bad thing. I know it kind of sucks, but it can't feel good to constantly be anxious. Throwing up after romance practice isn't a good thing, Gia."

Gia leans against the passenger door, refusing to meet my eyes. Sulking. "I know it's not good, okay? But I've been trying really hard."

"And it's okay to ask for help when you need it." We drive in silence for a minute. I keep glancing at her, but I wait for her to speak. It's hard to focus on the road, though.

"I guess I'm still thinking about Abuela," Gia finally says. "How I shouldn't give her any more ammunition against me."

"Well, that evil lady isn't here, and it sounds like your mom would rather die than let her get to you."

Gia makes a noncommittal grunt. She still stares out of her window.

"Dad's going to therapy," I add.

Gia looks at me out of the corner of her eye. "Do you think it's helping?"

I replay the last four weeks in my head. How hard he's working to change. How I'm stubbornly resisting but weakening every day because he really is better than before. "Yeah," I tell Gia, my voice soft. "It is."

Gia sighs but sits up straight. "Okay. I think I'll do it."

"Yeah?"

"Yeah." So she says, but her hands tremble in her lap.

"I'll go with you," I offer.

Gia raises her eyebrows. "You want to go to therapy too?"

"I mean, I can sit in the lobby or something."

Gia laughs, a relieved, happy one without a trace of fear. "Thanks, Nav. I'll see you there."

We drive for five more minutes in rosy silence, and I imagine us doing a bunch of things together, fun things like dates and hard things like therapy, and I've never wanted anything more. But then I put that out of my mind because I'm not supposed to be daydreaming about our nonexistent future together. I have to focus on now, because we're here.

I pull into a parking spot near the front and Gia perks up. "Oh, a museum?"

"Yep." I'm grinning already. The local Museum of Natural Science is practically empty because it's a random Thursday in June, so the crowd won't be overwhelming. And it's finally a non-exercise activity.

"I love museums," Gia chatters. She unbuckles her seat belt, and I follow her lead. "Have you ever been to the one in Washington, DC? With the T. rex?"

"Calm down, rich girl," I tease. I have actually been to that museum, back in elementary school. But I fell asleep in the gift shop, and Dad nearly had a heart attack when he couldn't find me. I tell Gia this story as we walk in and I pay for both our tickets. She shakes her head, smiling.

"You've always been a handful, huh?"

"I'm insulted by your insinuation." I stop walking when we're out of the reception area, staring intently at the free map. It's like I thought—we have to go through the rainforest and the desert before we get to where I want us to go. "All right, Gia, I'm gonna ask you a question I already know the answer to. How do you feel about taxidermy?"

Gia makes one of the ugliest faces I've ever seen, and I snort out a laugh.

"That's what I thought. I have a surprise, but you have to close your eyes until we get there."

Gia looks worried but nods. "Okay."

I hold out my hand, and she takes it. Her palm is warm in mine, and I try not to melt. "Eyes closed, ma'am."

Gia closes her eyes, and I lead her through the exhibits full of many, many dead animals. I've been here before, but looking at it again, there is *so* much more former roadkill in here than I remember. I get the educational value, but even I shudder as I look into the glassy eyes of a stuffed macaw. Gia would definitely die.

"Are we there?" Gia asks. She's holding my hand tight, and it's starting to get slightly damp against my skin.

"Impatient!" I round the corner out of the rainforest section, and we've arrived. The temperature instantly drops because there are no more harsh exhibition lights and the walls are painted dark blue. I lead Gia to the focal point of the room and squeeze her hand. "We're here."

I watch Gia as she opens her eyes. She blinks, then for half a second, she's in pure shock. I smile as her face fills with euphoria and delight, and then she turns all that joy to me. "Nav, you didn't."

I shrug, still smiling. "I'm sorry it's not a real aquarium. No sharks here." I glance at the giant tank of tropical fish in front of us. It stretches floor to ceiling, and so far behind the walls that we can't see the edges. In the dappled light, fish of all sizes dart through gently waving underwater plants. The only fish I recognize are Nemo and Dory, but there have to be dozens of varieties. One ugly flat fish skims slowly across the sand at the bottom. "But maybe not so bad?"

I glance at Gia again, and she looks so happy she might

combust. "I love fish. And this. And—" Gia cuts herself off, probably overcome with glee over watching fish swim around in circles.

I shake my head, still grinning. "I'm glad you like it, Gia."

Gia takes a shaky breath. We're still holding hands, and she squeezes mine tight. She looks me right in the eyes. "I can't believe you remembered. I only mentioned aquariums one time."

"Yeah, well . . ." I can't think of a smooth way to say *I remember because I might be in love with you.* "I'm putting my PhD in romance to good use."

Gia rolls her eyes, but she's still smiling like this is the best day of her life. She tugs me from tank to tank, her face lit by the watery glow. Like I hoped, there are only a couple of other people in here, so we practically have the entire Deep Ocean exhibit to ourselves. There are information placards attached to every tank, but Gia ignores them and starts telling me off-script facts about the fish. And I listen, really listen, even though I don't care if fish have been on earth for 450 million years or that lionfish are extremely poisonous but apparently delicious if prepared correctly (what maniac figured that out?). But I watch her nerd out about it, watch her eyes shine with joy and excitement, and I realize Gia was right. The aquarium is a really, really good date idea, because Gia is happiest in places where she can be unapologetically herself. And all I ever want to do is make her happy for the rest of her life.

The last tank, tall and round and lit from below, is full of jellyfish. They float in serene silence, barely moving, tentacles trailing gently beneath their mushroom heads. I watch them pulse, a little fascinated. Regular fish are boring, but these are cool. I sketch out a picture of them in my mind—no, a painting. I could do a killer watercolor of this.

"Do you like jellyfish?" Gia asks me.

"I don't like any fish I can't eat."

Gia shakes her head, grinning. "Then why are we here? It's supposed to be fun for you too."

I must be crazy, or it may be the low, intimate lighting, or the joy radiating from Gia, because I turn to her and say, "I wanted you to be happy, because you deserve it."

We stare at each other for several frantic heartbeats (if we're measuring by my own). Gia isn't smiling; she's looking right at me, her dark eyes unreadable. But then she laces our hands together and says, very softly, "I am happy."

I can barely concentrate. I battle the urge to rub her knuckle with my thumb, or pull her close and kiss her. Instead, I clear my throat and turn back to the moon jellies.

"That's good." Why is my voice so high pitched? I hate myself. "I'm glad. Should we go to dinner now?" Why am I cutting this short?! I *really* hate myself.

"Okay," Gia says, but doesn't let go of my hand. "Can we come back again?"

I nod, my heart about to jump out of my chest. I need to get into the summer heat and away from this low, romantic lighting. But I'm not strong enough to not make a promise I definitely shouldn't keep. "We can come back as many times as you want."

CHAPTER 29

I lead Gia back through the taxidermy graveyard sections, and soon, we're back in my car. Gia is practically radiating happiness as she buckles her seat belt.

"This is the best date I've ever been on."

"The best fake date," I remind her, though my voice cracks because my body hates me. If I'm being honest, this is the best date I've ever had too. Even if it's fake, and technically my first. I crank up the car and pull out of the museum to give myself time to recover. "Anyway, it's about to get better—we're going to dinner now. And you're ordering!"

Gia snaps right out of her happy haze. Her rigid posture and nervous fidgeting return in an instant. "Where are we going?"

I open my mouth to tease her, but she keeps talking.

"Don't say it's a surprise. I liked the aquarium surprise, but I absolutely need to know where we're going to eat if I need to order."

I'm reminded of when she got ice cream for us. I told her what I wanted, so she wasn't overwhelmed with options. And didn't she tell me once before she needs to see the menu ahead of time? I'm serious now too. "We're going to Abernathy's. It's a steak house, but they serve good seafood too."

Gia nods gravely and pulls out her phone. She stares at it

intently, like she's cramming for a final and her life depends on it. I chuckle to myself, but my amusement quickly turns to worry. I didn't even hesitate to accommodate Gia. I want her to order by herself, but not at the expense of making her anxious. It's not a big deal to change plans when Gia needs me to. But will Hallie know that? On Saturday, when they go to the movies, will she know that Gia needs to agonize over the options? Will she know that Gia sometimes needs to do her pep talk circle before doing something new? Will she know that Gia hates spaghetti with a burning passion?

Can Hallie love Gia the way I do?

This is dangerous thinking. I should absolutely not be thinking this. But Saturday plays in my head, my own horror version where Hallie does something on accident that hurts Gia, and I want to die. A little bit of panic tries to crawl up my throat, but I swallow it back down. I'm nervous, but Gia will be fine. Honestly, I think she's ready for the date. Even if Hallie doesn't do everything perfect, Gia will be fine. She's good about communicating her needs with me, and Hallie isn't an asshole, so I think it'll work out. But a terrible part of me isn't really worried if Gia's ready. It's worried if I'm ready to let her go.

I take a breath to steady myself. *Hold it together, Nav.* I just have to get through one fake dinner, and then it'll be too late to worry about it. Because, come the end of the night, Gia will be gone whether I like it or not. (Un)surprisingly, the thought doesn't comfort me; I'm an anxious ball of nerves when I pull into Abernathy's far too soon.

We're both tense, so I run around the car and open Gia's door for her. I bow mockingly and a smile replaces Gia's grim intensity.

"They say chivalry is dead, but clearly not," she says, eyes crinkled in amusement, and takes my hand. We walk to the restaurant together, and Gia opens the door for me, dipping in a clumsy curtsey. I laugh, already in a better mood. I put all those worrying thoughts in their own compartmentalization box and mentally duct tape it shut. One fake-date dinner, and that's it. That's my focus.

We walk in together, and I'm blasted by a rush of cool air. Abernathy's is a regular restaurant that pretends to be upscale, kind of like Red Lobster. Everyone goes here for fancy things like before-prom dinner or graduation, but it's thankfully almost empty at four thirty on a Thursday afternoon. We're quickly ushered into a booth by the door and left to wait.

I look at Gia, who's across from me. She's nervous; I can't see her legs, but I feel her bouncing up and down at a rapid pace. This is the hard part. I can't sit next to her or hold her hand for moral support.

"You okay?" I ask.

Gia meets my eyes, hers distressed. "Can you order for me?"

"No."

Gia sighs heavily. "You're the worst teacher."

"It's called tough love." My heart skips a beat when I say the word *love*, but I ignore it. "You studied the menu. You're fine."

Gia shoots a poisonous glare at me, and I respond with a

smile that shows all my teeth. Gia groans but slowly relaxes. "The food looks pretty good, at least."

"Please, Gia, you wound me. As if I'd pick a shitty restaurant! I have standards."

Gia snorts, rolling her eyes. She starts to say something, but I spy someone approaching our table.

"Look, here he comes! You've got this."

The waiter arrives and places two menus haphazardly on our table. He looks bored and uninterested, which is perfect for Gia. "What can I get you both to drink?"

I stare intently at Gia. If I go first, she might take the easy way out and say "same" to whatever I get. Gia begs me with her eyes, but I don't say anything. *You can do this. You can do this, Gia.*

The silence stretches long enough to become awkward. Gia's getting panicked, twisting her ring more and more. But miraculously, after a full ten seconds, Gia squeaks out, "Sweet tea."

I grin and give her two thumbs-up. She looks like she wants to both hug me and murder me, which is an excellent sign. I smile at the waiter. "Same for me, please. Thank you."

When he leaves, Gia slumps on the table. "I hate this. I hate this so much."

"You did good! I'm proud."

Gia looks up at me, her cheek squished against the linen tablecloth. "Really?"

"Really. Now sit up, you gotta order your meal."

Gia grumbles, but she cheers up when we open our menus.

"I'm so glad you didn't pick Italian. I feel like they always pick Italian in movies."

"You told me a million times that you hate spaghetti," I say, scanning the menu. Steak? No way. Salad? Also no way. Old faithful it is—chicken tenders and fries.

"You remember?"

I look up to Gia watching me with a sweet kind of wonder. Like I'd forget. "Of course. I'm not gonna take you to a place you hate." I pause, reflecting on that. "When Hallie asks you where to go, don't say 'anywhere.' She loves Italian food, so you'll be suffering at Olive Garden if you're not careful."

"I hate that place so much," Gia mutters. She looks at me, her eyebrows pinched together with worry. "Nav, do you think—"

We're interrupted by the waiter again. Gia fumbles through her order—grilled shrimp and a baked potato—but she does exponentially better than before. I'm beaming at her so much the waiter has to remind me to order.

"Chicken tenders?" Gia asks after the waiter leaves. "Really? You can get that at McDonald's."

"Here we go again, Food Snob Gia."

"I'm not being a snob! You can get chicken anywhere!"

"Okay, Miss Fancy Shrimp, if I can get it anywhere, I can get it here!"

We argue about nothing for a few minutes, and I'm grinning ear to ear. I don't know how it happens, but when I'm with Gia, hours turn into minutes. I never get tired of hearing her passionate arguments, even if they're about chicken tenders. I never get tired of being with her.

Gia sighs, finally defeated. "Fine, fine, eat whatever." She smiles at me, a soft, happy one. "Nav, can I tell you something?"

"Yeah, of course."

"I'm having a really good time."

I smile back at her, my cheeks warming in embarrassing pleasure. The dangerous thoughts from earlier strain to get out of their box, but I add another layer of mental duct tape to it. "So am I." It feels like gargling needles, but I add, "You'll have even more fun on your real one with Hallie. I'm just the stand-in."

Gia looks a bit worried. Uh oh. "About that . . ."

"No, no, we're not gonna be negative. It'll be great." A nasty voice whispers in my head that I kinda hope it isn't great. Or at least not as good as this one. I beat that voice into submission. I've really got to invest in better boxes. "Listen, even if it's not great, I'm still proud. You've done so well, Gia, seriously. I don't want you to feel any pressure; if the date isn't what you want it to be, that's fine. I'm not that worried about going to camp."

Whoa. Did I just say that? Before I have a chance to interrogate that thought, Gia waves her hand dismissively.

"Oh, don't worry about that. You're going to camp."

I blink at her, still in shock from what I said. "What?"

"Even if I bomb the date on Saturday, you did so much for me. And I know you really want to go." Pain crosses Gia's face, but it's gone so quick—maybe I imagined it? "So I already talked to Mami. I told her last night that I wasn't going and I wanted you to have my spot."

I stare at her, dumbstruck. "Gia, that wasn't the deal—"

"I know." Gia gives me a small smile. "I stopped caring about the deal a while ago. I know you want to go to camp, and you should. I will miss you, though." Gia seems so sincere that I want to cry. She doesn't even know how Saturday will go, but she did this for me anyway. Because it's what I told her I wanted. But the thought of leaving Gia for six weeks kinda makes me feel sick. Do I . . . do I even want to go to camp anymore? I haven't thought about it in days, because my head has been full of cotton candy thoughts about sunsets and aquariums and picking the perfect restaurant. Hallie leaves on Monday, *this* Monday, and I haven't even thought about what that means for me. I've been so consumed with all things Gia that I haven't faced the reality that going with Hallie means leaving Gia behind.

That compartmentalization box is wide open.

"Gia," I start. The truth is on the tip of my tongue and my heart is screaming for me to say it, and for once my brain half agrees. "I really appreciate this, but—"

"Nav?"

I blink and search for who's calling my name. Then I see Hallie, waiting by the hostess podium, waving enthusiastically at me.

And for the first time in my whole life, I am not happy to see her.

271

CHAPTER 30

"Don't panic," I hiss at Gia. She frowns and starts to turn around, but Hallie is at our table in seconds. No time to panic, at least.

"You snake! Coming to Abernathy's without me," Hallie says, laughing. She freezes when she rounds the corner and sees Gia. "Oh! Sorry, am I interrupting?"

Shit. This looks like we're on a date. Gia looks at me, eyes round with alarm. But she's not twisting her ring or trembling, so maybe she's okay? Or maybe she's in shock.

"No!" I say, my voice a little too loud. "No, not at all, just eating dinner."

"Yeah?" Hallie has a slight smirk on her face. Her sharp eyes look me up and down. "You look really nice, by the way."

She's making fun of me now! God, I want to kill her. Why did she have to show up here? Why *now*?

"What're you doing here?" I ask to distract her. Poor Gia looks like she's gonna pass out.

"Getting soup for Mom. She caught a cold, and you know how she gets." Hallie smiles, but I don't like how she's looking at me. She looks like a cat that caught the canary. "Let me leave you both alone—"

"You can wait with us," I blurt out.

Gia's eyes widen further, but I have no choice. I'm desperate here. I can't let Hallie walk away thinking Gia and I are dating. As much as I'd like that to be true, I don't want to ruin this for Gia. She deserves a fair chance.

"You sure?" Hallie's eyebrows raise in surprise.

"I'm sure." I scoot over so she can sit next to me.

"All right," Hallie says, and sits down. She smiles at Gia tentatively. "Hey, Gia. How are you?"

Gia looks at me, and for a second I'm scared she's dissociated right out of Abernathy's and she's in her room, playing *Briar's Blaze*. But I nudge her leg with my foot and she seems to come alive. After a painful few seconds, she says, "I'm good. How—how are you?"

Hallie looks at me, happy surprise on her face. I know I'm beaming. She's doing it. She's doing it! Four weeks of hard work culminate in a near perfect hello. It can't be normal to be on the edge of tears from pride.

"I'm good," Hallie says. "What're you two doing today? Hanging out?"

Gia nods robotically, so I rescue her.

"Yep, just hanging out."

"We went to the museum," Gia adds. She looks right at me, a warm blush on her cheeks. "I love aquariums, so it was a great surprise."

"*Nav* went to a museum? Willingly?" Hallie's eyebrows are threatening to join her hairline. She turns to me, slowly, and for some reason I feel like I'm in one of her favorite horror movies.

273

"Don't you usually fall asleep in gift shops?"

"That was one time," I groan.

Gia laughs, covering her mouth to dampen the sound. "She told me about that. She likes starting manhunts for her."

"Right?" Hallie laughs too. "An asshole from age eight."

"Younger than that, for sure," I say breezily.

Hallie leans forward, her head resting in her palm. She has her sharp eyes on Gia, and I recognize the posture—she's about to go on the attack. Shit. "So, Gia, I feel like I barely know you! Nav's been hiding you away. What do you guys do when you hang out?"

Oh, I'm gonna kill her. I'm absolutely going to murder my best friend. I stare at Gia intently, sending her a mental message to absolutely under no circumstances mention romance practice.

Gia seems to get the hint. Without a shred of nerves, she says, "Eat food, go to the park, sit by the pool."

"Oh, you have a pool?" Hallie seems interested. Since when does she like swimming? Ah, wait—she probably wants to test if she might.

"Yep! You should come over sometime and we can swim together."

Both Hallie and I are speechless. *Whoa.* Did Gia just invite her crush to her house in one smooth line? Is this a student-surpasses-the-teacher moment?

But Gia doesn't seem to realize what she said. She looks earnest and not at all embarrassed.

Hallie glances at me, but says, "Yeah . . . ! That'd be cool."

Gia aims her million-watt smile at me. "See, now you have to learn how to swim."

"Oh, I see how it is," I complain, but I kind of don't. I mean, I almost can't believe how well this is going. Gia is talking like normal, like she talks with me. And we're hanging out with Hallie and it's not awkward or painful or full of chattering teeth. My brain entertains this for a moment; us being a trio instead of two separate entities. For a magical moment, I think maybe I can have everything I want.

Gia and Hallie tease me for a few minutes about my hatred of the water, but I stand firm. Then, during a lull in our conversation, Gia nods at Hallie's hand and says, "I like your nail polish. That's a great color."

"Thank you!" Hallie sits up straighter in her seat and I swear I'm seeing things, but a slight blush tinges the top of Hallie's ear. "I like your dress. The strawberries are so cute."

Gia's face grows deep red, and she smiles at Hallie, and all my fuzzy feelings from before are gone.

"What's the matter?" Hallie nudges me with her knee, grinning. "You sad because we didn't compliment you?"

"Go to hell," I growl. I make sure my tone is joking but an unpleasant part of me kinda means it.

Gia laughs, but Hallie raises her eyebrows again, a sly grin on her face. She knows I'm mad, but she probably thinks it's because she and Gia are teasing me. But it's worse than that. I think I'm jealous. I'm actually jealous that my two best friends are happy and will continue to be happy together without me. I feel like a pathetic little worm. What kind of friend does this? Who thinks like this? Gia was waffling about therapy earlier, but *I'm* the one who needs it.

"Don't worry," Gia says, snapping me out of my broody thoughts. "I think you look great all the time."

My brain goes into blissful mode at her words, and Hallie laughs. "Look how happy she is. Just ask me for a compliment next time, dear."

"I'm a simple gal," I manage to croak out to save myself. I can hide my feelings from Gia, but Hallie is a dangerous wildcard. She'll figure me out if I'm not careful. "Don't you have to get some soup or something?"

Hallie holds her hands up in surrender. "I know when I'm not wanted."

"That's not true," Gia says, an anxious edge to her tone. I hate that I think it's sweet she cares about Hallie's feelings, and I also want to throw up.

"It's okay, Gia," Hallie says, that funny grin still on her face. "I have to get back anyway. See you tomorrow, Nav?"

I nod. I agreed to help her pack for camp. With a jolt, I realize I'll have to pack too. "See ya, babe."

Hallie waves and we wave back, and I watch her as she picks up her order and leaves. After she's safely gone, I slump against the booth with exhaustion. I feel like I attempted yoga again.

"Gia, you did it. You beautiful creature, you actually pulled it off."

Gia beams at me. "Only because you were here too."

"No, you really did great." I suck in a breath. I need to get myself together. Luckily I don't have to, because the waiter finally brings our food.

Gia and I get lost in Abernathy's above-average food and somehow we end up on the topic of whether zoos are ethical. Our silly argument lasts the rest of dinner and spills into the car after Gia pays for us both. (I insisted, but she shot me such a glare that I got intimidated and she'd paid the waiter before I knew it.)

I point my old rust bucket in the direction of Gia's mansion, a complicated feeling in my chest. I feel gross from the jealousy, proud of Gia's progress, and my dumb lizard brain is practically dancing from Gia's compliments. *You look good all the time.* That's going straight into the ego vault. But, weirdly, there's a layer of calm covering everything. Because even when my heart and brain are at war, when my emotions are out of control, just being in Gia's presence is soothing. And honestly, that's the worst isn't it? Gia means so much to me. I have to hold on to her, and that may require me letting her go.

"Everything okay?" Gia asks as I pull into her driveway.

"Yeah." I hesitate, then smile at her. "I had a really great time today."

Gia returns my smile. "Me too. I was so nervous about the date, but it was so much fun." Gingerly, she puts her hand over mine, and my heart sings with happiness and panic. I shouldn't be doing this. I shouldn't be so happy she touched me. I should pull away.

But I don't.

"I have something for you," Gia says. She looks less nervous now and more excited. "But I have to go get it."

"Okay." I'm pathetically disappointed when she moves her hand to get out of the car. I get out too, and we walk to the door together.

"It's a surprise," she says sternly. "Wait here."

I make a big show of huffing and rolling my eyes, but I'm grinning. Anyone with eyes could tell how much I like her. It's sickening. Gia darts inside, and I take the time alone to give myself a mental pep talk. Gia likes Hallie. She doesn't like me. Gia likes *Hallie*. Hallie is her dream girl. She likes Hallie's nail polish. She invited Hallie to swim with her. She said I look good all the time—okay, not helpful, brain.

Gia comes back, holding a sparkly bag decorated with "Happy Birthday."

I blink at it, some of my frantic thoughts subsiding. "It's not my birthday."

"I know, I couldn't wait until August."

I laugh. "Okay, what is it?"

"Open it!"

I take the bag from Gia, which is weirdly heavy. I take out the tissue paper and glimpse the top of a white stuffed animal. I'm not really into stuffed animals, but I'll be nice—

My thoughts screech to a halt when I pull it out of the bag. It's a Snuggable, but not one I've ever seen before. It's a white poodle with a lavender collar, and the collar has "Cuddles" written on it.

"I can't bring your dog back," Gia says. "But maybe it'll help to have something to remember her by? And they really do help you sleep. I have three."

I hug Cuddles-the-plush to my chest, overwhelmed with emotion. She didn't have to do this. She didn't have to listen to me whine about Mom, and order this custom dog for me. She didn't have to meet Dad because I asked, or stay at my tiny house rather than her mansion. She didn't have to do anything beyond our agreement, but she did.

Gia might not like me. But I can't ignore that I really, really like Gia.

I put Cuddles gently back in the bag. All logic has gone out the window—I'm running on pure emotion, pure euphoria, pure something that feels dangerously like love. "Thank you, Gia."

"You're welcome." She fidgets shyly. "Do you like it?"

"I love it." I take a breath, but it feels like I can't get any air. I need to get out of here before I do something stupid. "I guess I should go home."

"Oh." Gia looks disappointed, which feels like someone stabbing me right in the chest.

"This is part of the practice," I offer. "Hallie won't sleep with you on the first date."

Gia laughs, that adorable blotchy blush in full force. "So what happens next? After she drops me off here?"

My heart is pounding in my ears. It's all I can hear, though I know my breathing is too fast, bordering on ragged. "Well, she'll probably stand here, just like this."

Gia's laugh fades, and she's looking right into my eyes. "Yeah?"

"Yeah." I step closer, closing the distance between us. "And she'll say good night, but she won't want to go."

My chest is tight with longing, with the urge to do something I really shouldn't. My brain is screaming for me to step away, but I can't really hear it over the sound of my thudding heart.

I reach up and tuck a loose strand of Gia's hair behind her ear. "And she'll move your hair back, because she'll want to see how beautiful you are."

Gia gasps, a quick sound that sets me on fire. And I take her face in my hands, gentle, gentler than I've ever been. In my head, I'm narrating this scene, with Hallie standing in my place in two days, but that falls away. There's just me and Gia, here and now, warm summer heat and longing and the throb of my heart.

And I pull her to me, close my eyes, and press my lips to hers.

CHAPTER 31

For a second, I'm in blissful heaven, Gia's body flush against me, her lips pressed to mine, and everything is good and right in the world. Her hands cup my face, and she pulls me in closer, deeper, and I'm sure I'll never be this happy again.

A second after that, I realize what I'm doing, and that happy world comes crashing down.

I jerk away from Gia, gasping. What am I doing?! Gia's looking at me with wide eyes and I'm so panicked and ashamed and confused, I can't think.

"I'm sorry," I tell Gia, my chest tight.

"Nav—"

"I'm so sorry, Gia, I shouldn't have done that." I'm babbling, scrambling away from her. "Oh my God, your date is in *two days*, what have I done—"

"Nav, it's okay," Gia says. And her eyes are so pretty and reassuring, and for a second, I want it to be okay. But it's not okay, because I've done the one thing I didn't want to do, which was ruin our friendship.

"I have to go." I think I'm crying, or on the edge of passing out, because everything is blurry. I grab the bag at my feet and back away, stumbling off her porch. "I'm so sorry, Gia, I—"

"Nav, listen to me!" Gia calls, but I'm already scrambling into my car and driving away as fast as I can.

I can't think. I just drive, panic crawling up my throat like a demon out of hell. I want to vomit. I want to scream. Some sick part of me is delirious, wanting to drive back and kiss Gia again. It was everything I wanted. Her lips were so soft and sweet and she *kissed me back*—

No, no I can't think like this. But I am, our kiss rolling around in my head like a loose bowling ball. I've ruined everything. I loved ruining everything and I wish I could do it again. I've betrayed my two best friends in the world. I want to cry. I want to laugh. I want to puke. I might do that last one.

I don't even realize I'm at Hallie's until I'm ringing her doorbell. I'm breathing hard, like I've just run a marathon. Fuck, why is it so hard to breathe?!

Hallie opens the door, and her expression changes from curious to alarmed in seconds. "Nav? Nav, what's wrong?"

"I'm so sorry, Hallie." I still can't fucking breathe. "I ruined everything, I can't believe I—"

"Nav." Hallie's voice is close and urgent. She pulls me into a hug, one hand pressed firmly behind my head. "Slow down, breathe, okay? Just breathe."

I cling to Hallie, and slowly, the panic eases from unbearable to uncomfortable. The weight of what I've done finally settles in, and it threatens to crush me. I hold Hallie tighter, a slight whimper escaping my raw throat.

"It's okay, it's okay." Hallie holds me tight. "Are you hurt? Do I need to drive you to the hospital?"

"No," I mumble, my voice muffled by her shirt. It's wet,

which means I'm crying. I'd be humiliated, but I'm too busy being devastated. "I'm okay."

"You're obviously not." Hallie pulls away and searches my face anxiously. "What happened? You look like shit, Nav. Who hurt you?"

"Me. This is my fault." Fresh tears fill my eyes and I wipe them with shaky hands. I have to tell her. I have to come clean. "Hallie, I'm so sorry, but I kissed Gia."

I wince, expecting fury, but she blinks at me in confusion. "Umm, okay?"

"What?" I don't understand what's happening here. "How are you not upset? You're going on a date with her on Saturday!"

Hallie stares at me. "Wait, are you serious?"

"Are *you* serious? We had this planned for weeks."

"Wow. Okay." Hallie runs a hand through her hair, like she's exasperated. "Honestly, Nav, I thought you were dating Gia but were too embarrassed to tell me."

I stare at Hallie, open-mouthed. I can't even say anything. In some sick, twisted way, this is hilarious. Gia and I've been training nonstop for this date, and the whole time Hallie thought I was dating her. Even she could see my dumb love-sickness written all over my face, because of course she could. Someone starts laughing, and it takes a second to realize it's me.

Hallie hurries to continue, eyeing me uneasily. "I mean, aren't you dating? You're always at her house. When we fought at the party, you called her to pick you up. And didn't I walk in on a date earlier tonight?"

283

I can't speak. Hallie thinks Gia and I are together. It's so absurd and funny and heartbreaking I want to burst into tears again.

"It's okay if you like her," Hallie assures me. "We can cancel Saturday. And we should! Gia seems nice, but you and her are so good together. I felt bad about crashing your date today. You looked so happy."

"Hallie." My voice is hoarse and unsteady. "You have to go on a date with Gia. On Saturday. You have to."

"I don't understand. You kissed her, so you obviously like her—"

"Kissing her wasn't part of the plan!" All the pent-up emotion is pouring out of me at once. "Gia and I made a deal. If she gave up her spot at Carnegie Camp, I'd help her get over her anxiety of going on a date with you. Then you and me could go to camp together."

Hallie looks at me for a second, shock on her face. And then it turns into anger.

"Nav, what the fuck?"

"What?" I'm immediately defensive, on top of everything else. "I was trying to save our summer."

"Without asking me? Do you even care if I like Gia?"

"You said she was cute!"

"She is, I guess, but you know I wasn't looking for a hookup! You just wanted us to go on one date and you'd get everything you wanted?"

"Everything *we* wanted. We! We applied to go together!"

284

"Did you not listen at all when I said I wanted to try new things?"

"Yeah, *without me*. I heard that one loud and clear." I can't keep the bitterness from my voice.

Hallie looks like she wants to scream. She scrubs her face with her hands. "Nav, I love you, but you are so fucking selfish sometimes—"

"I know!" I'm shouting, and I don't want to be, but this hurts. "I know, okay? I know I made this all about me. I didn't ask you if you wanted me to tag along, and I was using Gia to get what I wanted. But it's not like that now. I started helping Gia, but I started caring about her too, and I got in deep. She's so good at talking with you now—she killed it at Abernathy's! And I'm so upset I couldn't stop being selfish for two seconds and I kissed her, because all I've done is fuck everything up. She deserves this, okay? She deserves to be happy, and that's not with me, that's with y-you."

Saying the truth out loud crushes me. I was in a blissful fog all day, but that's the bottom line, isn't it? I care about Gia more than I care if I'm happy. I care about Hallie more than I care about my own loneliness. But somehow I gaslit myself for an entire month that I could actually be happy in this scenario too. I fell in love, and look where it got me—pain and disappointment and grief, just like I expected. Just like always.

Hallie watches me for a moment, a complicated expression on her face. "Okay. Tell me this. Do you want to date Gia?"

I press my lips together so I don't blurt out a yes.

When I don't answer, Hallie continues. "Do you want me to date Gia?"

My throat burns and tears fill my eyes. But I force out a horrible, painful "That's the plan. That's how it was supposed to go."

Hallie puts both hands on my shoulders. Her sharp eyes are unreadable. "Nav, listen to me. I want you to go home and think about everything you just said. Everything. All of it. And I don't want to hear another word from your mouth until you figure your shit out."

I try to protest, but Hallie not-so-gently ushers me to my car. "Hallie, I—"

"Not a word," Hallie snaps. "I mean it. Go home, Nav."

I can't say anything, so I watch Hallie go to her porch, shoot me one last look, and close the door behind her. I watch her abandon me, and lose a second precious friendship in one night.

CHAPTER 32

I'm sick.

That's the only thing I can call it. I can't eat. I can't sleep. I stayed up all Thursday night, sobbing into my pillow. And then I tossed and turned in bed, feverish, heartsick, until I finally grabbed my early birthday gift and passed out around noon. Gia's right—those Snuggables really work. Cuddles-the-plush put me right to bed.

But the sleep didn't help. Because whenever I wake up, I think of everything I've ruined, everything I've lost. How much I wanted to hang on to them, and how they both slipped through my fingers.

Gia calls and texts me all the time, but I can't face her. I won't even look at my phone. I can't. I can't shower or snack or watch TV. I've stared at the wall for a whole day and a half.

There's a light knock at my door. "Naveah?"

Dad. I close my eyes, hugging the plush to my chest. It smells like lavender, but it smells like Gia's house too. I'm in hell.

Dad knocks again. "Naveah, it's dinnertime."

"I'm not hungry," I call, my voice weak. I haven't eaten since Abernathy's.

Dad doesn't say anything, but the next thing I know, my door is swinging open. I keep my eyes stubbornly on the wall.

Dad touches my forehead, his hand so gentle it shocks me.

"Are you feeling okay? You're a little warm."

"I'm fine." I blink against tears dangerously close to fleeing my eyes.

"No, you're not. Did something happen?"

I don't want to talk to Dad. I don't trust him. He left me. But . . . he came back. And right now, he's the only one who's still here.

"Maybe I'm not fine," I whisper, half hoping he doesn't hear me.

Dad is quiet for a second, then says, "I'll be right back."

I hear Dad leave, his heavy footsteps receding. He doesn't come back right away, so I close my eyes and wallow in despair. I miss Gia. I miss Hallie. I don't know if either will ever want to see me again.

Dad returns and nudges my back with something cold. "Come on, sit up. I brought you something."

Reluctantly, I turn over. I have to blink a few times to focus, but soon I can see Dad . . . and that he's holding ice cream in a mug. Ice cream that looks a lot like a Coke float. Vivid memories of me and Dad hanging out when I was a kid surface in my mind. Whenever I got into a fight with the neighborhood kids, or fell off my bike, Dad would make these Coke floats for me. Viciously sweet, horrible for me, but it always made me feel better. I haven't had one in years.

I sit up and take the mug, the handle cool against my skin. A wave of emotion threatens to drown me and I tear up again. I've cried more in the past two days than I have in years. In three years, in fact. "Thanks, Dad."

"You're welcome." He sits beside me on the bed. He gives me a spoon and digs into his own ice cream. "Start at the beginning."

Normally I'd be annoyed by his bossiness. But today I sniffle and say, "I kissed Gia."

"Hmm." Dad takes another bite of his ice cream. "Thought you said you were just friends."

I shoot a glare at him, and he smiles.

"Sorry. You kissed Gia. And that's a bad thing because . . . ?"

"Because she likes Hallie."

Dad's smile disappears. "Oh. I see."

And I could leave it at that, but I really do start at the beginning and tell Dad everything. The deal, the romance practice, falling in love with Gia a little bit every day until I was in too deep to know what to do. He listens, the only sound the scrape of his spoon against his mug. By the time I'm done with my story, my Coke float is mostly a Coke milkshake.

Dad sits still for a few seconds, like he's thinking. Then he says, "I don't think you're upset about kissing Gia. I think you're upset because things are changing, and it's scaring you."

I frown at Dad. "What? Were you even listening? I ruined everything—"

"Hear me out. Do you even want to go to Carnegie Camp?"

"Hallie and I applied together—"

"That's not what I asked. I asked do you want to go. You know it's not a real camp, right? You're not eating s'mores; you're studying and doing college prep."

I glare sullenly at my feet. "I don't really want to study all summer, no. But Hallie is going, and . . ." I trail off, the weight

289

of Dad's words settling around me. "And Hallie and I have never been apart that long."

"Bingo." Dad sits his mug on my bedside table. "I wanted to bring this up earlier, but I didn't know how. I worry about you and Hallie."

"What do you mean?"

"You two are close, and that's a great thing, don't get me wrong. But you can be codependent with her sometimes."

I don't say anything, considering his words. Codependent definitely has a negative connotation. But my friendship with Hallie isn't negative; it's one of the most important things in my life. "Hallie is my best friend. It's normal to spend time with each other."

"Yes, but not to the extreme you've been going to. I saw how disappointed and scared you were about becoming a manager. That's because you were worried about missing camp with Hallie, right?"

Damn, Dad should be a detective. But he's right. I was worried about camp, even though I've been aching to take Ethan's spot since I started at Sweet Teeth. Slowly, Dad's words sink in. I considered throwing away my dream to follow Hallie to a camp I don't even like. More than that—I watch Hallie's horror movies even though I'm not into them at all. Instead of being honest with her about how I don't want to exercise for fun, I follow her to yoga and hiking, and then end up fighting with her about it. I get anxious about her leaving me, but it's six measly weeks. When did I decide I couldn't be without her for that long? Dad warned me about spending too much time with Hallie, and though he was an ass about it, I think he's right.

"You're afraid of Hallie leaving you behind," Dad continues in my silence, "but you're changing too. You met a new friend and split your time. You worked hard at Sweet Teeth and were rewarded for it. I don't think you should be afraid. Friendships grow and evolve, and you don't have to be attached at the hip to still be friends. Growing up doesn't have to mean growing apart."

Hallie said the same thing. And though it feels like a disaster now, these four weeks were kind of amazing. We still hung out. Hallie visited me at Sweet Teeth, we had sleepovers, she went to Sarah's party with me, and we had fun. And I still had space to spend a ton of time with Gia and work too. Maybe it's okay if Hallie and I don't do everything together. Maybe it's okay to let some of my fear go. I glance at Dad, impressed and grateful. How did Dad get so good at giving advice? I should have asked him about this whole mess earlier.

"You're really doing well at therapy, huh, Dad."

Dad laughs. "My therapist thinks so, thank you. Now let's talk about Gia."

I sigh, but nod. That's the sorest spot. Hallie and I have been through a lot over the years; we'll probably be okay. But Gia . . . I don't know. I don't know how to fix this.

"I'm no romance expert; I'm just your dad. But I don't think you're being fair to Gia. You didn't give her a chance to tell you how she felt about the kiss."

"But she likes Hallie, Dad. That was why we started this whole thing."

"You liked Amanda Graceling in fifth grade and you changed your mind."

"That's different—wait, how do you know about that?"

Dad smiles. "What I'm saying is, you need to give her a chance to tell you her side of the story. You can't kiss someone and then run away from them."

"Well, that's what I did, so . . ."

Dad chuckles. "What are you going to do?"

"I don't know. I wish things didn't have to change. I hate change."

"I know. But change isn't a bad thing, not always." Dad takes a breath. "It will always hurt that your mother isn't here. I'm not trying to minimize that. And I get that you've made yourself a safe bubble to cope with not having her around. But nothing can stay the same, and you shouldn't want it to. Besides, things have changed already. You're a manager at Sweet Teeth now. You met Gia, and she changed you, like it or not. It's not all bad, you know?"

And, what Dad isn't saying, is that we're better. We're talking and close, like we used to be. I lean my head on his shoulder, and in my heart, I know I've forgiven him. For everything.

"Thanks, Dad."

"You're welcome." Dad wraps his arm around me and hugs me into his side. I feel warm and safe, and a lot better than I did before. "I think you know what to do, but just in case—stop avoiding your friends and apologize. And tell Gia how you feel. This isn't something you can get past without facing it head-on."

"Maybe I should go to therapy," I grumble against Dad's shirt.

"We can make an appointment if you want." Dad kisses the top of my head and hugs me tight. "Eat your ice cream, have a shower, and come eat dinner if you can. It'll be okay, Naveah. I promise."

Dad stays a little longer, but soon I'm alone. I pace in a circle, thinking everything over. Dad's right. I can't just cry alone in my room. I have to at least apologize to Hallie for using her. And Gia . . . though I feel sick about facing her again, I know I have to. I can't live my life without that adorable nerd in it. I have to tell her how I feel. I have to try.

I pick up my phone, and it's only on 12 percent. I also have a million texts from Hallie and Gia. I don't open them yet, because at the top of my list is a notification from Galaxy Cat.

Everything okay? We miss you ☹

I didn't log in yesterday. For the first time in over a thousand consecutive days, I didn't play that stupid game. I unlock my phone and go to the app, and I'm stunned. The counter in the corner, instead of counting the days Mom is gone, has been reset to zero. Three years of wishing, waiting, pining, are gone. I can't even remember what day we're supposed to be on. I stare at the counter, the new reality odd and uncomfortable. But somehow, the more I stare at it, the pain and worry fade into something that feels a lot like peace. Mom is gone, and there's no changing that. Maybe I should stop counting.

I close the app and delete it, finally getting rid of Galaxy Cat for good.

Then I go to my texts. Hallie has sent me several, but not nearly as many as Gia. Hallie's are mostly mild concern, until she texts that she talked to Dad and knows I'm at least alive. I touch Gia's name, heart pounding, sweat beading on my forehead. Let's get it over with.

Nav, please answer.

Nav?

Hellooooo

Please answer your phone! I'm not upset okay? But I think we should talk about this

I'm going to bed but call me tomorrow?

I'm getting really worried. Please let me know you're okay

Naaaav come on!

Okay I talked to Hallie and she said
you're alive. That's good but I need
to know if you're okay

I close my eyes. I made her worry, and I feel like shit about
that. Her anxiety has to be so bad. There's only one text left, so
I take a deep breath and keep going.

Hallie and I are going to meet at 7:00.
We're going to Ivan's. I just wanted
you to know.

Seven? I glance at the time and all the color drains from my
face. It's 6:57 right now.

I throw on clothes and shoes and fly downstairs like hell-
hounds are chasing me. Dad looks up in alarm as I charge down
the steps.

"I have to go," I say, grabbing my keys from the kitchen
counter. "They're on their date right now, I have to go meet
them."

Dad smiles. "Drive carefully, okay?"

"Okay," I say, already halfway out the door. "Love you, Dad!
Thank you!"

"Love you too," he calls, but I'm closing the door, jumping
into my car, and I'm gone.

CHAPTER 33

When I get to Ivan's, it's 7:13. And like some horror movie, I see Gia and Hallie, sitting at a table by the wide front window.

I almost die on the spot. They're talking to each other, Gia fidgeting nervously. They have a cup of ice cream each. They're on a date. I'm too late.

No. It's not too late. I have to tell Gia how I feel, now, urgently. I get out of my car and run to the door, and before I chicken out, I rush to Hallie and Gia's table.

Gia sees me first. She starts, and half stands up out of her chair. "Nav! Are you okay?"

"Hi," I say, suddenly conscious that I look like absolute shit. I'm wearing sweatpants, and I didn't wash my face, so I'm sure I have tear tracks on my cheeks. Wonderful, amazing, lovely.

"Very dramatic for you to show up here after ignoring us for two whole days," Hallie says. Her words are sharp, but there's amusement in her eyes.

"I know. I'm sorry about that. But I have to tell you something. Both of you." I take a breath. I wish I had Gia's fidget ring. "I gotta talk to Hallie first. Is that okay, Gia?"

Gia nods, worry creasing her brow, and sits back down. I take another shaky breath and face Hallie, looking into her eyes so she knows I mean it.

"I'm sorry, Hallie. I'm sorry I used you for my own gain, especially after a breakup I knew hurt you. I'm sorry I made fun of yoga and hiking, and I'm sorry I've been such a shitty friend this summer. I should have just hung out with you as much as possible before camp, and I shouldn't have been jealous and afraid."

Hallie nods slowly. She gives me a small smile. "It's cool, Nav."

"It's not cool," I insist. "I haven't been cool for weeks, and I treated you badly. For no reason, turns out, because I'm not going to camp."

"Really?" Gia says, pulling my attention to her. Her eyes are wide with shock. "But you were dead set on going."

"I know, but Hallie deserves this. Her grades are good, and mine aren't. And she wants to study all summer for some reason, and honestly I'd rather die." I look back at Hallie and grab her hands in mine. Hers are cold from the ice cream, and I use that feeling to ground me, to give me courage to say what I've known all along but was too scared to face. "You have fun, okay? I'll miss you, but I want you to have that space. I want you to experience new things, even if they're not with me. I want you to do this for you, because you earned it and you deserve it. And I'll be here when you get back."

Hallie's smile widens and turns warm. "I will. And I forgive you. Come here, you doofus."

Hallie stands and hugs me, and I hug her back with every amount of emotion I can muster. I'm still scared of change, and anxious that she's leaving, but now I have a new feeling: hope. I'm hopeful that Hallie and my friendship will be just fine. Nothing's permanent, but I feel encouraged to face whatever's next head-on.

"If you replace me with some nerd, I'll be so mad," I grumble into her shoulder.

Hallie laughs and lets me go. "Not a chance. You're stuck with me for life." Hallie's grin turns mischievous, and she nods to the side. "Now, don't you have something to say to Gia?"

I turn to Gia, who's waiting patiently. She spins her ring, turning it over and over, but she's staring straight at me. I open my mouth, but nothing comes out. My face is hot with nerves and I swear to God I'm about to pass out. I should have practiced or something.

"Can we go outside?" I manage to squeak.

Gia rockets to her feet. "Yeah, of course."

Hallie gets to her feet too. She gives me a sly grin. "Lead the way, Nav."

All three of us troop outside. I don't know how I will my feet to step out of Ivan's, but suddenly I'm not under harsh fluorescent lights and instead under the warm summer sky, one that's full of oranges and reds and Gia's favorite color. The sight calms my rapid heartbeat a little, and I manage to look Gia right in the eye this time. Now that I'm not so panicked, I notice Gia's wearing sweatpants too? And one of her famous animal-themed pajama shirts.

"You don't look like you're dressed for a date."

Gia seems surprised, then grins. "That's because I'm not. I met with Hallie to see if she wanted to storm your house with me."

I laugh, a deep one all the way to my belly, and I'm not so nervous anymore. Once again, Gia has made me laugh, eased tension from me, has been worrying about and looking out for me. The truth I've held on to slips out as easily as the laugh.

"Gia, I wanted to say I'm sorry for kissing you . . . but I'm not. I'm not sorry I kissed you."

Gia's eyes widen in shock, but I keep going.

"I like you, Gia. I like you a lot. And I tried to avoid it all this time, but I can't anymore. You're funny, and you're sweet, and you call me out on my bullshit. You get anxious, but you keep trying no matter what, and I love that about you. You're thoughtful, and kind, and when I'm with you, I feel so peaceful, like I'm just where I'm meant to be. I know you like Hallie, and that's why we started this, but I have to tell you how I feel. I . . . I hope that's okay." I finish lamely, conscious of the fact that I'm pouring my heart out in front of Hallie, who's standing behind me and eating ice cream like she's watching a soap opera.

Gia stares at me for a nervous second, and then that familiar uneven blush starts creeping up her neck. "Oh, Nav."

I wince. Here it comes. "You don't have to let me down easy. I know that—"

"Stop talking," Gia says.

I shut up, and Gia closes her eyes. She bounces on her toes for a second, then walks about ten steps away from me. I wait, and watch her do a tiny pep talk circle and come back. She takes a deep breath and then opens her eyes again, hers full of determination.

"Nav, I'm not sorry you kissed me either."

My heart soars with pathetic hope. "Y-Yeah?"

"Yeah. I told Hallie that I don't like her."

"She really did," Hallie pipes up from behind me. "Actually, she said, 'I don't find you remotely attractive anymore. Sorry about that.'"

"Oh God." I feel another laugh coming on, especially as Gia's face turns scarlet. That's such a Gia thing to say. But . . . but if she doesn't like Hallie . . . "Then why did we do all of this? The deal, and romance practice, and everything?"

Gia takes another deep breath. "I did like Hallie at first. But when we hung out, I realized I really didn't; I liked the *idea* of her. I liked the idea of love, you know? And I realized . . ." Gia balls her hands into fists, then breaths out slowly. "I realized that the person I liked was right in front of me. But she said she didn't believe in love, and she didn't date, so I didn't say anything." Gia's eyes shine with tears, but she's smiling. "But now I know she likes me back."

I stare at Gia, dumbstruck. She's talking about me. I said those things. She's liked me all along? "Oh."

"Oh?" Hallie teases. "That's all you have to say?"

"Shut up." I go to shove her and she dodges, laughing. "Go home, you voyeur."

"Let me have this. I love this cute shit." Hallie laughs, but she tosses her ice cream in the trash and heads to her car. "Fine, fine, I'm going to pack. Good for you, Nav! Sorry it took her so long, Gia!"

Gia smiles and I flip Hallie off, but I'm smiling too.

I look back at Gia after Hallie's car leaves the parking lot. "Do you . . . do you really like me?"

"Of course I do." Gia sighs heavily. "I've been going nuts. I tried to call off the deal several times, but you really wanted to go to camp, so I stopped. Then I thought if I dropped some hints, you'd figure it out."

"The dress," I say immediately. "On our date. It was the one you were wearing when we first met."

Gia's face fills with joy. "You knew! So wait, when we went on the date . . ."

"Oh yeah, I was pretty much in love with you," I admit. "I mean, come on. I looked at fish with you. Willingly."

"Oh my God." Gia looks like she's ready to faint. "This whole time, I thought maybe . . . but then I thought you were just a really nice person."

"I am nowhere near that nice. I would never look at fish for anyone else."

We grin at each other for a second, and I'm dizzy with the realization that this is happening. *This is happening.* Gia likes me, and I like her, and the truth is out in the open.

Gia steps closer to me, and before I know it, I'm closing the distance too. We stand there, inches apart, and Gia looks at me like I'm the only girl in the world.

301

"Can I tell you something?"

"Anything."

Gia smiles at me, and it's like being showered with pure happiness, all meant for me. "You're always there for me, Nav. I was so lonely when we moved here. And I thought a traditional love story was what I needed. But it wasn't. Falling in love wasn't anything like I expected. I didn't know it was bullying me into buying us ice cream, or playing different games together at the same time, or you coming to my house to help me clean up my puke." Gia winces at that and I laugh.

"Happy to clean your vomit any time."

"Stop! Don't ruin this," Gia groans. But she meets my eyes again and hers are soft and adoring. "None of this is what I expected, but I'm glad I get to do it with you. Umm, if you want." Gia's face is bright red, her eyes wide and hopeful, and my eyes fill with happy tears. Somehow, by making this deal with Gia, I got nothing I thought I wanted. But what I have now is so much better.

"I do want, Gia. And, if it's okay with you, you'll never be lonely again."

Gia hugs me, and I'm so overcome with emotion that I almost can't move. Gia makes sure I don't have to; she grabs my face and kisses me until I'm delirious with pure happiness and the taste of sweetness on her lips.

When we break apart, Gia looks lovingly into my eyes. And I look back, taking in her long eyelashes and pretty brown eyes and knowing she's here, she wants to be with *me* and no one else.

"You, my friend, are an excellent kisser."

Gia blushes, looking real pleased with herself. "I was worried because that's the one thing we didn't practice."

"I don't think my heart could have survived that." I want to kiss her again and again, but I'm still dazzled by the fact this is happening. "I can't believe this is real."

"You shouldn't be surprised, though." When I raise my eyebrows, Gia continues. "When we first started, you told me there were five steps to falling in love. We practiced all the steps."

Oh goddammit, she's right. I somehow tricked myself into falling in love, and that's the dumbest, best thing I've ever done. "You believe in my PhD in romance now, don't you?"

Gia rolls her eyes, but a laugh escapes. "Yes, Nav, I believe." She kisses me again, smiling against my lips, and though nothing worked out the way I wanted, I wouldn't change a thing.

EPILOGUE

Two Weeks Later

Shirley says something to me, knocking me out of the zone.

I look up at her, blinking against the harsh lights of the kitchen. I was focused on painstakingly frosting my newest experiment—strawberry-lemonade cupcakes. I've been at Sweet Teeth almost every day this week, trying new recipes (and burning some donuts, but we won't talk about that). Shirley has been asking me for ideas—me!—so I've been run ragged trying to train the new girl (way better than Ethan, but sometimes I miss the free Egg McMuffins) and also making every dessert in the store. Half the time I'm cursing my existence. But the other half, like now, I'm focused and driven and really, really happy.

I wipe my face with a towel, grimacing at the smear of pink frosting on the cloth. "What did you say?"

Shirley smiles at me. "It's three thirty. Time to go."

How did three hours go by so fast? I swear I was just scarfing down a PB&J Dad packed for me. I glance at my messy work-station. "Okay, let me clean this up—"

"No," Shirley interrupts me. "I'll clean, you go."

"But—"

"I insist." She pats me on the back, her hand a lot rougher

than I was expecting. "You've done great work today. I'll take it from here."

Well, okay. I take my apron off and box up my cupcake creation, and soon I'm in my loyal rust bucket headed to Gia's house.

The huge circle driveway is as familiar as my own home now. I pull in, park, and knock on the front door, and Jordan goes nuts. I smile. That's familiar too. The door swings open, and Jordan darts out, dancing at my feet.

"My sausage ball!!" I bend to pet her, but I keep the cupcake high above my head so she can't eat it. "Sorry, baby, no cupcakes for doggies."

"I appreciate that. She gets terrible stomachaches from people food."

I look up at the sound of Ms. Flores's voice. She grins at me, wearing some reading glasses and a nice shirt but old gray sweatpants. I thought she'd be super busy with the camp, but she was only gone for the first two days. She's been home a lot more often, to Gia's delight. I straighten and let her hug me.

When she's done squeezing me to death, she holds me at arm's length and fusses over my rumpled shirt. "Look at this, so wrinkled. Do you iron your clothes, Nav? I've tried convincing Gia, but you know she just takes them out of the dryer hot or something?"

I can't hold back a grin. "I do that too."

Ms. Flores rolls her eyes so far back in her head I'm scared they'll pop out of their sockets. "You children, I swear—and

look, Gia isn't even here to greet you! That girl, impossible."
Gia's mom mutters something in Spanish, but even I can tell Gia
is about to get her ass in trouble if she doesn't come downstairs.

"It's fine, Ms. Flores," I say, hoping to rescue her. "I'm sure
she's busy. I'll go to her room."

Gia's mom looks disapproving, but nods. "Fine, but you tell
her we're having a talk this evening. And the door stays open,
okay?"

I give Gia's mom a mock salute. She was delighted when we
told her we're dating, but I do miss the door-closed privileges.
"You got it, Ms. Flores."

Gia's mom lets me go upstairs and Jordan happily waddles
up behind me. Gia's door is ajar, and I hear the sound of *Briar's
Blaze* long before I nudge her door open with my foot.

Gia's still in her pajamas (flamingos this time), and she's
staring intently at the TV. Her green-haired dwarf balances
precariously on a thin bridge over lava, carrying some kind of
glowing rock. I wait until the dwarf is safely on the other side
and dancing before I nudge Gia's beanbag chair.

"Knock knock."

Gia turns to look at me, startled, ecstatic, and loving in
quick succession. "Nav!" She abandons her game and stands,
then pulls me to her. I'm laughing as she kisses me, her mouth
and mine smiling into each other. This part never gets old.

Gia pulls away first. "You're off from work already?"

"Some of us get up before noon," I tease.

Gia smiles, but she's distracted, looking at something above

306

my head. She reaches up and I feel a tug. She lowers her hand and shows me what she plucked out of my hair—a glob of pink frosting. "You made a new cupcake today."

"Hate it when you do that." But I'm grinning as I plop the cupcake box into Gia's hand. "It's strawberry-lemonade."

Gia opens the box right away; she knows the drill by now. I'm too shy to show Shirley my new ideas, so I roped Gia the Food Snob into tasting everything before I report back to Shirley. She approved the caramel/turtle/chocolate cupcake, but vetoed the pistachio creme (something about not wanting to eat green food?). I watch anxiously as she takes a bite, leaving a smear of pink frosting on the corner of her mouth.

"Hmm . . ." Gia looks deeply serious, which makes me more anxious. "It's kind of sour, but in a good way. And I like strawberries, so you get points for that. Eight out of ten."

"Only an eight?" I add mock anguish to my tone and Gia laughs.

"I'm sorry, I can't lie about food. Will a kiss make it up to you?"

"I guess it's a start." I kiss her this time, tender and deep, and she tastes like the strawberry cupcakes . . .

I pull away, frowning. "You're right. Something's wrong with that frosting."

Gia snorts out a laugh, and I swear I've never been happier.

Ms. Flores yells something in faint Spanish. We both turn to look, though I can't understand. Well, not yet. I've picked up on a few words, mainly food related. Gia yells back and rolls her eyes in an impressive imitation of her mother.

"What'd she say?"

"She said I better have my door open."

It's my turn to laugh. "She's super worried about me seducing her daughter, huh?"

Gia grins. "Too late." She kisses my forehead and I swear I'm melting. "Come sit down. I know you're tired."

"You just wanna get back to that game." But I'm not serious, because I am tired and I love that Gia knows that without me having to say anything. She holds my hand and pulls me to the Pokémon beanbag chair, and I rest my head in her lap while she plays one handed, her other hand on my back, tracing slow, soothing circles into my shirt.

Two months ago, I would have laughed in someone's face if they'd told me I'd be here, in a committed relationship, my head in my girlfriend's lap and allowing myself to be loved. It wasn't a concept I could fathom, much less dream of. My rules for myself were strict—hookups only, no getting attached, definitely no falling in love. I'm so glad I broke them all.

"Are you eating dinner here tonight?" Gia asks after twenty minutes of cozy silence. I have to shake myself awake because a minute longer and her circles would have knocked me out.

"No, Dad and I are going somewhere." That's something else I couldn't have dreamed of two months ago. Dad and I aren't perfect—we got into a fight yesterday over taking the trash out—but I don't feel uneasy or lost around him anymore. He's just my dad, and we're working hard to get to know each other again. Linda the therapist would be so proud.

That thought shakes me more awake. I look up at Gia, who's looking at me too, a soft smile on her face. "Are you nervous about tomorrow?"

Gia shudders and twists her ring around twice with her thumb. "I don't want to talk about it."

"You shouldn't be nervous. It's fine, I promise. I'm a therapy expert now."

"After two visits?!"

"I'm naturally gifted, what can I say."

Gia laughs, and I join in. After my chaotic confession, I decided I really do need therapy. I asked Dad, and he somehow got me an appointment for the very next day. So now I see Linda every Thursday, after work. It's fine, really. We talk about Dad a lot, and how I feel about dating Gia and missing Hallie. We haven't talked about Mom yet, but I don't feel so scared to now. Maybe someday we will talk about her, and maybe with my new support system (term courtesy of Linda), it won't sting so much.

Gia, on the other hand, dragged her feet the whole way and admitted to her mom that she wanted to try therapy again a few days ago. Ms. Flores scolded her for waiting so long to say anything and made her an appointment for tomorrow. An appointment Gia has been dreading like a root canal. But today she seems calmer, more determined and less I'm-about-to-faint.

"I'll be in the lobby," I tell her, because I promised. And because she waited in the lobby for me when I was debating

309

sneaking out of a bathroom window so I wouldn't have to meet Linda.

"I know." Gia bends down and kisses my forehead again, and I wonder how I ever went without forever.

My phone buzzes in my pocket, breaking me out of my happy daze. I fish it out and smile—Hallie is FaceTiming me. I accept the call and grin into the camera.

"Oh, *now* the scholar decides to grace us with her presence."

Hallie rolls her eyes, grinning too. The image is kind of grainy; apparently, they don't get great service in the middle of the woods. Thank God I didn't go. "Shut up, I'm on a break. Hi, Gia!"

"Hi, Hallie." Gia waves over my shoulder, but she's already focused on the TV again, her dwarf sneaking up on some sleeping jaguars or something.

"Why're you so sweaty?" I ask. Her face is shiny with sweat, and her hair looks soaked. She looks like they're making her do hard labor.

"It's July in Alabama?" Hallie acts like she's offended.

"You should be careful of heatstroke," Gia says, never taking her eyes off the TV. "Drink plenty of water."

"Yeah, listen to Gia! Why aren't you in your cabin?"

Hallie rubs the back of her neck, looking away from the camera. "Don't laugh."

"I'm not." I grin, poised to laugh.

"Well . . . there's this girl . . ."

"Oh, here we go." I don't laugh, but I can't stop smiling. I

310

was afraid of being separated, so afraid I nearly wrecked every single meaningful relationship I had, but I really had nothing to be worried about. Hallie is hundreds of miles away, but she still calls me whenever she gets a break, which is every other day so far. She's still falling in love with people, and still coming to me for advice. I changed, we changed, but the important things stayed the same.

I lean back on Gia's thigh, smile at my best friend, and settle in for some good old-fashioned romance practice, this time not involving me.

"Tell me everything."

ACKNOWLEDGMENTS

First and foremost, I have to thank my best friend, mentor, mother, father, best person in the world—Grandma. You are the greatest person I've ever met, and though we fight and get frustrated with each other, I hope we never change. Thank you for delicious grilled cheese sandwiches, listening to my depraved writing ramblings, and for being the best parent a girl could ask for.

Second, thank you to my agent, Holly Root. I'll never forget the sheer glee in your voice when we talked about Nav's first draft. It was the first time I felt true, pure hope that this writing thing might actually work out. Thank you also to my incredible first editor, Olivia Valcarce. I loved working with you on many projects, and I hope one day we can work together again. Thank you to Mabel Hsu as well, second editor extraordinaire, who swooped in and took Nav from pretty darn good to great. And to Clare Vaughn, third editor who arrived in the eleventh hour and handled the last-minute tweaks and changes. I'm lucky to have had all three of you on this special book!

Thank you to Nav's full Harper team: Natalie Shaw, Julia Feingold, Alison Donalty, Shona McCarthy, Gwen Morton, Danielle McLelland, Melissa Cicchitelli, Taylan Salvati, and Lisa Calcasola. And thank you to the entire Inkyard team. I am so grateful for you, and I hope you're doing well on your new adventures.

Immeasurable thanks to my best friend, Emily Chapman, for everything you do. Thanks for cheering me on and helping me brainstorm good date ideas. Thank you also to my dear friend Tas for three a.m. plotting sessions and an endless supply of dad jokes. I honestly feel like I can't write books without y'all.

To Belinda Grant—my great friend and unofficial editor!! You rock!! You cheered me on when Nav was just a messy "love triangle, but one leg is completely uninterested and the other two are idiots" idea. You were with me from the first draft of this book to the final draft, and I'm immensely grateful for this. Huge thank you also to Jacki Hale for being an excellent friend and sensitivity reader for Gia. Thank you for allowing my questions and cheering on our two dummies.

Paulette Kennedy, Marith, Kevin—thank you for being such great early readers. Your feedback was incredibly helpful in shaping Nav into who she is today. Thank you to my writing groups: the slackers, WiM, Scream Town, and AltChat 3.0. Laughter, memes, and especially strange two a.m. questions all helped me tell Nav's story. And thanks to several people for their friendship and encouragement: Gigi Griffis, A.Z. Louise, Jay, J. Elle, Mary Roach, Marisa Urgo, Meg, Lyssa Mia Smith, Rochelle Hassan, Thuy, Maria Tureaud, Zoe Zander, Rain Ashton, and Chandra Fisher. Y'all are the best, and I adore you!

Thank you to my family, particularly my two aunts, Sissy and Marteal, for showing me love and kindness. And the impromptu writing retreats (even if they resulted in a lot of watching murder mysteries and not a lot of writing ☺).

And finally, thank you to young Jessica, for staying. We've made it this long, and somehow, I'm happier than I ever could have dreamed. Thank you for hanging on so this can be possible.